"Baker's series debut brings Native American culture and big business together into a clash that can be heard across the mountains."

—*Library Journal*

A NORA ABBOTT MYSTERY

TATTERED LEGACY

SHANNON BAKER

MIDNIGHT INK
WOODBURY, MINNESOTA

FIRST EDITION
First Printing, 2015

Book format by Bob Gaul
Cover design by Lisa Novak
Cover illustration by Robert Rodriguez/Lindgren & Smith
Cover image: iStockphoto.com/9963181/ebettini

Midnight Ink, an imprint of Llewellyn Worldwide Ltd.

This is a work of fiction. Names, characters, places, and incidents are either the product of the author's imagination or are used fictitiously, and any resemblance to actual persons, living or dead, business establishments, events, or locales is entirely coincidental. Cover model(s) used for illustrative purposes only and may not endorse or represent the book's subject.

Library of Congress Cataloging-in-Publication Data
Baker, Shannon, 1960–
    Tattered legacy/Shannon Baker.—First edition.
        pages; cm.—(A Nora Abbott mystery; #3)
    ISBN 978-0-7387-4063-8
    I. Title.
    PS3602.A5877T38 2014
    813'.6—dc23
                        2014033922

Midnight Ink
Llewellyn Worldwide Ltd.
2143 Wooddale Drive
Woodbury, MN 55125-2989
www.midnightinkbooks.com

Printed in the United States of America

AUTHOR'S NOTE

Moab is a terrific place. I ask readers to remember that the Moab described in *Tattered Legacy* is seen through Nora's eyes, and she's got reasons to withhold her love. I've spent some time in Moab and Castle Valley and never once was I confronted by a dangerous group of locals, Mormon or otherwise. The people of Moab are warm and welcoming and, seriously, the landscapes are beyond amazing.

Since this is a work of fiction, I've taken a few liberties to arrange the world to suit my story. There is no Read Rock Bookstore. I created the store and the building and set it somewhere on Main Street. Thankfully, the Tokpela Ranch doesn't exist.

There is a campaign underway to expand the boundaries of Canyonlands National Park. It was this movement that prompted the very real Laura Kamala to produce a film to show lawmakers the benefits of expansion. If you're interested in more of the story—one not told through the point of view of made-up characters—I encourage you to go to greatercanyonlands.org.

The Southwest is full of amazing pictograph and petroglyph panels. As far as I know, there isn't a grand display in Fiery Furnace. Nor is there a design like the symbol Nora sees in her dreams. And though there is a Hopi Prophecy Rock and there are interpretations of its meaning, the rock where Benny takes Nora is fictitious.

Let me caution anyone not to do what Nora does and traipse off into Fiery Furnace in Arches National Park without a guide. It is a dangerous maze and a person could easily get lost. In the blazing high-desert sun. All alone. So thirsty.

The Castle Valley flood in this book is inspired by an actual flood in that area in 2009. By all accounts, and from the devastation left behind, it was a terrifying event.

The characters and groups I created in this book are not real. I don't hate Mormons or the LDS church any more than I hate Christians based on the Westboro Baptist Church or Muslims based on Al Qaida. This is fiction, so I had to come up with lots of gooey conflict.

Finally, the Hopi tribe is one of the oldest cultures in the world. I don't pretend to understand a fraction of their beliefs and customs. What I do know is that I've heard about some crazy stuff happening on the rez, and I have no reason to doubt its truth.

To Janet Fogg,
my hero.

ONE

WARREN EVANS FELT THE hand of God wrap around him, holding him straight and strong. Others might panic or lose their temper, but with God's help, Warren waited for the chaos in his head to subside.

He picked up his phone and resumed the conversation. "I see."

Barely controlled rage strangled his nephew's voice. "She figured it out. I don't know how. But she was going to expose us."

Warren leaned back, and the well-oiled springs of his chair whispered in his spacious office. He gazed out the window overlooking Central Park, the trees a mass of green. But his thoughts were in the canyon lands of his childhood.

The Promised Land.

The impossible red rock formations rising in majestic splendor under the vast sky, a blue never visible in New York City. He imagined the circling hawk and heard its cry echoing off God's canvas. He longed to see the hoodoos—the tall rock spires that marched across the high deserts of southern Utah—defending the castles of stone carved by wind and water, to feel the searing sun on his skin and taste the pure air.

Instead, he addressed his nephew in clipped tones. "Did you get the footage she's completed?"

"I'm working on it." Anger ebbed from his nephew's voice.

Warren clenched his fist, resisting the urge to pound it on the distressed surface of his antique oak desk. He stared at his hand, commanding his fingers to relax, then spoke with his characteristic authority. "That means you aren't sure she has it on tape."

His nephew swallowed. "She told Rachel she'd been to Fiery Furnace. We couldn't take the chance."

Fiery Furnace. Mention of the name sent a wave of longing through Warren. He should be in Moab instead of his corner office high above Manhattan's streets. With the end so near, they needed a steady hand, and he needed the strength and comfort of the land. The first lights announcing evening flicked on in countless other offices, but Warren sat in the growing gloom, straining to see the sky.

"I've done what needed to be done," his nephew said. "For you."

Bile burned Warren's throat. "For us. For mankind."

Pause. That hesitation of a nonbeliever. "And you'll lead us."

Those words hit like knives. Leading his flock had sustained him for years. But it would soon be over for him. Like Moses and even Martin Luther King, Jr.—though Warren hated to compare himself to a black man—Warren wouldn't enter the land of milk and honey with his people. God had told him that much.

But God hadn't told him who would lead in Warren's place.

Time was running out, and Warren needed to decide which of his nephews would inherit the kingdom.

TWO

Nora Abbott shut her eyes against the onslaught of icy water. She gasped in shock at the fury of the wave as it slapped at her face and knocked her against the back of the raft. Her feet slipped from the rubber strap that anchored her to the boat. Disoriented, she scrambled to her knees. The raft bucked and lurched, tossing her from side to side. She clutched the rigging threaded around the raft and braced herself to face downstream.

The raft crested the top of a swell and the canyon narrowed. Nothing but foam, frigid waves, and rocks ahead. The raft tilted to the right, banged against a boulder, and pitched forward, careening through another wave. It smashed into the canyon wall.

Nora popped from the waffling bottom. Her feet flew over her head. She clawed for the rope, but her fingers only scratched at slick rubber. A somersault catapulted her from the raft and she splashed into the freezing river, cracking her tailbone on rock.

Fighting for her breath in the glacial water, she succeeded in flipping onto her back with her feet pointed upstream. The life vest

3

offered neck support and her wetsuit and splash jacket kept her from instant hypothermia. She cooperated with the current until the canyon walls widened and the water calmed. She navigated to the bank, struggled for solid footing, and crawled out of the river moments before the raft crashed into the bank.

Cole jumped from the raft, nearly flattening her. He yanked on the rigging and the raft slid out of the water, coming to rest on the grassy bank. He spun around, breathless, his eyes wild, and focused on Nora, surveying her from head to toe. Apparently satisfied that she had indeed survived, he relaxed as his face split into a grin. "Whoo-hoo!"

Nora whooped in response, releasing tension. "I've never seen this river so full."

They'd pulled out in a small meadow—green grass lit by bright Colorado sunshine, edged in by pines and a few elms. The Rocky Mountains rose on either side of the Poudre River, where a heavy spring runoff raged. The rapids roared upstream, but peace reigned here.

They shrugged out of their life vests. Cole settled to the ground, pulling off Neoprene socks and wiggling his water-wrinkled toes. His sandy-colored hair dripped, and he pushed it back on his forehead.

Nora stripped off the splash jacket to let the sun warm her. She yanked the elastic from her ponytail and squeezed her shoulder-length hair, wringing out the river water. Stretching into the raft, she unbuckled the water bottle securely fastened to the rigging. She flopped down on the grass next to Cole and handed him the bottle. The sun kissed her and she tilted her head to catch its heat while the breeze teased a few strands of her drying, copper-colored hair into her face. "Whose great idea was it to play hooky today?"

He leaned back with easy grace. "You needed to get out of the office."

He was right. Probably. "What if Lisa needs something?"

"She'll figure it out." A mountain wren twittered, answered by more sweet birdsong.

Nora ignored the knot trying to form in her belly. "She called yesterday while I was Skyping with the board about forest restoration. I figured she'd call back if there was an emergency."

Cole's eyebrows raised in surprise. "That doesn't sound like you."

"It's killing me, but I'm trying to learn to delegate more."

He kissed her. "And you're making fine progress."

They watched the river race past. She stole a glance at Cole and found him smiling, his blue eyes twinkling. "What?" she asked.

He shrugged. "Nothing."

She landed a playful punch on his arm. "Talk to me."

He laughed. "I'm from Wyoming. Men aren't big on sharing feelings there."

"Says the man who insists I tell him everything like he's a therapist. Come on. It can't be bad—you're smiling."

He let his gaze rest on her and his smile faded. The blue of his eyes deepened. "I was thinking how damned lucky I am to have found someone who fits me so well."

His simple words took her breath with as much force as the icy river. "Me too," she whispered and kissed him.

They took a moment together, making out on the bank like teenagers. It was a perfect day—too perfect. At that thought, worry flooded in and Nora sat back.

"The film deadline is tomorrow. Lisa says she's almost done, but I haven't seen it." Reminding herself of the timeline sapped her of the exhilaration from the rapids and from her day with Cole. So much rested on the success of the film.

This was Nora's first big project as executive director of Living Earth Trust. She'd hired her college friend, Lisa Taylor, to create a feature film documenting Canyonlands National Park in Utah and the threats it faced. They were scheduled to screen the film for a committee of congressmen to advocate for expansion of the park's boundaries.

A flash of blue in the trees behind Cole made Nora gasp.

Cole twisted to look. He turned back to her. "What?"

She inspected the tree where she thought she'd seen the blue, then plastered on a smile. "Nothing."

"Is he there?" He studied her.

So much for brushing it off. Cole knew about her kachina. "No. I haven't seen him in months."

A blue jay squawked and fluttered onto a pine bough behind Cole, as if mocking her.

"That's good, right?" Cole asked.

Nora didn't miss him, exactly. "It's great. Who needs a visit from an ancient Hopi spirit? It's scary, and he always gets me into trouble anyway."

Cole didn't look convinced. "Except you'd like to see him."

There was no hiding from Cole. He knew her better than anyone and, surprisingly, still wanted to be with her. She'd struck a gold mine in him. "He made me feel like ... " She struggled for the words. "Like maybe I really am Hopi and, well ... " Exposing herself like this, even to Cole, made her hesitate. "Like I might belong."

"Belong to what?"

He actually seemed to take her doubts seriously. Once again, he proved she could trust that he really cared. "I don't look Hopi. I've got no evidence. But as long as a kachina shows up every now and then, I don't feel like a poseur."

Cole threw an arm around her shoulder. "You worry too much."

"I used to dream about him. And even though I've been dreaming about Hopi stuff, he's not appearing. And then I wake up nervous."

"I think you're dropping off to sleep nervous, fretting about Lisa's film."

She rested her head on his shoulder. "Probably. But these dreams are vivid. I'm standing in front of a petroglyph panel in the desert. There's this big design with concentric circles, like a bull's-eye, and lines shoot out from it."

"Like a sunburst?" Cole lowered to rest on his back, moving slowly so Nora lowered down, too.

She'd dreamed about it so often that she could see the petroglyph in detail. "Kind of, but not really. Instead of rays all around the circle, there are two parallel lines spaced evenly around it. Anyway, in my dream, I'm looking at it and feeling all this angst."

His voice vibrated in her head. "That's it?"

The sound of a telephone interrupted them. It was muffled, but Nora's ears pricked. She jumped up and raced for the raft. It rang again while she fumbled to unbuckle the dry sack from the rigging. She unrolled the top of the sack, but by the time she dug through the towels and lunch to find her phone, it had stopped.

Cole stayed on the ground with his hands behind his head. "You brought your phone along on your day off?"

Nora glanced at the caller ID. "I thought it might be Lisa."

"And?"

"It's Abigail."

"You don't want to talk to your mother?"

Nora switched the alert to vibrate and set the phone on the raft. She gathered up the sandwiches and apples and settled next to Cole. "She only wants to tell me about a new skin product or alert me to an executive position opening up in some bank. Besides, I said I'd take the day off to spend with you, and that's what I'm going to do. Sorry I weakened."

Her phone vibrated. Cole raised his eyebrows. Nora opened a plastic container and pulled out half a ham sandwich. "Abigail's nothing if not determined."

"You don't think it's Lisa?"

With determination, Nora said, "I'm taking the day off."

Cole sank his teeth into an apple. A muted Mexican tune played from the raft.

Nora listened in surprise, then grinned. "You brought your phone, too?"

Cole shrugged. He stood and hurried to the raft. "Guess it's my turn now."

He found it easily in the near-empty bag, swiped it on, and held it to his ear.

Nora took another bite of the sandwich, enjoying the salty ham after the exertion of their morning on the river. Slowly, Cole's influence had pulled her from her driven, make-every-moment-productive lifestyle to one where she took the time to enjoy what she loved: Cole and being outside.

She realized she hadn't heard Cole speak. She twisted toward him.

His face seemed to melt as it went from happy to serious to alarm.

Her phone vibrated again, and she debated. No. She and Cole still had a day off together, and she'd cling to that.

It only took seconds for Cole's shocked expression to harden with control. He had formed a plan and was ready for action. He lowered the phone and stared at a spot above her head, obviously working out details in his mind.

When she couldn't wait any longer, she asked, "What's wrong?"

"That was Mom. Dad had a stroke a couple of days ago and … " He gathered up the sandwich container and started stuffing things in the dry bag.

Nora followed, once again ignoring her phone when it started buzzing. "A couple of days ago and she's just calling you now?"

He didn't address that. "My brother is causing some trouble and I need to get up there and see what's going on." He picked up his life vest and shrugged into it.

"Your younger brother?"

"My only brother, Derek."

She retrieved her life vest. "What kind of trouble could he be causing?"

For the first time since Nora had known him, he snapped at her. "I don't want to talk about it. I've got to go home."

"Home? As in Wyoming?"

He inspected the raft to make sure it hadn't been damaged in the rapids. "Yes. I don't know much, but I need to get up to the ranch and see what's happening."

He secured the water bottle. Nora rolled the top of the dry sack. He strode away from her, crashing into the forest. "Pit stop."

Nora moved to buckle the dry sack when her phone went off again. Their day together had taken a bad turn; she might as well answer. She checked the ID. At least it wasn't Lisa with a problem. "Hello, Mother."

"Nora! Thank god. I've been trying to call you. Don't you ever check your phone? I've left you a million messages since early this morning." Abigail sounded distraught, but that could mean anything from suffering a paper cut to losing her house in an earthquake.

Damn. Maybe that's why she hadn't heard from Lisa. "This stupid phone drops messages sometimes. I don't know why."

"You need a decent plan with a legitimate company. Not that one you got for Trust employees because it's the greenest."

"Okay, whatever." Nora began with the usual questions. "Is something wrong? Is Charlie okay?" Abigail's fourth husband, Charlie, traipsed off into the mountains outside of their Flagstaff cabin nearly every day. So many accidents lurked in the wilderness.

"We're fine, dear. But . . . "

Something in Abigail's voice made Nora hold her breath. "What?"

"Sit down. Is Cole with you?"

"Just tell me, Mother."

"I don't know how to say this."

"Mother!"

"Okay, okay." Nora pictured Abigail waving her arms. She waited impatiently while Abigail drew in a deep breath. "Rachel called me."

"Rachel? Lisa's wife? Why would she call you?" Because Lisa couldn't.

"Nora, please; you're not making this any easier."

Part of Nora wanted to scream at Abigail to spit it out. Another part wanted to end the call and turn the phone off.

"Nora, I'm so sorry, but Lisa had an accident."

Nora's breath caught in her throat. "What kind of accident? Is she okay?" How soon could Nora get home and pack her car for the six-hour drive to Moab? How many days would this put the film behind schedule? Nora would have to take over and do whatever Lisa needed her to do. Together they'd meet the deadline. They had to.

Abigail made a clicking noise as if her throat refused to form the words. Nora tapped on the warm rubber of the raft, hating Abigail's struggle. "Is she injured? How bad is it?"

Finally Abigail's voice found the words. It sounded like they had traveled through a tunnel from the center of the world. They rang in Nora's brain, refusing to make sense.

"Nora, honey. Lisa's dead."

THREE

WARREN EVANS PUSHED HIMSELF to sit up. His weak fingers clasped the protein drink, and he raised it. The can's metal cooled his lips. The vanilla-flavored concoction touched his tongue, and he lowered his shaky hand to set the can in a shaft of sunlight on the desk. A drop of white splashed against the oak.

Nausea overwhelmed him, and he waited for it to pass.

He concentrated on the blueprints spread across his desk that detailed the masterpiece he'd created. With God's help, of course.

His calculations satisfied him that he'd provided perfectly. Three more groups planned to arrive in Moab today. He needed to contact his nephew to make sure everything was in place.

He paused and fought his stomach for control. And won. At least he'd already lost his hair and it wasn't coming out in handfuls everywhere. His new toupee pleased him. It had cost him more than his first house, but it looked natural. He assumed the housekeeper or one of her workers had vacuumed up the evidence of his weakness.

He knew for certain Christine wouldn't. She barely spoke to him these days.

Trying not to think about his wife of nearly thirty years, he sighed and reached for his phone.

Christine only wanted him for what he gave her in this life. She loved his wealth. She'd smiled and kissed him at every charity ball and political fundraiser from here to Hollywood, but she hadn't shared his bed for a decade. And when she'd learned of his illness, she'd only grown more distant.

She was a great public and business asset, but she'd provided him with no heir and gave him little comfort as he neared his end. Still, with the trust fund she'd handed over for his use after they were married, she'd been a fortuitous initial down payment on his fortune.

Now, with time dwindling, he needed to make sure nothing was left undone. Warren pushed speed dial and waited.

"Uncle Warren. How's New York?"

Warren lied, "I only have a moment. We're about to hit the back nine." Warren lowered his head and closed his eyes, willing himself not to vomit. His heirs didn't need to know about his illness.

"Weather must be good there." His nephew's voice held the slightest edge of resentment.

Warren forced a good-natured chuckle. "I know you're working hard. It's the curse of the young."

"Enjoy your rest. You've earned it."

Warren said, "I just learned another group will join the other two today. You need to meet them for initiation rites and instructions."

"I've already been in touch with them, and it's all arranged."

Warren liked the way his nephew took charge. Did he have the faith to lead the chosen? "And the film?"

His nephew paused. "I'm making some progress."

Warren clenched his teeth. "What about Rachel?"

More uncomfortable silence. "She's planning the funeral."

Acting as if she were a widow. When did homosexuality become so respectable? "She's vulnerable. Now is the time to approach her."

"I'll see her tomorrow at the service. I'll talk to her then."

Warren sat back. The chair used to fit like a power suit, with the soft leather caressing him like a lover. Now he felt dwarfed in its massive expanse and the leather chafed his skin. "Find the camera, too. Her last images could be damaging."

"I'll find them. What's going on in Washington?"

He couldn't blame his nephew for asking. Warren hadn't told anyone the timeline, and they didn't know the end would come sooner than they expected. "The debate is close. Stanley insists expanding Canyonlands will devastate the local economy. Ruben waves the letter from the Outdoor Industry Association defending expansion. Right now the congressmen on the energy corporation's payroll probably hold a slight lead."

His nephew sounded worried. "They can't see the propaganda on that film or we'll lose the homestead."

Warren's jaw ached from grinding his teeth. "I'm glad you see the importance of getting that film."

"You know you can count on me."

FOUR

Nora pulled up in front of the Days Inn in Moab. She'd risen before dawn to drive the six hours from Boulder to arrive in plenty of time for Lisa's funeral. She climbed from the Jeep into the bright sunshine and let Abbey, her aging Golden Retriever, hobble out and water a tire.

The sun lit the red rocks around her, chasing off the morning chill. Light air tickled Nora's senses, tingling with new-day freshness. Moab hadn't awakened yet, so voices and bustles didn't disturb the town as it stretched and yawned and readied itself for another day.

Lisa loved mornings like this. A thousand phone conversations had started with Lisa's breathless account of a sunrise bursting over the jagged purple La Sals or of the play of light on the red canyon walls. Lisa couldn't wait to be out in the majestic beauty of the towering red rocks.

Only three days ago—maybe a warm day, just like this—Lisa had gone for another shot of petroglyphs at the Moonflower campground. At dusk, the light faded, and she'd have put her camera away. Why had she climbed the ancient log scaffolding deep in the crevice? The

14

prehistoric site was restricted, and Lisa respected that kind of protection, especially the antiquities she cherished. It made no sense for her to cross the barrier and wedge herself in the incredibly narrow space where the Anasazi had set logs zig-zagging up the straight walls. They'd cut slices out of the logs, worn smooth by countless feet and centuries of weather, to create a ladder to the top of the deep canyon.

It seemed unbelievable that Lisa, mountain goat that she was, would lose her footing and fall. Even more unlikely was that the fall would snap her neck so cleanly, killing her instantly.

A stone stuck in Nora's throat. Instantly killed, like Scott. Only her husband's death hadn't been an accident. Nora pushed the thought away.

So many hikes, so many miles they'd covered together—Nora couldn't believe they'd never share another adventure again. Her throat tightened. How could Lisa be gone?

Nora stretched the kinks from her back and walked into the hotel. She approached the front desk and the young man behind it.

"I need a room for tonight."

He shook his head slowly. Any quick movement of his body might have caused his khaki chinos to slide the last half inch off his narrow hips and puddle on the floor at his feet. The company tie didn't quite cover a dark stain on his wrinkled Oxford shirt. "I'm really sorry, ma'am," he said. "This bike race's eaten up all the rooms. There's nothin' left anywhere around Moab."

Nora leaned on the chest-high counter in the cool, tastefully decorated hotel lobby. A teenaged girl clanked dishes while she straightened up what was left of the breakfast buffet in an alcove off the lobby.

Just one more problem. But one that would have to wait. She had a half-hour to get to Lisa's funeral, and though she'd hiked the trail with Lisa before, she didn't remember the exact location of the trailhead and how far up the creek the mourners would gather.

She left the air-conditioned lobby and walked into the hotel parking lot, the summer sun blazing overhead. Memory stalled her—her last conversation with Lisa, just days ago. She'd been updating her on all of the Trust's projects.

Nora had munched on her deli turkey sandwich and caught up with Lisa via Skype.

Lisa's eyes twinkled, even through the blur of the screen. She sat in front of her laptop in her renovated cabin in Castle Valley. She'd chosen Castle Valley because it was an enclave of like-minded liberals twenty miles outside of Moab. "This is an unbelievable experience. I'm learning so much! Not only about the land but about the history and about making a film."

Nora couldn't fault Lisa for lack of passion and energy. She swallowed the chipotle-laced turkey. "What about results? Is the film ready?"

Lisa laughed with the carefree delight Nora always envied. "You're so you—always cutting away the bullshit and going for the kill."

Nora slurped her coffee. "What about it? You're at deadline and thirty grand over budget."

Lisa looked startled. "That much? Wow. This is so worth it, Nor. This place—god, this place is gorgeous. You've got the funding, right?"

"Not millions, but enough for the proposed budget you just exceeded. That's not the point. I need something to show the board. Even more important, are you ready to take it to Washington?" The hard knot of worry balled in her belly, and she wadded up the remainder of her sandwich in the paper wrapper.

"I know the goal, Nor." Lisa ran a hand through her long mass of dark waves. She licked her full lips, chapped by days in the sun. "And I'll get it done. I sent you some footage."

"And it's as amazing as you've said. But you're spending a ton of money, and I haven't seen the whole thing."

Lisa rolled her eyes. "You'll be impressed by the dawn images, Fat Bottom-Line Girl. It's probably the shot that will seal the whole deal. How could anybody deny the park expansion after seeing it?"

"I know you're going all George Lucas out there, but you've got to wrap it up. Time is running out."

"Da, da, da…" Lisa sang the doomsday notes and grinned at Nora, the sunlight streaming in through her home office windows and highlighting her own glow. "Lighten up, chica."

Nora shoved the coffee away, suspecting it contributed to the sour burn in her belly. "Maybe I'll get Cole and we'll come to Moab next week. You can show it to me then."

"Speaking of Cole and gorgeous, how's that hunk o' burning love of yours?"

The air surrounding Nora brightened, and an irresistible smile replaced her responsible executive director face. "Cole is great."

"And he's still treating you like a queen?"

Movement behind Lisa captured Nora's attention. Rachel bent over a table and shuffled through a pile of papers. "Hey, Rachel," Nora teased. "Would you keep Lisa on task and get me that film?"

Lisa hunched her shoulders as if taking cover.

Rachel whipped her head toward the computer screen. She glared at Nora across the miles. "You're the boss. You do it."

Rachel spared one scathing look for Lisa and whirled around. Footsteps stomped and a door squeaked open, then slammed closed.

Nora raised her eyebrows and waited for Lisa.

Lisa shrugged and showed a toothy grin tinged with discomfort. "She's cycling. You know how emotional women get."

Rachel and Lisa had been together for three years. Last year, Nora had met them in Minnesota for their wedding. Same-sex marriage hadn't been legal in Utah at the time, but Minnesota had seemed like such a random pick. As far as Nora could tell, they were the perfect couple. "What's going on?"

Lisa's false cheer slipped. "She's had enough of the film, I guess."

Lisa glanced toward the door, then leaned closer to the screen and lowered her voice. "You gotta understand. Rachel's family has been out here forever. She's, like, fourth-generation Mormon. Obviously she's evolved, but it's not easy for her." Lisa's eyes twinkled as she teased. "Out here, everyone is on one side or the other. The hip, smart folks, like me, are for expansion, and the Neanderthals are on the other side."

"So Rachel doesn't believe in park expansion?"

Lisa was quick to respond. "Oh, she's on board. But it's causing her some grief, okay?"

"Her family is harassing her?"

Lisa shrugged again. "A little more than that."

Alarms jangled Nora's nerves. She tried to squelch the reaction—okay, overreaction. "Explain."

"The brakes went out of my old Toyota pickup last week. Rachel thinks someone tampered with them. But they were shot and needed to be replaced."

"Lisa!"

Lisa tossed her hair. "See? You and Rachel are more alike than you know. In fact, if you didn't have that strange preference for men, you and I might be married now."

Maybe for people with normal lives, no one tampered with brakes or plotted murder. But in Nora's world, these bizarre and dangerous things happened. "Be careful." But what she wanted to say was "Run!"

Lisa looked over her shoulder again. "Listen. I probably shouldn't say anything, and I promised myself I wouldn't until I get more information. But you know me, I can't keep a secret."

That wasn't entirely true. She'd kept her gayness from her family for over twenty years.

"But this is important. I was out at Fiery Furnace and I found this petroglyph—"

The door squeaked in the background.

Lisa jerked her head around. She turned back to the screen and the conspiratorial tone vanished. "Okay. Have a great week."

"Lisa, wait."

Lisa blew a kiss at the computer screen. "Love you, babe." She severed the connection.

————

Nora climbed into her dilapidated Jeep. Abbey wagged his tail and slapped his tongue in Nora's direction. She scratched behind his ears. "You're a good boy," Nora said, more to practice a solid voice than anything else.

Nora drove east out of town for several miles. The road ran along the Colorado River, which was usually wide and smooth here, a serene glide. Today, though, red silt raged, probably the result of a heavy rain upstream, swelling the banks. At least the water had a channel to travel here. In the open desert, it would cascade down any indentation and create dangerous flash floods.

She needn't have worried about locating the Moonflower trailhead. Cars and pickups and bikes spilled from the dirt parking lot to line the road.

Lisa had taken Nora on this trail before. It was one of her favorites. It wound next to a creek, along a valley of willows and cottonwoods. Then the trail climbed out on top of slick rock and, after a couple miles, dipped back into a box canyon with the sweetest swimming hole, complete with a rock slide. Nora and Lisa had spent a few lazy afternoons sunning on the rocks, swimming and talking about life.

They'd discovered the spot together on their first backpacking trip to Canyonlands. They later learned it was a favorite spot for locals. Nora remembered one sunny day when she'd had an epiphany about her life.

Nora had sat up on the warm rock. "I know what I'm going to be when I grow up," she said to a dozing Lisa.

"The first woman president of the New York Stock Exchange?"

"That," Nora agreed, "and an advocate for the environment. I want to do business *and* conservation."

Lisa rolled over and propped her head on her elbow. "You're not as confused as you think you are."

Nora would miss Lisa's way of clarifying her life.

Nora and Abbey climbed out and followed a group of three down the road, into the lot, and onto the one-track dirt trail. Watching the group ahead stung her. They were dressed in what Lisa referred to with rolled eyes as "Moab chic." One woman wore a short black skirt and leggings with Chacos on her feet. Another woman wore a green broomstick skirt and covered her head with a battered straw cowboy hat. The guy with them sported dreds that hung down to the middle of his back and were gathered in a tie-dyed bandana. He wore baggy shorts and a wrinkled T-shirt.

Deep drifts of fine, red sand covered the grass, burying smaller shrubs and piling around the willows. The destruction of a flash flood showed in the narrow canyon. It must have been a wild hour or so as the water screamed through, drowning anything unfortunate enough to be trapped on the canyon floor. Now the sand piled in drifts, still damp from yesterday's afternoon shower, and the clump grass and white flowers of the bindweed and evening primrose poked through the surface.

Vertical walls of sandstone rose high on either side, creating a slot canyon. Their variegated layers blended from yellows to reds with blackened surfaces near the top. The leaves of the cottonwoods rattled in the soft breeze with sweeping arms creating cover from the sun.

Nora and Abbey plodded after the others. She longed to feel the strength of Cole beside her, but he had his own problems to deal with in Wyoming. He'd been tight-lipped about that on the phone the last couple of days.

The day warmed enough that Nora removed her light jacket and tied it around her hips. It slapped against the back of her shorts as she trudged up the trail. Sand squeaked under her hiking boots with every step. She'd briefly considered dressing more formally but rejected the idea, knowing Lisa would think it pretentious. The burbling creek felt too cheerful for Nora's heavy heart. Even the air betrayed Nora's mood, smelling green and moist and full of summer's growth.

The three people ahead of Nora slowed behind an elderly couple making their way up the trail. Behind her, hushed voices of more people broke the silence. Bushes closed in on the hikers, and trees shaded the path. In a few moments Nora and the others entered a large clearing created by several slick red rocks. The creek, now back to normal after the flash flood some time ago, bubbled happily as it wound around the rocks and bumped against the cliff wall.

About fifty people crowded together under the willows and elms.

Rachel stood next to the creek. Her blond hair hung straight down her back. Her pale skin only highlighted her red-rimmed eyes and nose. Nora wanted to hug her, to tell her that it would be all right—but it wasn't all right. Rachel might love again. She might build a life full of exciting and fun challenges, might go on to be successful, and each day might radiate with happiness. But as Nora knew from her own experience after her husband's death two years ago, the pain would strike at odd moments. It would rush in like a black tide and wipe out the carefully constructed levy around her heart.

Not overly dramatic, huh, Nora? Okay, well, maybe that was all flowery and nostalgic. Nora and Scott had been headed for divorce, and it's likely that after they split, Nora would have felt a measure of the loss she felt now when she thought of Scott. But he hadn't had the chance to divorce Nora. He'd been murdered.

And Nora had stood on a mountaintop in Flagstaff, in very much the same way Rachel stood here.

Nora found a place at the back of the crowd so that Abbey could lie in the shade and not be stepped on. He settled under a bush, lowered his head to his paws, and dozed.

The crowd mostly consisted of outdoors types of various ages—from twenty-somethings all the way to gray-hairs. All wore hiking or casual clothes. Nora didn't spot any of Lisa's family, and she hadn't expected to. They'd turned their backs on Lisa when she'd come out her sophomore year, and as far as Nora knew, Lisa hadn't wasted any time trying to bring them back into her life.

A man about Nora's age in faded Wranglers and cowboy boots stood by himself. He held a black felt cowboy hat that left a ring around his light brown hair. His lips flattened in a look of irritation and he glared at Rachel. Another, more handsome man stood behind Rachel, close enough to touch her. Nora wondered if he was her brother, though with his dark wavy hair, trim and fit body, and alert expression, he looked like her opposite.

22

Rachel cleared her throat. "I'm happy to see all of you here. Moon-flower was Lisa's favorite place."

Rachel's composure impressed Nora. She'd barely been able to tie her shoes after Scott's death.

"There is nothing Lisa would have loved more than all of you gathered here in the sunshine."

Nora stared at the rock under her feet and fought the lump lodged in her throat. Someone sniffled. An older man put his arm around a gray-haired woman and pulled her close.

Rachel held her shoulders erect, her head high. "What I loved most about Lisa was her one hundred percent devotion to whatever she believed in."

Nora lost her fight for control and let the tears spill down her face.

A smile threatened Rachel's pale lips. "She'd spend hours watching the giant white flowers of datura open in the evening, delighted with the hawk moths that came to pollinate it."

Rachel swallowed and continued. "After hiking trails all over the world and covering almost every foot of her beloved southern Utah wilderness, Lisa died from a freak accident. How did the land she loved so well betray her?"

Rachel's voice wavered and she pulled her shoulders back. "When we backpacked together, I always headed out on a mission. I'd pop out of the sleeping bag ready to hit the trail, putting miles under my feet. Lisa loved to linger. She'd sit quietly with one more cup of coffee and watch the sun slide over rocks, shadows changing slowly. She'd pause on the trail to watch a toothpick-size lizard perform pushups or just to listen to the stillness of the desert." Rachel swallowed a hiccup. "I loved to spend time outdoors with Lisa because she forced me to stop and appreciate what I might otherwise zoom past."

Rachel swiped at tears. "Thirty-three years weren't enough for someone so vital and passionate. She should have had a lifetime to savor, more time to help the land she devoted herself to. And I needed more years to love the woman who brought me so much happiness."

A sob sounded from somewhere to the right.

Rachel's voice hardened and rang clear in the morning sun. "It was her passion for this place, southern Utah, that killed her."

The anger in her tone made Nora lift her head.

Rachel's eyes burned into her. "I loved Lisa. But she could be stubborn." This message seemed aimed at Nora. A subdued chuckle of agreement sounded from those gathered.

"She couldn't leave well enough alone." Rachel's glare was so fierce a few people turned to look at Nora.

Rachel started to shake. All at once, her knees buckled. The man behind her leaped forward and closed his arms around her. She leaned into him and buried her head on his shoulder. He spoke in a clear, strong voice. "Rachel would be pleased if you'd join us for a reception at Read Rock Bookstore on Main Street."

Rachel's eyes looked vacant in her pale face, as if she'd used up every bit of emotional strength she possessed. She dropped her head, and the man took hold of her hand, and led her toward the trail.

Nora glanced up and met the malevolent stare of the man with the black cowboy hat. His dark eyes bored a hole through Nora's forehead. He slammed his hat on his head, pulled it low over his eyes, and stomped away.

He must have picked up on whatever ill will Rachel had directed her way.

A small group of people spoke quietly, several of them with wet eyes, some sniffing. "Obsessed with the film." "Probably exhausted." "Wonder what will happen with the film?"

Most people dribbled away from the clearing with heads down. If they spoke at all, their words were too quiet for Nora to hear.

Eventually the mourners disappeared, leaving Nora shaken. She lowered herself to the ground, and Abbey rose from his spot under the tree. He sauntered over to her and accepted her caress.

Before Rachel faded, she'd been angry with Nora. Did she think Nora was responsible for Lisa's death? Lisa had begged Nora to fund the film. Had Lisa jumped in over her head, making her careless?

The sun danced through the branches. Humidity from a recent rain weighted the air and brought out the spice of sage and muted scent of damp sand. Life continued in an almost insulting way.

Nora wouldn't have been able to stop Lisa even if she hadn't funded the film. Lisa would have found another way.

Still, Nora's being here stabbed Rachel like a splintered arrow. Nora didn't want to cause her any more pain. She decided to quietly head back to Boulder.

She stood and brushed the dirt from her hiking shorts. A flash of blue caught her eye. Her heart jumped to her mouth, and she went numb.

Maybe her kachina was here in the sacred lands of the Southwest. With a growing hope that mingled with dread, Nora faced the spot where she'd seen the color. She stared in the bushes at the edge of the clearing and exhaled. No kachina. Her heart sank just a little.

But the blue hadn't been her imagination.

A wooden box with a beautiful inlaid band of blue sat on a rock by the creek. Nora approached it, Abbey at her heels. It sat alone, oddly at home in the natural setting. Sunlight danced along the inlay. Rachel had been so lost, she must have forgotten this.

Nora placed a hand on the sun-warmed surface of the box and sank to her knees.

It was Lisa.

FIVE

THE WEIGHT OF ABBEY's head rested comfortingly in her lap. Tiny wrens and warblers chirped and flitted amid the branches. The sun warmed the crown of Nora's head. The willows swayed gently, their wispy green leaves contrasting with the deeper green of the new grass peeking out from the sand. The creek chattered along the bend. To the life in the clearing, it was just another day.

The kindest thing for Rachel would be for Nora to skip the gathering at the bookstore and head back to Boulder. But Nora couldn't leave Lisa out here. She tightened her lips.

Nora shifted to stand, disturbing Abbey. He pulled himself up and shook, starting at his head and vibrating all the way to his tail.

"Guess we're going to Moab," she told him.

Nora picked up the polished wood box. Its heavy weight surprised her. The beauty of the intricate Native American inlaid border in blue and black suited Lisa's taste. It seemed impossible that Lisa's vibrancy and energy hsd been reduced to this.

Nora trudged up the path to the empty parking lot at the trailhead. The Jeep sat alone on the side of the road. Nora let Abbey in, placed Lisa's box on the floor of the passenger side, and climbed behind the wheel. She glanced up the quiet road and twisted to see the area behind her. Two lanes stretched in both directions, empty. About a quarter of a mile to the south, the road curved east. A slight rise to the north blocked the view after several yards. Nora hadn't seen any traffic on her walk from the trailhead. Like much of the area around Moab, this was a lonely stretch of road.

It was the emptiness Lisa had found so compelling. The vast swathes of rugged spires and canyons and stunning red rock formations resulting from millions of years of wind, ancient oceans, and the hands of the gods spoke to Lisa. She felt compelled to protect them from the modern world. Lisa raved about the archaeological sites with their petroglyphs and pottery shards much like other women might babble about their babies.

Nora inserted her key into the Jeep, and as she turned it, a squawking noise startled her. For a moment she thought she had a problem with her engine, then realized it was her phone. Fay, one of the staffers at the Trust, had programmed Nora's phone with bird calls. This one sounded like an angry raven. She reached into her pack in the back seat and pulled it out.

Along with the announcement for the incoming call, Nora noticed six new voicemails. She punched a button to answer.

"Etta here." The no-nonsense blast from the chairwoman of the Board for Living Earth Trust sent the usual ball of snakes into Nora's gut. "I've been thinking about Lisa Taylor and this situation."

Did Etta think the Trust should make a tribute? A grant in Lisa's name or tree-planting event would be nice. Maybe gather money from the staff for a memorial. "What situation?"

"The film, of course. We've invested well over a hundred thousand dollars so far. The committee vote is in three weeks, so they need to see this film tomorrow, if not yesterday."

Nora's grief left little space to worry about the film. "The screening is scheduled in two weeks. I'll be back in the office on Monday. Can I call you then?"

Etta exhaled. "Today is Thursday. I don't feel we have days to waste. How close was Lisa to completing the film?"

Nora stared out her windshield at the yellow wild asters and tried to sound like a smart and savvy executive director. She failed with her first *uh*. "I haven't seen much of the footage. Lisa wanted to edit it and show it to me when it was done so I'd get the full impact."

"Oh," Etta said and paused. "I would have thought you'd be in on the whole project."

Nora lowered her voice to sound more confident. "Lisa was close to being done."

"Good. Bring it back to Boulder. I'll meet you on Monday, and we'll see what we need to do from there."

The last thing Nora wanted to do was to confront Rachel and ask for Lisa's work. "I'm not sure I can do it that soon."

Etta's long-suffering sigh wafted from the phone. "I'll get an early flight from DC and be at the office Monday." Etta didn't wait for Nora's reply. The phone went dead.

Nora tugged on Abbey's ear. "You don't think it would be awkward to ask Rachel for the film on the day of her wife's funeral, do you?" Abbey's eyes drooped at the massage.

Nora tapped at the voicemail retrieval and entered her password. "Hey, Nor," began the first message. Her heart stopped, and her hand holding the phone turned to ice.

Lisa.

When had she called? And how had Nora missed it?

Lisa's voice sounded strained. "I really need to talk to you. You know those petroglyphs I told you about? In Fiery Furnace?"

Nora couldn't focus on the words. Lisa's voice sounded so alive. Nora's eyes came to rest on the box of ashes.

"The Mormons are—well, it's at the Tokpela Ranch. There's this—oh, shit. I've got to go."

There was some fumbling on the other end, then a breathless continuation. "I taped it all just in case. You'll know where the camera is. You know ... if I can't call."

Nora listened to the silence for a few seconds before the automated voice invited her to delete the message or save it to the archives. She pressed the archive number before it disconnected.

She replayed it again and again, noting the call had come in the evening before Lisa's accident. She checked the other five messages. All were from Abigail the morning after Lisa's accident. Nora was so changing her phone plan as soon as she got home.

"She sounded scared," Nora told Abbey. He opened his mouth to pant in the warm Jeep.

Fiery Furnace was a labyrinth of rock fins and canyons in Arches National Park. While Canyonlands encompassed a huge tract of land south of Moab, Arches was a smaller, if no less dramatic, park just a couple of miles north of town. Lisa had mentioned Fiery Furnace a few days ago. What about Tokpela Ranch?

She started the Jeep and turned the wheel to make a U-turn across the lanes and head to Moab. What should she do about Lisa's call?

Just as the Jeep moved into the middle of the road, a white pickup popped over the western hill. Instead of slowing, the pickup seemed to gain speed. The driver laid on the horn.

Electricity sparked in Nora. Her mind blanked.

The truck sped toward her like a flash flood in a slot canyon, arrowed at the very spot where she sat frozen, hands on the wheel.

She stomped on the gas and shot across the road, straight into the sandy shoulder. She slammed on the brakes before crashing into a stand of willows. Abbey tumbled from the seat to the floor, coming to rest on top of the box of ashes.

Still leaning on the horn, the pickup sped past her bumper, close enough to shake the Jeep. Nora turned in her seat, spotting the black cowboy hat of the driver as the pickup slowed, eased into the right lane, and continued around the curve and out of sight.

Not nearly as shaken as Nora, Abbey scrambled back on the seat. He wagged his tail and licked at Nora's face. She managed to avoid his tongue as she sucked in a breath.

Blood that had froze in those milliseconds of panic now thinned and surged. She concentrated on breathing. After a few seconds, Nora leaned over and righted Lisa's box. Thank goodness the lid was still nailed shut. She couldn't have faced her best friend's spilled ashes.

Nora put the Jeep into reverse. It revved. The tires spun in the sand; the Jeep didn't budge. She shoved it into first and hoped to rock it to gain momentum. More spinning.

"All this rock around here and I have to find a sand pile," she grumbled. Abbey didn't care.

Nora climbed out and located the shovel she kept in the back. She went to work. The six-hour drive, the exertion, and the sun stole any crispness that had remained from her shower a million years ago at her apartment in Boulder.

She dug a trench behind the wheels, found a few large stones to line it, and reversed the Jeep. It popped out onto the road and Nora and Abbey were back in business, sweaty, irritated, and craving a cool drink.

By the time they made it to the Read Rock Bookstore and circled around the block to find parking in the back, not many cars remained.

An alley ran between the bookstore and another building that led to Main Street.

Easing the Jeep into a spot shaded by the building that would catch enough cool breeze to keep Abbey comfortable, Nora frowned at her disheveled appearance. She rummaged in her overnight bag, found a brush to run through her hair, and scrubbed the dried sweat from her face with a hand wipe from a container she kept in her glove box. It was the best she could do for now.

She pulled Abbey's collapsible dish from the back, filled it with water from the jug she always carried in the Jeep, and waited while he lapped it up.

Moab was a small town of about five thousand that spread across the valley floor. Settled by Mormons, it had served as a rural supply center for the nearby ranchers. The population expanded with a uranium mining boom in the 1950s, then contracted again when it burst. Years later, its reputation as a recreationist's dream spread. Mountain bikers and four-wheel enthusiasts gathered, followed closely by the enviros and hippie types. Trust funders and wealthy retirees building second homes wandered in, drawn by the amazing scenery. Now it had a mismatched feel. Eclectic shops featuring sweat-shop-free items comingled with farm and ranch supply stores, tourist shops, outdoor gear, vegan restaurants, and old-time diners. If the population of the area mimicked the town structures, this was one schizophrenic community.

Nora picked up the box. "Be good," she ordered Abbey before cranking down the windows for the cross breeze and leaving him to nap. Most of the vehicles in the lot were covered with the red dust of Moab. The luxury cars and expensive SUVs probably belonged to the moneyed people who had moved here for the gorgeous views and then tried to protect them from the traditional uses of the people who had lived here for generations. The old beaters most likely carried the more earthy types, those with master's degrees in biology and environmental studies who worked for peanuts for conservation nonprofits. She made her way through the alley to the front of the store and scanned the street. She nearly dropped the box.

A white pickup. THE white pickup. It sat empty along the street. Nora changed direction and approached it. She placed her hand on the hood. Warm.

With new purpose, she strode to the bookstore and wrenched open the door.

Bookshelves had been shoved to the side of the cozy shop to make room for the reception. The dark wood that lined the walls was filled with hardcover, trade paperback, and mass market titles. It wasn't a big shop, but the inventory filled the room. An old-fashioned sales counter angled next to the front door, its surface cluttered with crocks full of pens and other bookish notions. Dreamcatchers, sand art, pottery, and other Native American art decorated the walls and shelves. Nora quickly scanned the space for kachinas but didn't find any. The relative dimness of the store felt cool and welcoming, inviting people to stay and browse.

The wood-planked floor creaked with the movement of Lisa's friends as they mingled. White plastic tablecloths covered two five-foot tables in the center of the shop. Remains of a cake, sandwiches, and chips lined one table. The other table held a basket for sympathy cards and the used plates, cups, and forks from the funeral refreshments. It wasn't fancy, but Lisa had never cared about finery. If she were here, Lisa would have a few words to say about the wastefulness of the plastic dinnerware.

No one turned to greet Nora. She walked into the hushed store.

Nora spotted a guy holding a black cowboy hat. He was the same one with the hate-filled gaze at the clearing. He stood with the man who'd led Rachel from the service.

Both appeared to be in their mid-thirties. Where White Pickup Guy looked about as old-school cowboy as Gene Autry, the other man looked more boardroom suave. He wore black suit pants, cut and draped to show a well-toned lower half. His fresh-from-the-laundry blue shirt fit his broad shoulders perfectly. The conservative cut of his wavy dark hair and the tie knotted neatly at his neck gave him a professional air.

Their conversation didn't appear friendly. The dapper guy spoke, and his handsome face drew down in a frown. The cowboy looked at him dismissively. With one more muttered word, the clean-cut guy strode away.

Nora stomped over to White Pickup Guy. "Did I do something to make you mad?"

The cowboy's thin mouth turned up in a smirk. He stood several inches taller than Nora's five-foot-seven frame and looked as ropey and tough as a dried stalk of corn. Nora suspected the deep tan on his face and neck ended where the V of his shirt hit his chest. Not one gleam of friendly showed in his eyes. "Don't know what you're talking about."

Nora's heart banged away and heat radiated from inside out. "At Moonflower, you nearly killed me."

He spoke in a low, slow voice, reminding her of Cole—except Cole had never sent goose bumps over her flesh. Not the scary kind, anyway. "I didn't see anyone out there. Rachel sent me back for the ashes, but they were gone." He nodded at the box Nora held.

She hugged the box to her. "You ran me off the road and I had to dig out. You never saw me?"

His dark eyes bored into her. "Tourists, such as yourself, don't understand the local ways. They tend to get in the way and sometimes end up getting hurt." His words came straight out of a spaghetti western, but the threat behind them felt real.

Unnerved, Nora answered with bravado. "Next time, I'll call the cops."

He threw back his head and let out a guffaw. "You do that." He stuffed his hat on his head and sauntered away, cowboy boots thudding on the wood floor of the Read Rock.

Anyone watching wouldn't see her tremors. Probably. Why had she thought going head-to-head with a stranger would be a good thing?

The well-dressed guy appeared at her elbow. He raised an eyebrow in humor. "Wow. Not many people stand up to Lee like that."

She watched the cowboy's broad back. "Lee who?"

"Evans. A longtime local family."

The door closed behind Evans.

A well-established family who wouldn't want Canyonlands' borders expanded? "Does he have a ranch?"

The man at her elbow nodded and held out his hand. "I'm Darrell Burke." He said it as though they were having a casual conversation at a cocktail party.

That's when she realized she still held the box containing Lisa. Nora's face burned even more. "I'm, uh, I'm Nora Abbott."

His face opened into a warm smile. "That's obvious. You're not from Moab, and since Lisa's family disowned her, you have to be her best friend, the famous Nora Abbott."

She opened her mouth to say something but had no response. Even though he was a stranger, he made her feel comfortable.

He laughed quietly. "Lisa told me a lot about you."

Had he said his name? Nora's brain tilted on overload. Between losing Lisa, the voicemail, and the lunatic cowboy, she wasn't at the top of her game.

Lisa's box weighed heavy in her hands. She stepped over to the plastic-covered table littered with used plates and cups to set it down, hesitating. It seemed disrespectful to plop it down next to red Solo cups with dregs of lemonade and plates holding half-eaten ham sandwiches, but she didn't know what else to do with it. The sun-drenched clearing by the creek felt more appropriate. Maybe she should have left Lisa there after all. She hugged the box harder, glad she hadn't left Lisa for Lee Evans to find.

The nice guy didn't comment on the box but kept his eyes on her. "So Lee ran you off the road?"

"Right into a ditch." She set the box on the table.

"Lee has a temper. Most folks avoid provoking it. Lisa didn't." He looked pointedly at the box.

Nora asked the obvious. "If Lee didn't like Lisa, what's he doing at her funeral?"

He lifted his chin, indicating something behind Nora. "He and Rachel used to be close."

Nora turned to see Rachel standing across the room. She was speaking to a blonde woman in a silk summer suit, her back to Nora. Rachel crumpled and fell into the woman's arms. The sight brought Nora to tears.

Nora knew how Rachel felt and almost wished she could fall into comforting arms, too. In fact, if she couldn't feel Cole's arms around her, the woman holding Rachel might make a good substitute.

The handsome man followed Nora's gaze. "This is going to be a hard time for Rachel."

Nora nodded, not trusting her voice.

They watched the pair, and he spoke. "I thought I knew just about everyone in Moab, but I don't recognize that woman."

"She's not from around here," Nora said.

"You know her?"

"That," Nora started across the room, "is my mother, Abigail Podanski."

SIX

ABIGAIL STOOD A TRIM five foot six with a soft blonde bob—the perfect shade and cut to make her appear fashionable and age appropriate. She wore a beige silk suit and scuff-free heels. She and the man talking to Nora—what was his name?—would fit right in at a luncheon on Capitol Hill but were too formal for Moab.

Nora's natural inclination would be to take off in the opposite direction. But for one of the few times in her life, she actually felt happy to see her mother. After an uneasy relationship that often bordered on outright war, Nora and Abigail were forging a new bond. Well, working at it, anyway—a few ignored calls notwithstanding.

Rachel sobbed silently against Abigail's shoulder.

Nora inched around to stand in front of Abigail. "Mother?"

Abigail made eye contact with Nora. She continued to pat Rachel's back and murmur to her, "I know, dear. I've lost three husbands. I understand." In between all of this, she managed a smile of acknowledgement to Nora.

Rachel pulled away from Abigail. "Lisa thought of you as her mother."

Nora didn't know whether to wait for Abigail to break from Rachel or wander away and give them space. She backed up and into a warm body. "Excuse me."

The nice guy took hold of her elbow to steady her. "I can't even imagine her loss." His eyes filled with compassion.

Nora stepped away from him. "You must be a good friend of Rachel's."

He studied Rachel. "It's hard to get to know someone as guarded and private as Rachel. I knew Lisa better. We worked together on some land-swap issues over the years and now on this film project."

A light clicked on inside her brain. "Oh, Darrell Burke—congressman. I'm sorry I didn't recognize you earlier."

He brushed it aside. "I'm not here campaigning."

"You were helping set up distribution of the film to the congressional committee. Lisa told me you made a lot of progress."

His eyes rested on the box halfway across the room. "It was a passion Lisa and I shared. This land needs someone to protect it from over-grazing and mining, and even from too many tourists. I just wish I could have protected Lisa with the same effectiveness."

What a strange thing to say. "Did Lisa say anything to you about needing or wanting protection?"

He laughed in that sad way people do at funerals. "As if she'd allow anyone to take care of her, except maybe Rachel. She was a real force for the environment. I don't know that there's anyone who can take her place around here."

Lisa was irreplaceable, but they had to do something. "You've arranged for the committee to screen the film?"

He inhaled. "I hate the thought of cancelling it."

"Don't. We can make it. Lisa's work shouldn't be lost."

Darrell sounded sad. "As I understand it, the film isn't finished."

Nora ignored the spike of panic in her heart. "The film can make the difference in the vote."

"Still," Darrell said. "There's no one to finish it, edit it, and get it out in time."

"Don't cancel that screening." Nora watched Rachel and Abigail, wondering how and when to ask Rachel for a copy.

Darrell continued. "Obviously, I'll still lobby for the park expansion. I've got some favors to call in. We're not out of fuel yet." Nora liked the warm way his attention seemed totally focused on her, as if this problem were his only concern. She'd heard certain politicians had the ability to make everyone feel unique, and despite knowing that, she still felt a little special.

Her phone vibrated in her pocket. She glanced up at Abigail, who was the one usually calling. But Abigail still had her arms around Rachel. Nora pulled out the phone and glanced at it. A little thrill raced through her, as it usually did. "Excuse me," she said to Darrell. "I've got to take this."

She spun away and headed for the door. She punched the answer button and stepped into the sunshine, letting the door close behind her. "Cole." She exhaled his name with a mingle of sorrow, hope, and longing.

She felt his support through the phone. "You sound stressed."

She found a spot of shade under the store awning and leaned against the stucco wall. "I wish you were here."

"I'm sorry. I know this is tough. How are you?"

Nora watched an ant scurry along the sidewalk. "I'm okay. Abigail is here."

"That's good." A long pause followed.

When Cole didn't continue, she asked, "How's your father?"

"He's in the hospital in Sheridan. He's not doing well."

Another brick piled on their load. "How about your mother and brother and the ranch?"

Silence fell as the little ant darted on its erratic path. Finally Cole spoke. "When do you think you'll be home?"

Nice nonanswer to her question. Things must not be going well. "That's hard to say. I need to get Lisa's film. I'm hoping to do that this afternoon and head out later. There're no hotel rooms here so I'll probably stay in Grand Junction overnight."

"Isn't the film digital—on the cloud or something?"

Nora nodded as though he could see her. "Probably. But I don't know where. I need to talk to Rachel about it." Nora sighed. "It's bad timing to bug her today."

"Then don't. Come home. I can get away from here for a day or so and meet you there."

She craved being next to him. "I'd love to. But I really need to get that film."

"It can't wait a few days?"

The ant wound back around. He didn't seem to be making any progress. "Etta called and jumped all over me. This is a big deal."

"That woman doesn't have any compassion for people—just the environment." Cole knew about Etta from Nora's conversations.

Nora nodded again. "I pushed for this film. I guaranteed the board that spending a hundred thousand dollars would give Canyonlands its best shot at Congress. I've got to see it through."

"Maybe you can do a scaled-back version. You ought to let Rachel have a day at least." He sounded like Darrell.

"You're right. But … " She wanted to suck that last word back.

"But what?"

Might as well tell him. "I had a voicemail on my phone that I didn't get until today. It was from Lisa."

"When did she send it? Why didn't you get it before now?"

Another ant joined the first. "Don't know. Abigail's probably right about the service I contracted."

"What did Lisa say?"

"It wasn't so much what she said, it was how she said it. She sounded scared. Then she hung up abruptly."

He sounded concerned. "Scared? What about?"

One ant scurried away, leaving the other on its own. "She said she taped whatever she had to say, so I guess I can get the camera and find out."

There was no smile in his voice. "If you think it seems fishy, take it to the cops and let them deal with it."

Again, the pause felt uncomfortable. Good thing they didn't have to carry on a long-distance relationship because they both were bad on the phone.

The door of the Read Rock opened, and a group of people came out and headed for the parking lot.

"I'd better go," Nora said. "I'll call you when I know more."

"Right."

"Well, bye."

A slight pause. "Nora?"

"Yes?"

"I love you." He hung up.

Nora stood in the shade of the building. The ant must have dashed from her sight when she wasn't looking. A chill ran across her skin. While it was always nice to hear those words, Cole didn't use them often. Like, maybe once before.

This meant something.

But what?

SEVEN

THE SUN SHONE BRIGHT on Central Park and streamed across the thick carpeting in the office, but Warren stuffed his arms into his cashmere cardigan and shuffled to the thermostat on the wall. He pictured healthy cells decked out like gladiators swinging their broadswords to cut down the pale cancer cells.

The image didn't hold up. He hated to admit the warriors had dwindled to only a few holdouts backed onto the cliff face. The cancer army stood poised to run them through. *I only need a few more days.* Maybe God would listen to his plea.

His desk seemed miles away across the expanse of his office. The plush carpet felt like deep sand under his feet as he focused on the leather chair behind his desk. He loved this office. He'd chosen everything in it to fit his needs and desires. Christine and her platoons of decorators ruled over the rest of the penthouse, but no professional decorators had set foot inside his office. He allowed the cleaning lady in and, reluctantly, Christine.

He succeeded in making it to his desk. The beat-up oak monstrosity had belonged to his grandfather. It had sat in the corner of the sitting room for half a century until Granddad passed over. By then, Warren could have afforded any world-renowned artist to customize his desk. But he wanted this reminder of his roots in Utah. It helped him to remember that possessions were only vanity, and in the end, they didn't matter. His grandfather was a righteous man, dedicated to both the church and his many children, grandchildren, and great-grandchildren. Warren had no doubt Granddad waited for him on the other side. But like everyone who had come before him, Granddad depended on Warren to complete the task God had set before him.

Warren dropped his head and leaned heavily on the desk. His focus strayed to the architectural drawings spread on the rough surface. He pictured the actual structures the lines represented with satisfaction.

No one else could have done what Warren had accomplished. Why would God call him home before he saw it through to completion?

The answer was obvious.

Humility. God fulfilled his promise through Warren. Together, they'd done the impossible. Warren would be rewarded, along with all his ancestors. He just wouldn't lead the final exodus.

Who would?

Warren had it narrowed down to two of his nephews. Neither of them had Warren's strength or his brain. Why hadn't God provided a successor for such an important job?

"My goodness, it's like an oven in here!" Christine swept into the room, pulling Warren from his plans.

The heels of her pumps left mini craters in the carpet as she swished across the room in her flowing black pants and jacket like a queen strutting around her chambers. She adjusted the thermostat.

Warren straightened and strode to the chair, costing himself too much in an effort to appear strong. "I thought you were having lunch with Amanda Reynolds."

Christine folded her arms, her back to him as she studied a framed five-by-seven-foot artist's rendering of the solar system. "That was hours ago." She tilted her head one way, then the other. "I don't understand why you have this here."

Of course Christine wouldn't appreciate Warren's fascination. "Reminds me of our place in the universe."

She spun toward him. Warren wished he could capture the energy she wasted on her quick movements. "It seems out of place here."

"Can I help you with something?" On a good day he could indulge in chatter. This wasn't a good day. Christine didn't enter his sanctuary often, so she must have a reason.

She ignored his question and wandered over to an amateur's painting of an old-fashioned white barn with red rocks in the background. "Has Bourne Financial weathered the recession?"

Money. She wanted to know if the giant financial conglomerate Warren had created would keep her in style. "Yes."

She left the painting, crossed to the far side of the room, and stood in front of a slab of sandstone he'd had extracted from a Utah cliff. Unknown hands had etched designs into the rock more than a thousand years ago. "How much do you think this petroglyph panel is worth?"

Heat rose to his face and his heart beat faster. "It's not worth much since I can't sell it on the open market."

She kept her back to him. Christine had a head for numbers. She had come to his office to appraise his treasures and see what she might expect in a payoff when the cancer finally won. "It came from your family's ranch, didn't it?"

He wanted to rise from his chair and pull her away from the panel. Her calculating eyes felt sacrilegious—especially as she focused on the figure of a person in what appeared to be a boat. "Doesn't matter if it was private land. You can't cut into a petroglyph panel and remove it from the rock. It's a violation of the Antiquities Act."

"So you having this here is illegal?"

He didn't answer her. She knew this. Maybe she wanted to drive home the point that she knew his secrets. That brought a smirk to his face.

"So why did you want this petroglyph? It just looks like a bunch of stick people with big heads. It's not nearly as remarkable as the drawings of horses or deer."

An electric shock of pain made a circuit up Warren's spine to the base of his skull. He closed his eyes against it and waited for the worst to pass. "What's on your mind, Christine?"

With practiced nonchalance, she started toward him. Her voice sounded young and lilting. "My goodness. You have such an interesting mix in here. I don't know much about decorating"—he scowled at her blatant lie—"but I think they would tell you to pick a theme. You have this barn picture that looks like a first-year art student with little talent painted it, then kachina dolls and pottery on shelves and the strange mix of astronomy and rock art."

"I'm not interested in what a decorator thinks." It came out as a short-tempered growl. "What is it you want?"

Her lower lip protruded. "I haven't seen you much lately. I thought maybe we could catch up."

Clouds brushed across the sun and the shafts of light on the carpet disappeared, as if God was toying with a dimmer switch. "Actually, I'm glad you're here." Her practiced grin made her face sparkle as if she delighted in this news, when Warren knew it was nothing more than the effort of a consummate actress. "We're going to Moab Saturday."

Her well-shaped eyebrows shot up. "I can't make it. I've got two committee meetings."

"You'll have to reschedule. Darrell Burke is running a close race, and we need to throw our weight behind him."

She shifted into a sympathetic tone. "It's Utah, dear. Darrell is Mormon. I can't see there's a crisis."

Bile rose in Warren's throat, and he waited it out. "Darrell isn't traditional and can't count on the Mormon vote. He's going to need our help."

"You should concentrate on you now. The chemo's made you weak, and you shouldn't be running around the country." She paused for effect. "Darrell needs your money, not your personal testimony."

He didn't have the strength or the will to parry with her. "Tell me why you're here."

Her lips tightened and her dark eyes lasered in on him. She lowered herself to a leather-covered client's chair opposite his desk and stared at him. "I don't know how to bring this up," she began.

He watched her struggle for the right words that wouldn't make her sound like a vulture. Maybe he held a modicum of responsibility for what she'd become. Thirty years ago she'd been a vibrant, loving young woman. She'd grown up in New York in wealth and privilege. She hadn't even finished her undergraduate degree at Columbia, something she was certainly smart enough to complete, when they met at one of her father's cocktail parties.

By that time, Warren had already accumulated his first million. But he'd divvied up those profits into investments and needed a cash flow so he wouldn't miss out on the opportunities opening before him. More than that, he needed a wife. Back then he had considered a career in politics, and that required a bright, well-connected, impeccably raised woman by his side.

That was before he'd found his true aptitude lay in creating huge wealth. That kind of money could buy whatever politics he wanted without him having to suffer public scrutiny.

Warren had only loved one other woman. Puppy love, really. Christine, with her fine breeding, dark beauty, and social ambition was a completely different species than the naïve, simple blonde of his college days.

Christine and her trust fund entered his life at the right time. He gave her value for her money, though. She wanted an ambitious man, one who would provide for her, not only financially but give her the kind of notoriety and status even money couldn't assure.

It sounded cold in retrospect, but he'd loved her. He thought she'd loved him. Through the years of toil, when he'd spent eighteen to twenty hours a day amassing a fortune whose dimensions only he knew, the disappointment of no children and the demands of great wealth had evaporated their affection, leaving only a functioning business arrangement.

Finally, Christine spoke. "What has the doctor told you?"

He leaned back in his chair. "I've got cancer."

She tilted her head in annoyance. "Yes, I know that much. But you won't allow me to accompany you to your appointments or consultations with your medical team. I have no idea what's going on."

"You mean, you don't know how long you have to wait for me to die."

Her shoulders slumped the tiniest bit. "I've upset you."

"No. This disease upsets me."

She pushed herself from the chair. "I'll go."

He waved her down. "You want to know how much money you'll have when I'm gone. Is that it?"

A flush rose to her cheeks, but she remained where she was and nodded. "I don't like talking about this, but I'm ignorant of our holdings. I'd hate for the estate to wither from neglect after you've gone."

She made it sound as though her concern was for his legacy. "Don't worry. I had Darrell draw up papers for a generous fund for you. The rest is not your concern." He'd left her more than enough to last into her dotage.

Her face tightened. "That's generous of you to take care of me, but what about your businesses and investments?"

"It's all down to one holding. And the rest will go to the church."

He didn't need to wonder how this news struck her. The pale face and wide eyes revealed shock. "One holding? How is that possible?"

He smiled at her. "I've invested in an important project." The most important since Noah's nautical venture.

"What project?" Her voice sounded strangled.

He pushed his chair from his desk with shaky arms. "It's time for my medication. Please excuse me."

He envied her quick jump to her feet. Her flushed face indicated the panic that must be raging inside. "It's not fair that you don't share the details of the estate with me."

"I've left you a hundred million dollars. If you live frugally, it should last. The houses, of course, are in both our names, as well as the yacht, art, plane, and cars."

She nodded, cool as January snow. "And the bulk of the estate?"

"Invested in the family ranch." He watched her, fascinated by her self-control.

She drew in a long breath. "Your entire fortune is invested in a cattle ranch?"

He grinned. "It's a very nice ranch."

EIGHT

THE LITTLE BELL ABOVE the door tinkled and the wooden floor creaked as Nora walked into the Read Rock. The musty smell of old books lingered in the cool air, making the shop feel comforting after the blazing sun outside.

Nora realized she'd been holding her breath. She let it out and inhaled. She'd never heard such heaviness in Cole's voice. He had to be hurting about his father, but he didn't want to talk about it. She'd give him time before she pushed. Maybe he knew how much Lisa's death pained her and wanted to give her support. She wanted nothing more than to hurry back to him and feel his arms around her. But first, she needed to get a copy of Lisa's film. According to Lisa, she'd completed everything except one video session and the final edits.

Darrell stood in front of her, all warm sympathy again. "You're frowning. Are you worried about the presentation to the committee? Don't be. Even without Lisa's film, I'll make a great case for expanding Canyonlands' borders."

No simple presentation would pack the wallop that viewing the iconic landscapes would. Lisa had created time-lapse footage with stars and sun trading places and views of pristine sunrises juxtaposed with damage from tar sands mining.

If there was no film, Nora might as well start sending out her résumé again. Just the thought of leaving the Trust hurt. Nora's position at Living Earth Trust was so much more than a paycheck, even a much-needed one. For twenty-five years, the Trust had done good work for the environment. But recently, it had been tainted with scandal and murder and corrupt leadership. In the last few months as executive director, Nora had worked endless hours repairing its reputation. She'd flown from coast to coast meeting with past and potential donors. She'd staked her personal integrity, taking responsibility for the programs and policies coming out of the Trust. Another disruption could finish the Trust, and all the good work would stop. Nora would lose the anchor of a job that gave her life meaning.

Darrell's voice brought her out of her funk. "It'll be okay. I can be very convincing. You can come with me, and together we'll make the committee understand the importance of preserving this area."

Maybe Darrell was right. Probably he wasn't. "I'll get a backup of the film and figure out how to edit it," Nora told him.

Darrell looked skeptical.

The door opened again. The sunshine outlined a slightly stooped, thin man with a halo of unruly hair.

Nora grinned. "Excuse me," she mumbled to Darrell, leaping around him and running the two steps to fling herself at the grizzled old man. "Charlie!"

His arms circled her in a bear hug. "You are a vision of loveliness."

She loved the way he always spoke, as if acting in a melodrama. "I didn't know you were here, too!"

He patted her arm. "It's tough when your friends leave this world. Your mother and I thought you'd need us with you."

Nora squeezed his hand. "I'm glad you're here."

He scrutinized her. "How're you holdin' up?"

Why did he have to ask? Her throat closed up, and she fought tears.

"Nora. Dear." Abigail spoke from behind Nora.

Nora didn't anticipate her reaction when she turned to see her mother. She stepped into Abigail's comforting embrace, probably surprising them both.

Abigail patted her back. "There, there." Her soft words lasted only seconds. She took Nora by the shoulders and held her at arm's length. Abigail reached up with a tissue that had magically appeared in her hands and dabbed at the tears streaming down Nora's face. "Since you don't wear makeup, at least you don't have black streaks." Yep, typical Abigail. Thank goodness some things didn't change.

Abigail lowered her voice. "You have to be strong for Rachel. She's going to need you now." Then she turned to Charlie. She placed her white hands on either side of his Velcro face and planted a solid kiss on his lips. "Thank you for parking the car, dear."

Charlie glowed in his worship of Abigail.

Darrell approached them. He held out his hand to Abigail. "Hi. I'm Darrell Burke."

Abigail slipped her hand into his and smiled. "Abigail Podanski. This is my husband, Charles."

Charles? Nora raised her eyebrows at Charlie. He had been one of her closest friends for years. But once he'd laid eyes on Abigail, he'd been a goner. No one, ever, in a million years, would think of him as Charles. No one, that is, except her mother.

Charlie locked eyes with Nora, shrugged, and gave her a little grin.

Darrell shook Charlie's hand. "Were you friends with Lisa?"

Abigail's mouth tightened. "What a lively spirit. I can't believe it's been snuffed out. How did you know Lisa?"

Nora tuned out while Darrell explained. She looked around the bookstore. All the guests had disappeared, leaving only their little group and Rachel.

Charlie nudged Nora and tilted his head toward Rachel. Rachel stood alone, her eyes unfocused.

She should go speak to Rachel. Nora understood how confused and alone a person felt, how you quit thinking and doing ordinary things when your spouse dies. When Scott died, Charlie and Abigail had helped Nora.

Nora took a tentative step toward Rachel, then another, and soon stood directly in front of her. She opened her mouth to ask about the film but couldn't do it. "Can I drive you home?"

Rachel's head snapped up and her eyes focused. The sorrow turned hard. "You..."

Abigail appeared and took Rachel's hand. "It looks like everyone has gone. Charles is bringing the car around. We'll take you home."

Rachel gave Abigail a tired smile. "Thank you."

Abigail linked her arm with Rachel's and they started for the door. Abigail looked back at Nora. She raised her eyebrows, indicated the box on the table and Nora, and gave her head a "come-on" wag. Translation: Bring the box to Rachel's house.

Great idea. It sounded like Rachel blamed Nora for Lisa's death. The last thing she needed was for Nora to traipse into her home uninvited.

And yet, there sat Lisa. Since Nora had brought her from the creek, it seemed like her responsibility to look out for her the way Lisa had always looked out for everyone.

Nora remembered the first week of their freshman year at CU. She'd been in the communal bathroom on their dorm floor, brushing her teeth. Someone was taking a shower. A pale girl from several doors down crept into the bathroom. She slipped into a stall. Within seconds, the sound of sobbing wafted over the stall walls.

Nora didn't know what to do. She couldn't pretend she hadn't heard the poor girl's misery, but knocking on the stall door seemed inappropriate. She stood, paralyzed by indecision.

Water turned off in the shower and the curtain swished aside. A petite girl with dark hair that curled despite the weight of the water drenching it wrapped a towel around herself. She strode to the closed stall door. "My name is Lisa. What is it, honey?"

"Please. Go away." The girl's voice barely carried in the echo chamber of the tiled bathroom.

It was as if Lisa broke a barrier and Nora was able to act. She joined Lisa at the stall door. Together they talked the girl out of the stall and coaxed her to talk.

Charlotte came from rural southern Colorado and trusted everyone. The attention of an older guy thrilled and flattered her. Until the creep got himself invited to her dorm room, didn't understand the word no, and nearly raped her.

As soon as Lisa got the story, she stomped from the bathroom, not bothering to dress. Nora bounded after her, and they burst into Charlotte's room in time to confront the weasel.

It still tickled Nora remembering Lisa, with the towel barely covering her, giving the shocked creep what-for.

Nora and Lisa had been friends ever since.

Curtains concealing a passage at the back of the bookstore parted and a tall woman peered out. She scanned the store, eyes resting briefly on Nora and dismissing her. She flowed out of the back room and into the store. She appeared to be around fifty and had the face of someone used to being outdoors: weathered and wrinkled, browned by the sun. Her gray hair was shorn short enough that it spiked at the top of her head, and the large hooped earrings she wore dangled nearly to her shoulders. She wore a long skirt and blouse in the deep reds, oranges, and golds of a desert. She appeared solid and strong under the rich fabric.

She moved with purpose but didn't hurry as she reached under the counter and pulled out a trash bag. She started at the refreshment table, tossing the disposable dishes into the bag.

Nora felt she should say something. "Can I give you a hand cleaning up?"

The woman didn't look up. She wound the plastic table covering, careful to keep the crumbs from spilling out. "I can do it."

"You must be Marlene," Nora said.

The woman stopped moving. She raised her eyes to Nora. They were dark and full of suspicion. "That's right."

Nora tried to look harmless. She didn't know why Marlene should be worried. "I'm Nora Abbott. A friend of Lisa's."

Marlene studied her. "The one who gave her the funding for the film."

Nora nodded. "She loved this bookstore. She told me she spent a lot of time here."

Marlene turned pale. A moment passed, and she started to breathe again. "I'm going to miss her."

She moved on to the next table. Nora met her there and picked up empty plates and cups. She stuffed them in Marlene's trash bag. "She told me this place was her office away from home. She liked to come here when she felt stymied."

Marlene's mask of control slipped. Her smile looked heavy, like sand after the tide. "She was so smart. So quick-witted. She had that sort of energy people envied." Marlene stuffed the table covering into the bag. "You knew her a long time, didn't you?"

Nora nodded. "Since freshman year. Sometimes we wouldn't see each other for a while, but every time we talked, it was like picking up the conversation mid-sentence."

Marlene nodded and tied the bag. "She was special."

Nora followed Marlene to the sales counter. "It was really great that we could work together on this film."

Marlene stared out the front window. "She was committed to it. Maybe more than she should have been."

"What do you mean?"

Marlene turned her focus to Nora. It felt as though her dark gaze seeped inside of Nora, exploring her worthiness. After a moment she spoke slowly. "It caused problems between her and Rachel."

That landed heavy on Nora. "She didn't say anything to me about it, but I had suspicions."

Marlene raised one eyebrow. "It's hard to overcome your up-bringing."

Lisa had said the same thing.

Marlene moved out from behind the counter and flipped one of the tables over. Nora worked at folding up the table legs. "Because she's from here?"

Marlene hefted the table and set it against the wall. "Rachel loved Lisa. The Mormons aren't so big on lesbians. Until Lisa showed up, no one knew Rachel was gay. But suddenly, here is Lisa with all these liberal notions of protecting land that's been in their hands for generations, *and* she scoops up one of the local girls."

"People around here didn't like Lisa, is that what you're saying?"

"No, what I'm saying is that people around here hated Lisa."

"But so many people came to the funeral."

Marlene smiled. "The people who loved Lisa aren't locals. They're the transplants, the newbies, the outsiders. They aren't Mormon. They love this land just as an art aficionado loves Rembrandt. The old-time Mormons love it as a member of the family."

Nora gave Marlene a questioning look.

"It's this way: The environmentalists want to preserve it. Tread gently on the trails, gaze at the arches and hoodoos. Sit quietly and contemplate its beauty. The Mormons want to live on it, work it. Fight with it to give them sustenance, care for it so it stays healthy and productive. Do you see the difference?"

Nora summed it up. "Conservationists want to put it in the parlor and cover it in plastic, and locals want to sit on it and watch TV?"

Marlene laughed. It changed her whole appearance. She went from stern and formidable to friendly and accessible, and Nora could see why Lisa had found refuge in this place and with this woman. "Not exactly how I would put it, but you get the idea."

They moved to the next folding table, the one that held Lisa's ashes. Marlene clenched her fists, her face suddenly pasty.

Nora reached for the box and transferred it to the counter next to the cash register. "You weren't out at the creek, and you didn't come out of the back room while everyone was here."

Marlene busied herself with clearing the table. "I'll say goodbye to Lisa in my own way."

Fair enough. Marlene seemed a curious mixture between stern and loving, restrained and straightforward. "Did you and Lisa talk about the film?"

Marlene brought her eyes slowly to Nora's. "She talked about it to everyone. You know Lisa—whatever churned in her head frothed out her mouth."

"She said she only had one more shooting session and she would wrap it up."

Marlene dumped the table over and Nora hurried over to help fold up its legs.

Marlene straightened and stared out the window again. Maybe she waited out waves of pain to keep from breaking down. "Everything she did was the most important thing. The next moment, there would be a new most important thing. She leaped from peak to peak." Marlene hefted the table across the room.

Maybe Nora wouldn't have to bother Rachel. "She didn't happen to leave a backup here, or do you know where she stored them?"

Marlene slammed the table on the floor and spun around. "How should I know? If I felt like chatting about Lisa and her life and her work, I'd have joined the gathering at the creek or at least come out of the back room. I lost my friend, and I don't feel like being social."

Nora's face burned. Her whole body felt on fire from Marlene's anger. She hurried across the room to retrieve the box. "I'm sorry. I'll go."

Marlene geared up. "You all come in here with your tears and sorrow. You tote around her ashes as if they were a gym bag or yoga mat. You'll go home to your lives, doing what you were doing before this incident disrupted you. But I'll be here. Missing her every day."

Nora didn't want to spook the majestic Marlene during her meltdown.

"She's not going to fly through those doors, nearly sending the bell sailing across the room. She won't open new shipments of books and oooh and aahhh with me, falling in love with every title. No more sharing tea in the mornings or a bottle of wine on a winter evening." The hot tears Marlene refused to shed coursed down Nora's face.

Marlene's shoulders never sagged; her backbone remained straight, chin raised. "You didn't see her eyes light up and hear her words tumble out faster than she could keep up when she came in after a day of shooting or scouting locations. You don't know what I'm going to miss. Every. Single. Day. For the rest of my life."

Nora's voice filled the silence. "She loved you, too."

Marlene broke. Like an avalanche on a rocky mountain, first one boulder broke loose, followed by a few more, gaining momentum and power. Marlene folded over and gasped, massive sobs shaking her.

Nora placed a hand on Marlene's heaving back, keeping watch while the big woman mourned. After several minutes, the sobs tapered off and Marlene straightened, only slightly less regal.

Nora strode to the sales desk and found a box of tissues. She pulled out several and hurried back. Marlene accepted them and wiped her eyes.

If it were anyone else, Nora might lead her to the oak library table and sit her down, pat her hand, or rub her shoulders. Instead, she stood silently and waited.

Marlene focused out the window again. Tourists meandered outside the door. She inhaled deeply. "Lisa was right. You're a good person."

Nora allowed a smile. "You know, she was my best friend."

Marlene nodded.

"And at least a dozen other people who showed up today called her their best friend, too," Nora said.

Marlene dabbed the last of her tears. "She was that way, wasn't she?"

"I need to go out to Rachel's. Are you going to be okay?"

Marlene tilted her head and gave Nora an are-you-kidding-me look. "Leave that door open on your way out. I've got books to sell."

Nora understood drawing all that pain and anxiety deep inside to form an impenetrable ball of strength. "Sure. I hope you don't mind if I call you."

Marlene frowned at her. "Why?"

Nora traced the bright blue band on the box. "You might have some insight into what Lisa had planned. I've got to finish the film."

Marlene came around the sales counter to face Nora. "That's a bad idea."

"Sort of like someone taking Hemingway's unfinished novel and publishing it. I know I won't get it the way Lisa would have wanted, and heaven knows it won't be as good. But I need to finish it."

Marlene's weak moment had definitely passed. "Are you some kind of idiot?"

Nora was lots of kinds of idiot but didn't know which kind Marlene meant.

"Do you honestly think Lisa slipped and fell? Use your brain. Someone didn't want her to finish that film, and they found the most effective way to silence her."

NINE

THE SPOTLESS BENTLEY EASED to the curb and Warren braced to step out, knowing his neuropathy would shoot pain into his feet. "I won't be long, so circle around."

Ben nodded. "Sure thing, Mr. Evans."

Ben's easy manner and friendliness saddened Warren. He'd always liked Ben, ever since he'd brought him here from Salt Lake City thirteen years ago. Back then, Ben had been a homeless runaway, just one of the countless others Warren had given a hand up.

Warren pulled himself out and patted the top of the car to send it off. He pushed aside the stinging in his feet and strode through the bustling crowd to the glass doors and into the plush office building. He rode the elevator twenty-one stories up and exited to one of his shell corporation's headquarters. The attractive receptionist, who had no idea what business was transacted there, greeted him. "They are in the conference room waiting."

Warren liked to personally greet the new immigrants whenever possible. A good leader took the time to know his followers, and even though Warren wouldn't go forward with them, giving them individual attention would create a more cohesive group.

He entered the window-lined conference room with a grin. "Welcome to America. How was your flight?"

The straight-backed man looked exhausted. From the carefully vetted application and extensive Skype interviews, Warren knew Hans had made a respectable fortune in construction in Germany. At forty-five, he'd never had any serious health issues, left behind no siblings, and his parents were deceased. His wife, Katrina, likewise had no extended family. They had brought their four children with them.

Katrina and the children looked equally worn out by the overnight flight from Germany. Two boys, ages six and eight, sat together in one leather chair. The oldest, a girl of thirteen, blinked bleary eyes at Warren. Katrina leaned back in another chair with their youngest, a cherub with pink cheeks and dark ringlets who stretched across her lap, sleeping.

Hans jumped to his feet and shook Warren's hand with enthusiasm. "Mr. Evans. I'm honored. I had no idea you would meet us personally." His English, though precise, was heavily accented and halting. Warren insisted all the immigrants speak English.

At the sound of voices, the little girl opened her eyes. She flashed an immediate smile and sat up, rubbing a hand across her nose. With that minor transition between sleep and play, she slid off her mother's lap and hopped to the two boys. Her little tennis shoes twinkled with lights in the heels.

Hans glanced at her but didn't give her his complete attention. He seemed oblivious to the precious gift of his daughter. Abundance bred thoughtlessness. If he could, Warren would have scooped her up just to hear her giggle. He'd tousle those soft curls, tell her a story, grant her every wish.

Hans's eager eyes sought Warren. "You are a man of true vision. I can see that God speaks through you." His voice sounded sincere even if his words felt prepared.

Warren tried to deflect adoration. "God speaks to us all if we listen. As scripture tells us, we all have the capability to become brothers to Jesus Christ."

Hans nodded eagerly. "Yes. Yes. I believe and that's why we've come to join you."

Katrina's worried smile showed a little less enthusiasm, but joining her husband demonstrated obedience, a trait lacking in most modern women.

Warren's feet throbbed and he needed to return to the penthouse to rest. "You'll be met at the airport in Denver and given keys to a vehicle big enough for your family and luggage. Maps to Moab will be inside."

"Thank you, Mr. Evans," Hans said.

"It's best if you go straight to the compound. But if you get lost, my nephew's phone number is included with the maps."

Katrina stood and thanked Warren with a more fluid English than Hans. "I have studied the scriptures, taking special interest in those you pointed out. I see how the timing is perfect, how this is what God asks of us. I appreciate you allowing us, our children, for inclusion."

The praise the immigrants heaped on him made him uncomfortable. "There are still a couple of days until the solstice, so enjoy the beautiful scenery. The compound is isolated, but be vigilant and stay out of sight."

They thanked him again and Warren turned to leave.

Before he pulled the door open, he gave in to his desire. Even though it cost him the pain of several extra steps, he went to the little girl and placed his hand on her head. To Hans and Katrina, it probably looked like Warren was blessing her. In reality, the feel of the soft curls and skin still warm from sleep blessed him.

TEN

Despite the blazing mid-day sun, Nora felt chilled. Clutching Lisa's ashes, she trudged around the bookstore to the parking lot. Local antagonism over the feds snatching more land ran high. Lisa had been accosted in restaurants and lambasted in the local paper. But would the locals feel threatened enough to kill her?

Marlene's ominous insinuation had to be the fallout from grief and anger.

Still, Lisa had sounded scared in that voicemail.

Nora shivered in the shade as she stood in the alley next to the bookstore. She glanced up to see if clouds had moved in for an afternoon monsoon rain. A flash of blue in her peripheral vision made her freeze.

Someone had scribbled graffiti on the side of the bookstore, too high to reach on foot. In blue spray paint they'd imitated countless rock art figures throughout the Southwest. This collection of drawings consisted of big-headed figures with antennae, the profile of a saucer-shaped boat with a person sitting in it, and some giant human-type figures holding goats or antelope in their hands. Toward the bottom the symbol from her dream jumped out at her. Three concentric circles, sort of like a target, with six sets of two parallel lines radiating outward. It looked like a weird sunburst. Goose bumps rose on her arms.

Oh, for heaven's sake. Her imagination was up to its usual mischief. Shaking her head, she crossed the lot to the Jeep. She balanced the box on her hip, pulled the Jeep key from her pocket, and unlocked the door. Abbey uncurled himself from where he'd slept in the passenger seat and stood. He delicately stepped over the gear shift, wagging his tail in greeting. He stuck his nose toward Nora for a hello pat and jumped from the Jeep.

Darrell popped around the corner of the bookstore. His face lit up when he saw Nora. "Hi again."

Nora couldn't help but notice Darrell's good looks. If he hadn't gone into politics, he would have made a terrific movie star. Even his saunter spoke of assurance laced with an animal sensuality. A comparison to John F. Kennedy hit her. Women voted for Kennedy in droves because of the same qualities she observed heading toward her across the broken blacktop of the parking lot.

Abbey lifted his head at Darrell and stepped up to greet him. Darrell bent down and offered Abbey the back of his hand to sniff, then rubbed him behind the ears. "This your dog? He's a handsome old guy."

Nora glowed with affection for him. "Abbey's like any gentleman—the gray around the muzzle only adds to his distinction."

Darrell laughed. "I'll remember to resist the Grecian formula when my time comes. Abbey? But he's a male?"

Unbidden, Nora's mind flashed to an older Darrell with a smidgeon of salt to go with his pepper-dark hair.

Cole. She loved Cole. An immediate rush of warmth surged through her again. Strong, capable, kind, and funny Cole. She missed him even though it had only been a few days since they'd gone in different directions. No wonder he'd said he loved her on the phone. He was feeling that tug, too. "He's named after Edward Abbey."

Darrell considered that with a tilt of his head. "The conservationist. That makes sense. Are you staying in Moab tonight?"

Nora motioned for Abbey to climb into the Jeep. "I've got to go to Castle Valley. Abigail and Charlie took Rachel home, and I'm still on Lisa duty." She indicated the box.

Sadness fell on Darrell's face. "I can't wrap my head around Lisa being gone."

Nora placed the box on the floor in the back seat and wedged a backpack and fleece pullover around it. "I'll get in touch when I find the film."

He stepped to her door after she climbed in and said, leaning over her window, "I'm available for whatever you need."

"Thanks." She turned the key. A weak sound like the final movement of a wind-up toy rose from the engine and faded. She twisted the key again, and this time a click greeted her. One more twist resulted in the same click.

Darrell raised his eyebrows. "Sounds like you've got trouble."

She tried once more. Nothing. Drat—and lots of other words she didn't want to blurt out. Slamming the steering wheel wouldn't solve her problem and would only make her look like a spoiled brat in front of Darrell, so she clenched her fists in her lap. She reached for her pack to find her phone. "I'll call Abigail and Charlie."

Darrell put a hand on hers to stop her from dialing. "Don't do that. I'll take you to Rachel's."

"But it's twenty miles."

He chuckled. "Yeah, I know where it is."

Of course he did. This was his district. She hated to impose on him but couldn't stand the thought of prolonging Rachel's ride by making Abigail return for her. "Okay, thanks. That would be great. I saw a Conoco station a couple of blocks up the street. Can we stop there and see if they can work on it?"

He opened her door and she slid out.

He pulled his phone from his back pocket. "That place will gouge you. They feed off tourists. I know a better place." He dialed and arranged for a tow while Nora let Abbey out and grabbed her pack that contained an extra change of clothes and the barest of necessities. If Abigail was true to form, she might have scored a suite somewhere in town where Nora could crash on the sofa for the night.

Darrell slid his phone into his pocket. "All arranged. Ready?"

He led them to a shiny dark blue Toyota 4Runner.

"I'm sorry about Abbey," Nora said. "You probably aren't used to hauling dogs around in your backseat."

Darrell grinned at the dog. "I live in Moab. Keeping a vehicle clean is a challenge I deal with regularly." He pointed a key fob at the back window and it slid down. He reached in and pulled out an old blanket.

Nora set Lisa's box in the back and tossed her pack beside it.

Darrell spread the blanket in the backseat, let Abbey jump in, and he and Nora settled in the front seat.

The 4Runner sported leather seats and a black interior. It felt like riding on a cloud compared to Nora's geriatric Jeep.

Darrell glanced at her. "So tell me about Nora Abbott."

She gave him a sideways glance. "Going all politician on me?"

He tilted his head back and laughed. "Got me."

"Why don't you tell me about you instead?"

He shifted his eyes toward her. "That's a boring story."

"We've got a half-hour. Bore me."

ELEVEN

Nora admired the beauty of massive red and black cliffs as they rose on either side of the highway that wound along the Colorado River east out of Moab. She inhaled the heated afternoon air that blew in the open window. Willows, Russian olives, and tamarisk lined the banks and whipped in the afternoon wind. At this point in its journey, the Colorado hadn't gained the power and wildness that was its trademark as it made its way through the Grand Canyon. But it ran high enough to accommodate adventurers in their colorful rafts bouncing in the waves.

Rain clouds built in the distance to fuel the over-active monsoon rains of this season.

"That's a big sigh," Darrell said.

Nora dug for a smile. "I was thinking about all the river trips Lisa and I took together."

Darrell laughed. "I joined her on a trip last year. We were having trouble getting funding for the Canyonlands film, and she decided to invite a few potential donors for a river trip."

"Since she ended up coming to the Trust for money, I'm assuming the trip didn't go well," Nora commented.

He gave her an irresistible grin that promised whatever adventure he cooked up was sure to be fun. "It started off great. We had sunshine and a light breeze to keep the bugs at bay. But things went downhill pretty fast when one of the older gentlemen kept ordering Lisa around like she was a waitress."

"Uh-oh."

"You know how everyone takes turns with chores on a river trip? This guy didn't do anything. Two nights before we pulled out of the river, we were sitting around the campfire after dinner. Lisa and I had just finished cleaning up the dishes and settled in with the group when this old duffer raised his empty glass and nodded at Lisa to get him a refill of wine."

"Did she toss him into the river or just his sleeping bag?"

"Actually, Lisa smiled as sweetly as I've ever seen and took his cup. I thought maybe she would sacrifice her pride for the good of the film."

Nora laughed.

"Yeah, I didn't know her very well then."

"So what did she do?"

"She walked back with the last two bottles of expensive cab he'd brought along. When I saw the look on her face I jumped up, but I was too late. She lifted the bottles and poured them on the rocks of the fire ring."

Nora could envision Lisa's fiery eyes. "He was lucky."

"Classic Lisa." Darrell laughed. "It took all of my people skills to keep him from decking her. I'm not sure he ever understood what he'd done wrong."

"Lisa was okay with you defending her?"

The twinkle in his eyes showed his shrewdness. "She didn't know about it and I wasn't going to tell her. As far as she knew, he realized his error and donated much less than she'd hoped."

"I see why you're a successful politician."

"Ouch." He grew serious. "I didn't do it for a vote. I'm pretty sure I lost that one. I did it because we needed the cash for the film. It's important work."

"Yes. But politicians tend to do what's expedient for their careers, not necessarily what's right."

Red cliffs blackened by unrelenting sun rose in majestic splendor on Nora's right. Rows of tourist cabins nestled in a grassy meadow that led to the river on the left.

Darrell glanced at her, then back to the road. "You're right, of course. And I'll admit to a little hedging here and there. Quid pro quo. But not on something this serious."

"A sincere politician?" The resignation in his eyes made her regret she'd teased him.

"People never trust my integrity. But I was raised to do what I believe is right. We lived on a ranch and worked hard. I learned that if you ever want to gain a person's trust, you've got to do what you say. There's no faking true belief."

"You've never taken a stand you didn't believe in just to get the votes?"

His dark eyes, full of good humor, flicked to her again. "Not on the big issues. And Canyonlands is huge. If we destroy the land, it can't be replaced. And the cultural sites, the rock art, and archaeological treasures are beyond value. I can't compromise on that."

"What makes you so committed to this place?"

"It's in my blood," he said. "My family is from around here. I believe in my legacy as a son of Utah."

She tried to gauge his sincerity.

One eyebrow cocked up in humor. "You're doubting me."

"How could I question you?" she teased. "You're our voice of Canyonlands. Single-handedly, you're carrying our message to Congress."

He waved his hand in a come-on motion. "And I'm ruggedly handsome and completely irresistible."

No denying Darrell was attractive, but he couldn't compete with Cole for her heart.

He grew serious. "I was born here. But what most people don't know is that my mother was one of three wives."

"Polygamists?" She couldn't hide the surprise in her voice.

He nodded with a sad smile. "It's not in my official bio, so this is between you and me. When I was fourteen, my father kicked me off the ranch. He'd picked my half-brother as successor and didn't want any other men around the place."

"Fourteen?"

"It's pretty young. But I got some help to get to Salt Lake City and I managed to finish school. That's when I met Warren Evans."

"THE Warren Evans? Bourne Enterprises Warren Evans?"

Darrell grinned.

"With a friend like that, I'll bet you don't have to set up many campaign fundraisers."

A slight frown creased Darrell's face, then disappeared. "Warren may be wealthy, but he's frugal. Probably has to do with his Mormon upbringing. He didn't give me cash outright, but he buried my embarrassing past so deep no one will find it. Now my bio simply says I was raised by a single mother." He eyed her. "Again, this is not for public consumption."

"Why are you trusting me with this? We just met."

He chuckled. "I'm an amazing judge of character. That, and you're Lisa's best friend. That's good enough for me."

She frowned at him.

"Okay. I feel like maybe you understand what it's like to not always fit in."

How did he know this? She squirmed, not comfortable with confessions. "Maybe I've never really felt like I belong, but my upbringing wasn't nearly as traumatic as yours. I'm sorry you had to go through that."

He shrugged. "Makes me stronger. Why did you feel like an outsider?"

He had a way of making her want to talk, which was unusual for her. "Sounds cliché, but I didn't have a father. I didn't fit with the geeks, even though I got good grades. I didn't fit with the druggies, and I wasn't an athlete."

"What happened to your father?"

Her father. Now that was a mystery. What was he like? If he'd had the chance, would he have loved Nora, nurtured and raised her? "My mother manufactured a tale about a young man who fell out of love and left. She wanted me to dislike him so I'd never search out my roots."

"Why would she do that? Is he a celebrity?"

Nora shook her head. "I've never been able to decipher Abigail's thought process." The truth turned out to be more complicated than the fiction. "My father was a Hopi. Don't ask me where my red hair comes from; that might be a mystery I never solve."

He considered the news. "Did it bother you to find out you're Hopi?"

"No. It's strange, though. In the last couple of months I've been able to spend a few weeks on the mesas in northern Arizona. My new cousin, Benny, has been trying to teach me the responsibility of being Hopi."

"As I understand it, Hopi are pretty secretive."

"They've been really nice to me on the rez, but they won't tell me about their secret ceremonies." She watched the clouds building for an afternoon monsoon storm. "I try not to worry about it too much. I have a job that fits me and a boyfriend I love."

Darrell lifted an eyebrow. "What inspired you to be an environmentalist, and what brought you to the Trust?"

"It certainly wasn't the way I was raised."

Darrell nodded. "Abigail? She seems lovely."

"She's not the fire-breathing harpy I saw her as while I was growing up. And I could do a lot worse. But we've had our difficulties. Right now, I'm trying to be a grown-up and appreciate all the good things about her."

"That's enlightened."

Nora couldn't claim success. "It's progress."

He laughed. "So Abigail isn't a conservationist. What happened to you?"

"I grew up in Boulder, so me being an environmentalist is sort of like a baby beluga knowing how to swim."

He accepted that and kept probing. "But you're more on the business side than the science side."

"I owned a ski resort in Flagstaff and decided the best way to turn a profit was to make snow." She didn't see any reason to address the whole Hopi-kachina-visiting-her-and-choosing-her-to-protect-the-sacred-mountain issue.

"After realizing my misguided ways could have led to disaster, I decided to work for an environmental protection organization."

He gave her a sideways glance. "You wanted to use your powers for good."

"Exactly." She paused. "Or to be honest, to make reparations for the damage I almost did."

"Guilt."

She hesitated. "Maybe. But I'm proud of the work we do at the Trust. We're making strides on the pine beetle problem in the mountains and we've done a lot of research on cattle grazing impacting the way ranchers are using their lands."

"And Canyonlands," he prompted.

"Yes, Canyonlands. This is my first big program for the Trust. All the other projects were in place when I became executive director. But Lisa's film and the campaign to enlarge the park is on me."

He kept grilling her. "So you need to make it succeed or your career is toast."

"No. I need to make it succeed because it's important."

"And your career has nothing to do with it?"

She realized the trap she'd fallen in and laughed. "You're good."

That charming twinkle hit his eyes. "I know."

He flipped on the signal and turned right, skirting along a rock ridge. The black face of the rock absorbed the afternoon sun.

"So now you're back to guilt," he said.

"What are you talking about?"

His eyebrow shot up again as if he questioned her declaration of innocence. "You facilitated Lisa in her dream of creating this film and saving Canyonlands. She died trying to fulfill the quest, and now you feel you need to complete it for her to make her death meaningful."

Maybe Darrell was a politician because he was so insightful or maybe he was insightful because he was a politician. Whatever chicken-or-egg scenario, he dug too deep inside Nora for her comfort.

His mentioning Lisa dying in association with the film brought back Marlene's hint that Lisa's death wasn't an accident. The message Lisa left on her phone seemed ominous, too.

He glanced at her. "I didn't mean to upset you."

She felt her scowl and lightened her expression. "I was thinking about a voicemail Lisa left me that I didn't get until this morning."

He turned off the highway onto a steep one-lane road into Castle Valley. "That must be bittersweet to hear her."

The massive hoodoos called Preacher and Nuns that marked the edge of Castle Valley glowered down on them. "She said some things that don't make sense."

Darrell slowed in anticipation of turning off the highway. "Can I hear Lisa's voicemail?"

Nora cued it up, and he listened while they wound through the sleepy enclave of Castle Valley.

Castle Rock, the reason for the settlement's name, towered above them on the left. It looked like a fortress built to defend the community from the outside. Castle Valley, a small community of houses, filled the grassy valley. The original settlement snuggled in a green expanse shaded by old growth elms, cottonwoods, and willows. The rest of the houses were scattered along the scrubby valley floor between towering canyon walls.

Large tracks of undeveloped high desert terrain separated the houses, isolating them with scrub oak and juniper shrubs. The residents ranged from the very wealthy—retired or living on trust funds—to aging hippies who had accumulated enough to afford a modest home to the young people keeping close to the land with little more than a sleeping bag and camp stove. But the people who lived in Castle Valley were Moab's outsiders. They didn't own cattle or raise crops. They didn't run the gas stations or the hometown grocery store.

Darrell handed the phone back to her. "She sounds upset. She said she'd hide the camera. Do you know where?"

"I don't have a clue. Lisa could be so dramatic."

Darrell agreed. "She could overreact. That's for sure."

73

"If I had any insight to Lisa's brain, I could find the film and camera myself. I hate asking Rachel to get me the film."

They turned onto a gravel lane and continued for a mile.

"Give her a little time. If there are copies, she'll come around eventually."

Eventually. The word dropped like lead in Nora's stomach.

Darrell pulled into Lisa's winding driveway. The cabin hid behind trees and shrubs, not fully visible from the top of the dirt driveway with its deep ruts. After several yards, they rounded a slight curve. Abigail's champagne-colored Buick sat close to the front porch. Lisa's rusting black Toyota pickup was parked in the weeds next to the cabin, and Rachel's Passat snuggled behind it.

Several other vehicles lined the side of the dirt driveway heading to the road. Didn't this funeral ever end?

Nora's phone rang, and she answered. The garage mechanic explained the damage was a minor problem with her starter, but they needed a part that couldn't be delivered until late that afternoon. She hung up. "Damn."

Darrell raised an eyebrow. "Trouble with your Jeep?"

She shook her head. "Not really. I'll have to stay overnight, though."

"You need a ride back to town?"

No crisis, just annoying. "No, I'll get my mother to take me."

"Okay." Darrell eyed the vehicles parked on the road. He pulled the key from the ignition. "At least Rachel didn't have to come home to an empty house."

No one stood on the front porch so they all must be inside. "I suppose they're Rachel's family."

Darrell opened his door and climbed out. "I doubt that. They're not exactly supportive of her lifestyle."

"You'd think the outside world of the rich and artists and all those left-leaning people moving into Moab in the last twenty years would have desensitized the locals to lesbians. But I guess it's hard for old timers to change."

"It's not just her marrying Lisa."

Nora picked up the box and climbed from the 4Runner. She let Abbey out to trot off. "They're mad about expanding Canyonlands?"

He swung the door closed and came around the vehicle to walk with her. "To them, it feels like she's trying to steal their land."

Lisa's cabin was not one of the tonier houses in Castle Valley, but Nora had loved it from the moment she saw it ten years ago. Made of native logs, the front porch ran the length of the cabin, raised from the front yard by three steps. The railing around the porch made it look like a set piece in a spaghetti western.

Lisa had given her heart to the old place, renovating it room by room. She still needed to do some work on the foundation and re-place some windows, but she'd succeeded in creating a perfect home for her and Rachel.

Lisa had placed four Adirondack chairs on the porch. Before Rachel and her artistic talent, an ordinary forest green paint covered the chairs. Now they bore bright images of nature scenes and animals, sort of like useful totem poles.

Darrell's kind eyes touched her. "Are you going to be okay?"

No. "Yes."

"If you're sure, I'll head back to town. I have to make some arrangements for a community meeting in Moab on Saturday afternoon. If you're in town, why don't you stop by?"

Life continues. "Of course. Thank you so much for bringing me out here."

Darrell's smile warmed her like a cozy fire. "I'm glad we met. I'm looking forward to working with you." He placed a hand briefly on her arm.

She watched him climb back into the 4Runner and reverse down the rutted driveway.

A pair of hiking boots with dried mud caked on their soles sat next to the door. Nora caught her breath at the sight. She knew they were Lisa's by the size. For a short woman, Lisa had unusually big feet. They'd been the subject of many jokes over the years. Nora stood on the grass, unable to move.

The front screen door squeaked open. Charlie appeared. "Nora?"

She forced her eyes away from the boots. "Yep. Coming."

Charlie stepped onto the porch and waited for Nora to climb the stairs with the box. She nodded toward the door. "Is everything okay?"

Charlie rubbed his grizzled chin. He spoke in a falsetto. "There's not a stitch of food in the house. And it's inconceivable the neighbors haven't brought casseroles and cookies. And not even any coffee."

His Abigail imitation made her laugh.

"And," he continued in the same voice, "there's only one roll of toilet paper."

"Sounds like Abigail will get it set straight. It's her superpower."

Charlie nodded. "The only good thing is that everyone will have to up and leave soon and let poor Rachel have some peace."

Nora stared into the darkness on the other side of the screen and heard a murmur of voices. "Maybe she doesn't want peace. It's tough to be alone."

Charlie followed her gaze.

The weight of Lisa's box pressed into Nora. Maybe asking for Lisa's film would actually be good for Rachel—help take her mind off her grief.

That was a stupid thought. Rachel didn't want to think about the film.

"I'm being sent back to town with this." He held a long list written in Abigail's perfect penmanship.

Maybe Nora should help Charlie with his mission.

"Nora," Abigail called from inside the house. "I need you."

No escaping now. Nora raised her eyebrows to Charlie. "I've been summoned."

"We live to serve," he said. For Charlie, that was true. The moment he'd seen Abigail when she stood in the parking lot of Nora's ski resort in Flagstaff, he'd handed over his heart.

She watched Charlie take the steps and hurry to the Buick on legs kept spry by his daily forest ramblings. He climbed into the car, looking as out of place as a can of Pabst Blue Ribbon at a champagne brunch.

Nora scanned the yard and spotted Abbey investigating the pines on the other side of the driveway.

Nora missed Lisa. The girl she'd stayed up all night with, watching old movies and talking about how they'd change the world. Lisa always felt comfortable in her own skin. She knew herself and felt confident about her place in life. Lisa might not have told her parents she was a lesbian until her sophomore year at CU, but she'd never hidden it from them. It hurt Lisa that her parents couldn't accept her, but she understood, even at that young age, everyone lives their own life.

It angered Nora that Lisa's parents had turned away. Lisa didn't have time for anger. She had things to do. Nora admired Lisa's confidence.

Spring break their sophomore year Lisa had planned a backpack trip in Canyonlands. It would be her first time visiting southern Utah and she'd been talking about it for a month.

Nora sat on Lisa's bed in the tiny dorm room while Lisa laid out her supplies and gear on the other bed. "Come with me, Nor. We'll have a blast."

Nora's feet itched to be laced into her hiking boots. "I can't. My mother and Berle have an Easter brunch planned, and Abigail commanded I attend."

Lisa put her hands on her ample hips. "That's Abigail's deal. What would you rather do?"

Nora could almost feel the chill of dawn and the first burst of sun over the horizon. "You know I'd rather go backpacking."

Lisa flipped her dark waves over her shoulder. "Then get your pack. We leave first thing in the morning."

"Abigail would have a fit. I'd pay for this for the rest of my life."

Lisa clicked her headlamp on to check the battery. "Only if you allow it."

Nora leaned forward, feeling the inkling of possibility. She sat back. "You don't know Abigail the Terrible."

Lisa shook the canister of fuel for the camp stove. "It's your life, chica. Abigail has her own."

Nora stood, jumpy at the thought of outright rebellion. "Yeah. But I should—"

Lisa spun around. "Should? Do you want to live your life for everyone else? Who are you?" It wasn't rhetorical. Lisa stared her down, waiting for an answer.

Nora's face burned. If she backed down now, she'd look like a weenie. She could defy Abigail and go backpacking. "Okay. I'll do it."

Lisa didn't budge, didn't smile. "Nope. You're not invited anymore."

"What?"

Lisa shook her head. She picked up a packet of dehydrated beef stew. "You're only going because I bullied you into it."

Tongues of frustration licked at Nora. "I love backpacking."

"So why does it take me badgering you to go?"

"I'm going now. That's good enough."

Lisa turned back to her gear. "Of course you can come with me. I'm super excited to have you, and we're going to love it. But you really ought to figure yourself out, chica."

The clatter of dishes sounded from inside the cabin, and Abigail's voice wafted through the open screen. "Why don't you lie down, dear? You've been through so much today." From the volume and tone, Abigail was sending a message to people that it was time for them to leave.

Rachel mumbled something.

Nora addressed the boots silently. "I'm still trying to figure out who I am."

Abigail opened the screen door and stepped out on the deck. "Come in here. Rachel needs you."

Rachel probably had tons of friends she'd rather talk to than Nora, a woman she barely knew and had never really connected with. Still, if Abigail thought Nora could help Rachel, she ought to give it her best shot. Maybe she'd be able to gently ask about the film.

Abigail met her on the porch. She lowered her voice in conspiracy. "Try to get rid of those people. Rachel needs to rest."

"Who are they?"

Abigail threw a disgusted glance at the screen and the low voices inside. "Environmental activists, from what I can tell. They're discussing their next meeting and protest with no consideration of Rachel."

"Where are you going?" Nora asked.

Abigail descended a step. "I can't send Charles to the store on his own. He gets the store brand or organic or local or who knows how he decides. It's rarely on quality and taste."

"So I'm supposed to clear the house and wait for you to get back?"

Abigail hurried down the remaining three stairs. "That and comfort Rachel."

Nora balanced the box against her belly, opened the screen door, and stepped inside.

Nora hadn't been to the cabin since Lisa and Rachel married. Significant differences from when she'd been here last jarred Nora, but once she thought about it, she realized the changes were normal. As Lisa and Rachel twined their lives together, their house would morph from simply being Lisa's to theirs. And now, just Rachel's.

The screen door opened into a sunny great room. Hardwood floors stretched out, bright Navajo rugs spread at odd angles. Heavy leather furniture added to the lodge theme. Frameless canvases of desert flowers, much like Georgia O'Keeffe paintings, hung on the walls. As was evident with the porch chairs, Rachel's painting style here was unmistakable.

The kitchen sat off to the left, a breakfast bar separating it from the great room. French doors framed an office at the far end of the room. Lisa's massive pine desk, reclaimed from an old government office and refinished by Lisa's determined hand, sat littered with papers and file folders. Her laptop rested amid the debris, the top up as if Lisa had momentarily walked away.

Stairs led off the left of the doorway, heading up to the three bedrooms on the second floor. Even though Lisa had bought a four bedroom, she'd ripped out a wall, installed another bathroom, added a balcony, and created a romantic master bedroom with an incredible view of Castle Rock as a wedding gift for Rachel.

Rachel stood in the kitchen, hands on the breakfast bar, staring across the great room at a window between two of the giant flower paintings. Her eyes didn't seem to focus on the mountains in the distance.

Two thirty-something women flanked her. They seemed focused on their conversation with the two men standing in front of the mantel of the fireplace. A gray-haired woman and man sat on the leather couch.

A lively discussion filled the room. "I think we need posters showing tar sands damage and we don't make a sound."

"Yes! Like those pro-life posters of half-aborted babies. Demonstrate the evil. A picture is worth a thousand words."

"That's stupid. We should do like PETA. Remember when they splashed blood on women wearing fur?"

"It was paint. And that won't work."

The arguments flew around the room with everyone stepping on each other's sentences.

Nora crossed the room, the floor creaking as she passed Rachel's line of sight. "I'm going to set this in Lisa's office."

Rachel's eyes slowly focused on Nora, and she gave a short nod.

"Why bother with a protest around here, anyway? These people have their minds made up."

"Besides, they aren't the people voting."

"Heath's got a point. We should go to D.C. and picket on the Capitol steps."

"Not everyone is a trust funder and can fly all over the place."

Nora entered the office. To the right, another set of French doors opened out onto a low redwood deck without rails. Abbey lay on the warm wood, dozing in the sun. He acted as though he'd been here dozens of times and knew his way around, which, of course, he had— just not in the last couple of years.

The deck was one of the first things Lisa had refinished after buying the cabin over ten years ago. The plumbing hadn't been up to snuff, and smelly carpet had covered the floors. The windows were tiny and leaked with the slightest breeze, but Lisa installed the French doors and built the deck because she needed contact with the land and sky. She loved the view of the La Sal Mountains and, most days, wasn't content to see them from behind the doors.

Her desk faced the doors, which she kept open in all but the worst weather. She loved watching the jagged peaks, purple in the morning, turn green and brown and black as the sun played against them. She said their grandeur reminded her to be humble.

Like the sculptor who finds the image hidden in stone, Lisa had discovered the beauty of the cabin. But Nora had to admit Rachel's art and decorating touches made the home bright and comfortable. More than once Lisa had raved about how Rachel had improved her life: "I had no idea how much I needed a wife!"

A wood-burning stove nestled in the corner opposite the deck. An antique pine cabinet sat along the wall, its surface scattered with piles of papers. Nora pushed several file folders out of the way and set the box on the desk. Lisa couldn't look at the view anymore, but somehow, placing her ashes there made Nora feel better.

Voices rose, reminding Nora of Abigail's orders. She spun around and returned to the living room. Rachel no longer leaned on the counter between the two women. Nora glanced around the room and out the screen door. Rachel sat on one of the Adirondack chairs, leaning forward, her face to the mountains.

Nora held her hand up. "Thanks for being here for Rachel. I know she appreciates your concern. But it's been a long day. Please call and visit again."

A couple of the people looked confused. Some seemed to take Nora's words at face value and got ready to leave. At least one woman scanned the room for Rachel, and when she realized Rachel was no longer with them, looked stricken and ashamed.

Nora ushered them out the front door. The storm clouds blotted out the sun and a few drops plopped onto the porch roof. While they said their goodbyes and offered to help Rachel in any way, lingering on the porch, Nora returned to the office.

She stood in the center of the room, feet planted on a blood-red Navajo rug. Her eyes scanned the surface of the desk and the shelves, traveling to the cupboard doors and across to a pine filing cabinet. Where would Lisa keep copies of the film?

Soft raindrops pattered on the deck. Nora hesitated. Lisa still lingered in this house, in the office, and Lisa hated anyone messing with her stuff.

Lisa and Nora had shared an apartment the last two years of undergrad in Boulder. It drove Nora crazy the way Lisa cluttered the tiny space with her books and papers, socks, sweaters, shoes—everything. Nora would gather all of Lisa's things from the common space and deposit them in Lisa's bedroom. That led to a major confrontation and a compromise. Nora wouldn't mess with Lisa's stuff if Lisa would try not to clutter the living room.

"This office is like you, Lisa—messy, beautiful, and bright." Nora wrapped her arms around herself.

Outside, Abbey stood and shook. The rain didn't appear too serious so Nora left him to enjoy it.

She ran her fingertips along the edge of the desk while her eyes took in the chaos of papers on top. Lisa worked in a whirlwind, often losing items or forgetting appointments. Rachel's hand kept order in the rest of the house, but this office belonged to Lisa.

Nora slipped around to the desk chair and sat in front of the opened laptop. "Where did you put the film?" she spoke, even if Lisa couldn't hear.

Abbey stretched, circled around twice, and flopped down again.

Without the film, Nora's best option would be to collect photos and write narration for Darrell. That seemed like a poor solution. Even with the amazing landscapes, a slideshow seemed stagnant. To stir the committee's passion, they needed movement, light, breathtaking sights, and ugly images to demonstrate the threat.

Nora slid her finger on the laptop's touchpad and waited for it to wake up. She surveyed the pinion and juniper outside. The sun broke out, highlighting individual raindrops. The tangy smell of sage drifted through an open window.

The sound of car engines indicated the activists must be on their way.

Nora glanced through the file icons on the computer's desktop. Nothing indicated a film project. She found the directory and looked through that, too. She opened a few files that might have contained some portion of the project. Nothing. No notes for narrative, no digital pictures, and certainly no film.

Abbey no longer sprawled on the deck. Nora pulled herself from behind the desk and crossed the room, peering out the doors in search of him.

She located him by the movement of ginger hair against the scrub and sand. He trotted toward the front of the house. Maybe Charlie and Abigail had returned. If so, they hadn't been gone long.

Nora popped open the doors. She stepped out on the deck polka-dotted by drying raindrops. It took her a moment to recognize what she heard.

Rachel's voice sounded irritated. A man responded, matching her heat. Nora jumped to the edge of the deck, ready to dash to the front of the cabin if necessary.

The sight of Lee's white pickup stopped her. She inched a ways before she spotted Rachel and Lee standing in front of the hood of the pickup. Lee held Rachel's hand and only a couple of feet separated them. Lee's head bent and Rachel's raised face was only inches from his. Nora couldn't see their expressions, only their profiles. Their anger dropped away and they stood, motionless. They communicated without words. These were not the movements of strangers.

Nora backed up and retreated to Lisa's office. She clicked the door closed and stood in front of it, staring into nothing, trying to understand what she'd seen. Her eyes slowly focused on the Navajo rug. She lifted her gaze to the bookshelves next to the wood stove.

She already suspected Lisa's death might not have been an accident. Maybe Lee killed Lisa so he and Rachel could be together, Nora thought wildly. Right. That made sense because people always killed someone instead of just asking for a divorce. Sheesh, Nora. Jump to conclusions much?

Her eyes came to rest on the jumble of loose pages and books, pamphlets, and magazines scattered on the bottom shelf. Wait. What was that? There, thrust between stacks of papers, she caught sight of a DVD case, the slim black edges barely visible.

Nora rushed across the room and squatted down. She snatched the case, excited to see the DVD nestled inside. Lisa's bold handwriting dated it May 28. No year. But if it was this year, this DVD was only three weeks old. If it was a backup, it would only be missing images from a couple of shoots.

Hope swelled in her chest. This might save the day.

Nora lunged for the laptop, fingers running along the sides, looking for a disc drive. Damn. The newer machine didn't have one. Desperate, she jumped from the desk and rummaged through the debris scattered across its surface.

She yanked out a drawer. The wood stuck. Nothing but files and notebooks. She shoved against it and tried another drawer. This time she hit pay dirt. An external drive sat amid discarded phones and charger cords.

Nora pulled it out, sweeping her hand through the dead and dying electronics. She came up with a USB cord and quickly attached the driver to the computer and inserted the DVD.

This was it: Lisa's work. Something for Nora to hold on to.

Nothing but a whirr of digital and black screen. Nora's heart shriveled.

The screen flashed bright and suddenly sprang to life with a broad view of the cliffs. Time-lapse photography took the scene from dawn to midnight in a matter of seconds. Stars shone bright, then faded as the sun swept across the sky and reemerged. The image faded to a creek, the same spot Lisa's box had rested just that morning. Again, the images on the screen shifted to show a trampled, barren creek bed eroding away and leaving desolation behind. A gushing black flood of tainted water showed the uglier side of tar sands mining.

Lisa's film. Edited but without narration. Nora and Darrell could finish it. No one with a heart could turn down the chance to protect this iconic landscape. Lisa had done it!

"What are you doing?" Rachel's ragged voice demanded as she stood in the doorway between the living room and kitchen.

Nora jerked and sucked in air. "You scared me."

"This is Lisa's office. She'd hate for you to be in here."

Nora couldn't point out that someone, sometime would have to be in here and pack up Lisa's life. Maybe sharing the news that Lisa's work would go on might help Rachel. "I found it."

Rachel's face blackened like a storm cloud. "Found what?"

Nora spun the laptop around to face Rachel. "The film. I suppose it's missing the last bits, but we can totally use this."

"Where did that come from? There were no backups."

Nora pointed toward the bookshelf. "I found it, buried."

"No! No more. Leave it alone." She leaped forward. Before Nora could stop her, Rachel grabbed the computer and jerked it off the desk. The attached player dangled from the upraised computer. Rachel brought the laptop down on the side of the desk with all the rage of an abandoned wife. "I won't have it!"

She raised her arms and smashed it again and again.

Nora kept her eye on the external drive that swung back and forth, occasionally smashing against the side of the desk. As long as Rachel's temper tantrum focused on the laptop and left the player alone, the film would survive.

Rachel grabbed the cord of the player. She yanked it from the computer and threw the laptop with enough force that it crashed against the bookshelf and fell to the floor, separating the screen from the keyboard. She held on to the drive and ejected the DVD.

"No!" Nora cried as she lunged across the desk.

Rachel gritted her teeth and, using both hands, brought the disc down on the corner of the desk and leaned her weight on it. It bent slightly, then snapped with a popping that might as well have been a BB to Nora's heart.

TWELVE

RACHEL STOOD IN FRONT of Nora, panting with spent rage. Her flashing eyes dared Nora to challenge her.

Heat surged through Nora, her hands clenched in their urge to throttle Rachel. The film. The only copy she knew existed. All Lisa's work—her passion, her talent—destroyed in a tantrum. She stifled the frustrated scream, fighting to understand Rachel's grief but really wanting to smack her.

"Why did you do that?" Nora barely restrained her temper.

Tears glistened in Rachel's eyes. "Forget about the film."

"But it was Lisa's dream!"

Rachel flung her arm in the air. "If you'd never given her funding, she'd have had to give it up. She'd be alive now."

There it was, the familiar guilt drenching her. Nora fought to keep from drowning in it again. "Her death was an accident."

Rachel spit her words at Nora. "You keep believing that."

Marlene had said it, now Rachel. Nora kept her voice slow and even. "I understand how you feel."

Contempt dripped from Rachel's words. "You don't know anything about how I feel."

Sadly, Nora probably understood more about it than either liked to admit. She knew because her husband had been murdered. It had felt like her heart had been ripped out, leaving a raw, bloody hole. She'd barely been able to breathe, let alone believe she'd ever smile or laugh again.

Nora stepped toward her, intending to reach for Rachel's hand or put an arm around her.

Rachel stepped back. "I won't have anything to do with that film."

Nora nodded. "Okay. I … " She was going to say she understood but stopped herself. "Saving Canyonlands meant so much to Lisa. She believed, and I do, too, that her film would make all the difference with the committee. I'd like to finish it for her."

"It's not safe to continue." Rachel's thin lips disappeared in her anger.

"What do you mean?"

Rachel skirted Nora and stomped into the living room. "You have no clue what it's like around here. The Mormons—my family and everyone I grew up with—believe they own this land. And why not? They came here when it was empty. Nothing."

Sure, empty—except the indigenous people scratching out their existence, migrating and living off the land. The first people to live around here were the Anasazi, and the Hopi believed they were descended from the Anasazi. That would make them Nora's ancestors. The Anasazi wrote their history on the rocks everywhere throughout this place. They built shrines across the land.

Rachel spewed in her rage. "My ancestors were persecuted. They were chased from New York to Illinois and Nebraska. They only wanted to live their lives in peace. They sacrificed every luxury to move west and settle here. It was a hard life, but they survived. And now you do-gooders, who think you know what's best, are trying to steal their sanctuary."

Nora kept her voice calm. "Protect it, not take it away. We're only trying to keep it alive and safe for future generations."

Rachel glared at her and let out a bitter laugh. "Sure. Because the Mormons are stupid and haven't been good stewards for the last hundred and seventy years."

Nora didn't mention the riparian areas ravaged by tromping hooves. Overgrazed, arid pastures that blew sand, creating such severe dust storms that highways had to be closed down. "Things can't stay the same way they've been. The land won't last."

"The Mormons believe in stewardship. Joseph Smith wrote about taking care of the land and the animals so we'd have abundance."

"We're trying to use science to conserve the land," Nora explained.

"From what you call over-grazing. What they call making a living," Rachel countered.

"Grazing cattle out there is inhumane. There's not enough for them to eat."

"These people, my family, only want to raise their children the way they were raised."

"Expansion of Canyonlands can't destroy a livelihood that doesn't exist because the land has been exhausted."

Rachel's hands shook and tears glistened. "It's their land, and people who don't understand their way of life are trying to steal it. Do you know what that's like? It'd be like social services barging into your home and taking your child because they don't agree with your religion."

A kinder person would not say anything. "Is that why someone killed Lisa?"

Rachel's eyes widened until Nora thought they'd pop like water balloons. "Don't say that."

"Lisa climbed like Spider-Man. She wouldn't have fallen from that ladder."

Rachel dropped to a brightly padded Morris recliner and buried her face in her hands. Nora sat on the sturdy pine coffee table in front of Rachel and tried to peer into her face. "You said as much yourself."

Rachel lowered her hands and stared at Nora with dead eyes. "Leave it alone. You can't bring Lisa back. If you keep after this, you might have an accident, too."

"So you're just going to ignore that someone might have killed Lisa?"

Rachel glared at her.

Nora stood. "I'm going to the cops."

Rachel jumped to her feet. She took two steps toward the galley kitchen and spun around. "Don't do that."

"Why not?"

"Because the law around here is Mormon. They'll take care of their own, but if you go telling them what to do, you'll only get in trouble. And I mean big trouble."

"I can't just leave it alone."

"I'm begging you! Go back to Boulder and the Trust and find another project. The planet is a mess—surely you can find another way to spend your time and money."

"If I could find a copy of Lisa's film, I'd be out of here right now."

"There is no copy. I destroyed them all."

"They weren't yours to destroy! They belong to the Trust." Nora wanted to hit something. She placed her palm on her forehead, trying to think. "Did she put anything in a safe deposit box, maybe? Or store it in the cloud?"

Rachel lowered her eyebrows. "It's not like home videos of a birthday party. This stuff can't be put in the cloud. And believe me, I've thought of every place Lisa might have stored a backup. I've destroyed them all. Every one."

"There was that one on the bookshelf."

"You won't find another. Go home."

"But if Lisa was murdered…"

"She wasn't!"

"Who wasn't what?" Abigail interrupted, opening the screen door on the front porch.

Rachel startled and spun toward Abigail. "You're back."

Abigail's sandals clicked on the wood floor, then thudded on a Navajo rug, then clicked again. Charlie dogged her, balancing several grocery sacks. "Put them on the counter, dear."

Charlie obliged and retreated to gaze out the window.

Abigail pulled gourmet coffee from one of the bags, followed by a bottle of white wine. "You said 'she wasn't' and sounded all worked up. I asked who *she* was and what *she* wasn't."

Rachel shrugged. "Nora thought Lisa planned on going to D.C. to screen the film and represent the Trust, and I said she wasn't."

Abigail bustled about the kitchen putting the groceries away. It looked like she'd bought all the basics. It's true that Abigail's presence often turned Nora into a raving lunatic, but sometimes she knew just what to do. In this case, it was making sure Rachel's kitchen was stocked. "I have to agree with Rachel. Lisa, while I adored her, would never have been good presenting her case to Congress."

Abigail set a bag of pasta in a cupboard. "Nora, you can be very cool, almost standoffish. You should be the one to make a professional presentation, and Darrell can supply the charm."

Nora ignored the insult nestled in there. Rachel's lie had slipped out so easily. She must have plenty of experience with them. She could be lying about more backups.

Charlie spoke softly. "Don't see your Jeep anywhere."

A stab of annoyance flashed. "It's not going to be fixed until tomorrow. Can you give me a ride back to town?" Nora asked.

Abigail inserted a corkscrew into a bottle of Chardonnay. "We can drop you on our way home tomorrow."

Rachel sat on a barstool made from pine and covered with a woven cushion similar to the Navajo rugs. She rested her cheek on her hand and watched Abigail.

"I need to go tonight."

"Why tonight?" Abigail asked. The cork extricated from the bottle with a cute little pop. "Your Jeep won't be done until tomorrow."

"I need to get a hotel room."

Rachel pointed to a stemware rack above the sink. Abigail slid three glasses off and placed them on the counter. "All the rooms are booked. There's a big bike race or somesuch and not a room to be had."

"Then I'll get my camping gear from the Jeep and sleep outside."

Abigail poured the wine and handed a glass to Rachel. She picked up the other two and walked around the counter to hand one to Nora. "That's silly. Rachel has kindly offered to let us stay here. You know, Lisa always said since I gave her the loan for this place, I could stay anytime I wanted. Rachel won't mind if you take the other room, will you, Rachel? And I'm sure Lisa would want us to be here."

Rachel took a sip of wine and lowered her glass. She glared at Nora. "Feel free to stay as long as you like."

THIRTEEN

THE CHILL OF EARLY morning pricked Nora's nose. She sat huddled on the front porch in a soft throw she'd found on the couch. The glow over the tips of the La Sals hinted at the sun's arrival. She drew the throw, with its earth tones and gentle pattern, closer around her.

Abbey sniffed and explored the yard, stopping to pee on an Apache plume shrub beyond Abigail's Buick. Nora tucked her feet under her in the Adirondack chair. She'd chosen the chair painted with mountains and dancing yellows and blues of swirling Van Gogh skies. Small birds flitted from the gnarled branches of the scrub oaks and the meadowlarks had just let out their first blast of song.

Nora's mind had been spinning in circles all night. She'd fought the blankets and finally cried uncle. She'd plodded down the stairs, intending to go through Lisa's office again. She'd no sooner clicked on the desk lamp when Rachel had appeared and stood in the doorway with her arms crossed until Nora retreated to the front porch. Rachel had gone back upstairs but Nora didn't want to upset her any further, so she left the office alone.

She'd been sitting on the deck for the past few hours. Cole would be stretched out in his family's house in Wyoming, no doubt flat on his back, sleeping that deep sleep he fell into almost every night. She longed to cuddle next to him.

Her brain switched to Etta and her threats. She loved her job but hated the dance to keep the Board of Directors happy. After that, she felt the weight of Lisa's death. Had someone killed her to keep her from finishing and distributing her film? Rachel said local law enforcement wouldn't help. Nora had no proof and only a vague suspicion, so taking it to another agency, like the FBI, wouldn't do any good. Wrapped in frustration and helplessness, she tried to distract herself by trouble-shooting an upcoming public education event the Trust planned to sponsor next month in Boulder.

But an image of her kachina popped into her head. His absence felt like rejection. Maybe she'd been fooling herself into thinking she could be a part of the tribe when really, she'd never be anything more than a tourist.

Unable to stay still for another second, she threw off the blanket and scurried into the house. Trying to be as silent as possible, she leaped up the stairs and ran to her room. With growing urgency, she rummaged in her backpack until her fingers finally closed on the small leather pouch. She pulled it from the pack and raced back to the porch.

Her hand shook as she reached into the pouch, pinched at the corn dust inside, and brought it out. She faced the mountains and held her breath.

Three … two … one.

The sun flared over the peak. Nora inhaled and tossed the corn dust into the air.

A real Hopi would sing out loud. She'd express her gratitude to the spirits for creating the world and pledge herself to protecting it.

Nora gazed at the sun over the mountains, inhaled the fresh morning air, and kept her mouth shut.

"What are you doing?" Abigail's voice preceded the squeak of the screen door opening.

Nora jumped and spun around. Heat rushed to her cheeks. "I couldn't sleep so I got up early."

Abigail stood on the porch in one of her velour workout suits, this one a brilliant turquoise. She held two thick pottery mugs with swirling browns and deep reds adorning the sides. She must have been brewing coffee in the kitchen when Nora raced upstairs. Nora had been so wrapped up in her own angst she hadn't even smelled it. Abigail narrowed her eyes. "Did you just toss corn into the air?"

Nora shoved the pouch into her shorts pocket. She sauntered back to the chair and picked up the throw. "Is that coffee I smell?" she said.

Abigail handed her a mug. The warmth of the coffee penetrated Nora's palm and the moisture from the aromatic steam greeted her. "Thanks."

Abigail lowered herself into a chair painted with a red armadillo, purple javelina, and yellow ground squirrels. She sat on the edge and clutched her mug. "You and that old fool, Charles."

Nora raised her eyebrows. "What about Charlie?"

Abigail waved her hand in dismissal. "He was up hours ago. He said he couldn't sleep and went trudging off like he does."

Nora scanned the yard. "I didn't see him."

Abigail sipped her coffee and stared ahead. "He wouldn't disturb your vigil. He's like that."

Nora nodded. "Abbey must have gone with him."

They sat in silence for a while until Abigail said in a tight voice, "I don't suppose there's anything wrong with saying thank you for this sunrise."

Nora sat in her mountain chair, careful not to spill the coffee. "This porch is the reason Lisa bought this place."

Abigail spoke quietly. "I remember that first summer she lived here. No running water, the stairs threatening to cave in. I believe a family of skunks lived under the porch."

The coffee tasted a little like heaven, though not a big chunk of heaven because Abigail had made her usual anemic brew. Still, it was good enough that Nora felt a pang for enjoying it, knowing Lisa would never drink another cup.

That kind of maudlin attitude wouldn't help anyone and certainly didn't honor the spirit of her friend. "It was really nice of you to loan her the money for this place."

"I was happy to do it."

That wasn't exactly how Nora remembered it. To Lisa's face, Abigail was all generosity and graciousness, but to Nora, Abigail complained about the foolishness of buying a dilapidated shack and fixing it up herself. She argued that the house sat on a flood plain, although no one living could remember a flash flood so violent it would rush though this wide valley. Abigail had told Nora one reason she lent Lisa the money was to distract her from the ridiculous notion of being a lesbian. If she focused on something else, she'd get over it and find a man, her mother reasoned. Abigail had progressed a long way since then.

Nora closed her eyes to the sun's warmth. "She loved it here."

"I've never liked Moab."

Nora watched Abigail's tense face. "I didn't know that. Why?"

"Bad juju." Abigail twisted her mouth in distaste.

"What do you mean?"

"The vibes. I just don't like it."

It surprised Nora that Abigail noticed anything beyond the retail experience of a place. "I didn't know you spent any time here."

"A little."

"When?"

"What is this? Twenty questions?" Abigail snapped.

Nora sat back, puzzled at Abigail's reaction. "Sorry."

After a pause, Abigail said, "Your father and I visited once."

Nora sat up. Abigail didn't offer up much about Nora's father. "When?"

Abigail gazed at the mountains. "Not long after we met. He loved it here and wanted to show it to me. We backpacked in Arches and spent some time in Canyonlands."

Nora nearly choked on the coffee. "You…" She couldn't picture it. "You backpacked?"

Abigail frowned at her. "I wasn't born being your mother. I was young once, too."

In principle, that made sense. Nora could see Abigail as a high school girl in Nebraska, being head cheerleader and dating the football captain. She could imagine her in college giggling with the girls on her dorm floor. What she couldn't fit into her brain was her mother sweating under a pack and sleeping on the ground, covered in the red dust of the Southwest.

"So you and my father came up here? What did he show you?" Nora grabbed hold of any knowledge about her father. She longed to know more about him, and these rare snippets from her mother were all she had.

Abigail waved her hand. "Oh, I don't know. We hiked around and it all looked pretty much the same to me. I was young and just happy to be with him."

"Did he tell you anything about the landscapes or traditions? This isn't typical Hopi land, so I wonder why he brought you here and not the mesas."

Abigail clucked her teeth. "You've been to the mesas. They aren't much to look at. I suspect your father felt reluctant to introduce me to his family. They weren't likely to approve of me."

Nora waited. There had to be more.

"He did what you just did, though. Every morning he would get up ridiculously early and say prayers to the sunrise and throw corn dust into the air." Abigail shook her head. "I'm glad you don't grunt and moan like he did."

"Singing, Mother. They call that singing."

Abigail waved it away. "Yes, I know what they call it. What I call singing is the Beatles or Neil Diamond. And throwing corn is odd."

"You and Berle used to go to church every Sunday. What's the difference?" Berle was Abigail's second husband, the man she'd been married to the longest—unless she and Charlie stayed together for another twenty years.

Abigail gave her an incredulous look. "How can you even compare the two? Sunday services at Boulder Presbyterian were conducted at reasonable times on the day of rest. Not at sunrise, except for one day of the year, of course."

Maybe Abigail wasn't as progressive as Nora hoped. Nora reached across to Abigail's chair and took her hand. "Thanks for coming. It's good to see you and Charlie."

Abigail looked startled by Nora's affection. She eyed Nora closer, as if checking for fever. "Lisa was special to me."

They sat, silent for a moment, probably as long as Abigail could stand. "But this whole thing she was doing, this film. I don't understand what it's about."

Nora sipped her cooling coffee. "She was making a film to screen for the people at the Department of the Interior and to Congress to show them how important and fragile Canyonlands Park is and how desperately we need to enlarge the park boundaries."

Abigail sat up, as if spoiling for a fight. "That's silly. You've got Arches Park," she pointed behind them, toward Moab. "There's Escalante and then Canyonlands. The whole darned state of Utah is practically a giant park."

Who knew Abigail harbored such resentment for conservationists? "Actually, Mother, there's one point four million acres of public lands surrounding Canyonlands National Park that need protection." Nora heard the edge in her own voice. It was the defensive hue that colored her words since she'd first berated her mother for crimes against the rainforest when Nora was in fourth grade.

Now, Nora and Abigail were grown women. They could be friends. The kind of people who respected each other and could engage in civil discussions.

Nora started again. "The original proposal for Canyonlands, way back in 1936, was for one million acres."

Abigail's mouth set in disapproval.

"But it was whittled down to 338,000 acres before Congress voted. That's about a third of its original size."

"Even if it's desert wasteland, you can't restrict such huge portions of land."

"So many cultural resources and relics lay just outside the park with no protection."

Abigail waved her hand in the air again and made a dismissive noise with her lips. "Do you really believe there aren't enough petroglyphs and pot shards protected already?"

With clenched teeth, Nora said, "Do you really believe we need to preserve *Romeo and Juliet* since we already have *Henry the VIII*?"

"That's not at all the same thing." Abigail stood up and reached for Nora's empty coffee cup. She retreated into the house.

Nora watched the light play on the mountain range, the shadows deep on Castle Rock. She leaned her head back on the chair and closed her eyes. The bird chorus erupted in full sunrise crescendo. Even the flies and other insects buzzed in their morning busyness.

The screen opened again and Nora smelled coffee. Abigail must be back with a second cup. "I'm going to stay," Nora said, more to herself than to Abigail.

"Good idea. Enjoy the sunrise and have another cup of coffee. I'll start breakfast." Abigail set the coffee cup on the wide arm of the chair.

Nora sat up, eyes on the changing light of the mountains. "No, I mean I'm going to stay here in Moab."

"Now what's the point in that? As I understand it, there are no copies of Lisa's film so there's no reason for you to be here."

"I have to do something about this," Nora replied.

"About what, the film?"

"Find it, yes. But..."

"What?"

Nora wanted to take back the "but" she'd uttered. Abigail didn't need to know Nora suspected Lisa's death wasn't an accident. If the local police wouldn't help, she'd have to do it on her own.

Abigail frowned, "This isn't..."

Nora jumped up, letting the blanket fall to the porch. "Where is Lisa's camera? She said I'd know. They might have destroyed the film but not the camera."

"They who?"

Nora grabbed Abigail and coffee splashed from the mug. She pulled her mother close and squeezed. "I'm going to finish this for Lisa."

She jumped toward the door, ready to get started.

Rachel stood just inside the screen, coffee cup suspended halfway to her mouth. She glared at Nora for half a second, and then whirled around.

FOURTEEN

Fueled by determination, Nora hurried from the porch. The screen banged closed behind her, then opened and tapped closed to let Abigail in.

Nora rushed into the office and stood in the middle of the room, the wool of the Navajo rug warm under her feet. She placed a hand on the cool wood of Lisa's box. "What were you trying to tell me?"

If Lisa were murdered, the logical suspect was a local landowner with a grudge against environmentalists. While Nora didn't know many people who fit that description, one face popped to mind.

Lee Evans. Those hate-filled dark eyes focused on her at the funeral. He ran her off the road and pretended it was an accident. Was he trying to scare her and make her go home? Had he done the same to Lisa? When she wouldn't back down, had he created an accident?

He'd been out at the cabin yesterday having a serious conversation with Rachel. Rachel wanted Nora to drop the film project and go home. Was she protecting Lee? If so, why?

A cold wind blew across Nora's brain—an affair! Both Marlene and Lisa mentioned Rachel's upbringing and how hard it was for her to give up her old life. Maybe she was trying to go back to it.

Lisa's message said she'd recorded something on film. Her voice had sounded terrified. Whatever she wanted to tell Nora was on that camera, and Nora needed to find it soon.

She glanced quickly around the office, but didn't see a camera sitting anywhere. She hadn't expected it to be in plain sight. She shook her head at the pile of papers on the desk and lowered herself to sit. The bottom left-hand drawer squeaked as Nora tugged on it. Inside, a mass of file folders, envelopes, and odd bits of articles torn from newspapers and magazines tumbled in an orgy of clutter. She shoved it closed and tried for the drawer on the other side.

The stairs creaked and seconds later Abigail appeared in the doorway. She'd traded her velour running suit for beige slacks, a T-shirt with all sorts of shiny bling attached, and flats. For Abigail, even a few days away from home required an extensive wardrobe. Even if Nora had expected to stay longer than overnight, she wouldn't have packed much more than a change of clothes. As it was, she was reduced to wearing the same shorts but had donned a clean T-shirt and underwear. "Would you like more coffee?"

"Yes, please." She looked around for her cup, couldn't remember where she'd left it, and shrugged at Abigail. She returned her attention to the desk and started arranging the piles of papers. None of them had to do with household expenses. Rachel must handle all that. Lisa's papers mostly dealt with environmental issues. Articles about climate change and the benefits and challenges of sustainable energy tangled with maps of Utah in various iterations. Topo maps, park boundary maps, historic renderings. Black Sharpie circles pointed out various locations. Next to many of these, Lisa had scribbled dates and times.

A few articles about Mormon history and beliefs were scattered amid the environmental information clutter, although it really didn't fit Lisa's MO. Maybe she was studying the local culture to better deal with the opposition. Or maybe she wanted to understand Rachel better.

A raven squawked in Nora's pocket. It startled her and she reached for her phone, checking the ID and hoping it was Cole. Disappointed, she answered. "Hi, Fay. You're up early."

Fay directed the open space programs for the Trust. "Weed Warriors. We were going to do this on Saturday, but a few people couldn't make it so we bumped it back a day. I've got a ten-person crew to pull Russian thistle along the road, and we wanted to get it done before it gets hot."

Nora knew that but had forgotten.

"Sorry to bother you. But I checked the Trust voicemail, and Etta Jackson left a long message about being here at eight on Monday morning and bringing a couple other board members."

A giant sour ball burned in Nora's stomach. She'd known about Etta's trip but not about her bringing a brigade. "Thanks for letting me know." After hanging up, Nora clenched her fists and stared at the La Sals. That left her three days.

Abigail walked into the office and placed a steaming cup of coffee on a spot Nora had just cleared.

Nora picked up her cup. "Thanks." She took a sip and, with effort, kept from making a face.

"I used that hazelnut creamer you like," Abigail said.

"When did I tell you I like flavored creamer?"

Abigail walked over to a bookcase and gazed at an owl's wing. She must not have realized it was a real wing and not an artist's rendition. "Oh, maybe that wasn't you. It wouldn't make sense that you'd like flavoring. You only want that whole grain, tasteless stuff, vegetarian and quinoa."

"Pronounced *keen-wa*, Mother. Not like the city in Portugal. And I'm not a vegetarian. I just prefer food that wasn't manufactured in a lab." Nora eyed the coffee, gauging whether she could stomach the sweet to get at the caffeine. She decided not to risk it.

Abigail spun around and sashayed to the French doors. "How long do you think you'll stay in Utah?"

Nora eyed the mess on the desk. "Not sure."

Lisa might not be the most organized person, but she would have at least stashed a copy off-site. The work had consumed her for years. And the camera—where would she have hidden that?

"Can't you work from Boulder? Load up Lisa's files and take them with you." Abigail swayed as if listening to calming music. Her air of casualness was entirely too practiced.

"When are you going home?" Nora stacked the maps on one corner of the desk, the random articles on another, the Mormon stuff, unrelated pictures, and ads in yet another pile behind Lisa's box.

"This morning. As soon as Charles gets back from his walkabout. We'll drop you off to pick up your Jeep." Abigail sipped her coffee and hugged herself with the arm not holding the cup.

Nora studied a photo of a rock art panel. It showed the typical snake squiggles, running antelope, and big-headed people with spears. An ancient hand had carved the weird sunburst image into the corner of the panel. Nora tossed the photo into a pile with several other pictures of rock art panels.

Abigail rocked on her heels. "What about Cole? Doesn't he miss you? You shouldn't leave him alone too long."

Nora sat back in her chair. "Have you talked to him lately?" Abigail and Cole had a whole relationship separate from Nora. They'd conspired last year to get Nora together with Cole.

Abigail frowned. "No. Why? Is something wrong?"

Nora shook her head. "He's in Wyoming. His father's health is failing and there's something going on with his family."

"There's something else, isn't there? What is it?" Abigail advanced on her.

"Nothing." Nora picked up a map of northern Arizona and dropped it on the map pile. "It's just…"

"Just what?"

Nora sipped her coffee and nearly gagged. She'd forgotten about the creamer. "He sounded funny on the phone. And he said…" Nora trailed off, knowing it was going to sound silly.

"He said what?" Abigail's impatience surfaced.

Nora pushed her hair back. "He said he loved me."

Abigail stared at her.

"I know, you think that's good, but it's not like him. It's weird. To me, it sounded like one of those things like, 'I'll always love you, but it's over.'"

Abigail brightened. "Don't be stupid. Cole telling you he loves you obviously means he's going to ask you to marry him."

Wait. What? Marry him? Nora shook her head. "No. He's probably upset about his father."

"Nora." Abigail sounded exasperated. "It means a proposal. I have experience with these things and I just know."

It isn't as if she hadn't thought about it. "No. It's too soon. Besides, if he wanted to marry me, he'd discuss it with me." Nora went back to sorting Lisa's papers.

Abigail might be all giddy and excited about a wedding, but not Nora. Something was up with Cole, and Nora braced for the worst. When it hit, having her mother around wouldn't be a bad thing. "What's the big rush to go to back to Flagstaff?" Nora said without looking up. "I haven't seen you for a while."

Abigail spoke into the French doors. "Don't you need to get back to work? Charles and I can come up to Boulder in a few weeks, after things settle down."

This jumble of papers seemed daunting. Nora's battered emotions clenched again when she thought of all the note-taking systems she'd offered Lisa over the years. She'd sent her day planners, lovely little notebooks, custom-made sticky notes, yellow legal pads, anything to help Lisa organize her life. As far as she knew, Lisa burned it all at summer solstice and danced around the bonfire naked.

Rachel wouldn't help her with this mess. Maybe Marlene could give her some insight. Nora glanced at the clock. She calculated. If she left here in fifteen minutes, she could get to town when the Read Rock opened.

"I'd think you'd work much better at your own office instead of this foreign environment."

Nora noticed the tension in Abigail's voice. "Why do you want me to leave?"

Abigail whirled around, a too-bright smile on her face. "Oh, it's not that. Not that at all."

This behavior seemed odd, even for Abigail, who often baffled Nora. "You're itching to get out of here and are trying to get me to leave, too. Why?"

Abigail kept her false cheer and opened her mouth as if to deny it.

Nora narrowed her eyes. "Tell me."

Abigail bit her lower lip. Not a good sign. She set her cup on the edge of the desk, inhaled, then exhaled and folded her arms in front of her. "I just don't like being here. It reminds me too much of Dan."

Dan. Nora's heart jumped. Abigail hardly ever used her father's name. "How long were you here with him?"

Abigail's eyes lost focus, as if she watched her past. "Not more than a week. But the air feels charged with him. It makes me miss Dan, and that feels like cheating on Charles."

If Nora moved, it might stop Abigail mid-story. "Charlie understands he isn't your first love. He had a whole life before he met you, too," Nora assured her.

Abigail brought her focus back to the room, all business. "Of course he did."

Nora paused to let the last sentence drop. "Maybe you need to remember it all. Live it and embrace it, and then you can let it go."

Abigail tilted her head and narrowed her eyes. "What are you up to?"

Nora stirred. "Stay here with me. Let's spend some one-on-one time together. We'll drive through Arches Park and you can tell me about my father." Arches—where the rock formation Fiery Furnace stretched across the mesa.

Abigail shook her head. "Oh, no."

"Why not?"

"I don't want to remember. There's no good to come from dwelling on sad things. I don't like being here."

Nora stood and squeezed around the desk to stand in front of her mother. "Don't you think you owe me something? Shouldn't I know my father just a little?"

"I barely knew your father. We weren't together more than two years. I've got nothing much to tell you."

"Tell me what you remember," Nora begged. "Please stay."

Abigail studied Nora for a long time, but Nora doubted Abigail saw her. Eventually her eyes focused and she said, "No."

FIFTEEN

When Charlie hadn't shown up from his morning march, Nora had begged Abigail to drive her to Moab. She'd picked up her Jeep and drove through the quiet town to the parking lot behind the Read Rock, making sure Abbey would be cool and leaving the Jeep's windows down. As she turned off the street, movement ahead caught her eye and she drew in a sharp breath. A battered stock trailer disappeared around a corner a few blocks away. The vehicle pulling it eased behind a building but before it did, Nora was sure she identified a white pickup.

So what? There were probably twenty white pickups in Moab. It didn't mean Lee Evans was in town. Even if Lee was, what difference did it make? Just because he was sinister and opposed to everything Nora strove for, and he'd run her off the road yesterday, didn't mean he was dangerous. Okay, it might mean that. She wondered just how violent his temper could be.

The sun already blasted down even though it was still too early for shoppers to line the streets. A dented, dusty late-model black Suburban was the only other vehicle in the lot.

Nora hurried through the alley, eyeing the graffiti rock art. She thought about taking a picture to give to Lisa for her collection before remembering Lisa was gone.

The sign in the front window of the Read Rock said they opened at nine, but when Nora tried the door at 9:10, it didn't budge. Marlene didn't seem like the type to open late. Nora peeked through the window.

The curtain to the back room rippled. Marlene probably worked in the back and didn't realize the time. Nora banged on the door to alert her. A moment passed and Nora banged again.

After another few seconds, the curtain swept aside. Marlene burst through, glanced over her shoulder at the back room, then hurried to the front door. She unlocked it and frowned at Nora. "What do you want?"

Surprised at the abrupt greeting, Nora stammered. "I, uh, wanted to talk." What a stupid thing to say. She'd meant to start off on a more friendly note and ease into the topic of the film project, even though Marlene made it clear yesterday she didn't think Nora should pursue it.

Marlene didn't step aside to let Nora inside. She tilted her head, as though fighting not to look behind her. "Sure. There's a café down about two blocks. I haven't had breakfast. I'll meet you there."

She shut the door and locked it again. Nora leaned toward the glass and watched Marlene hurry to the back room.

Nora was still puzzling over Marlene's strange behavior ten minutes later as she sipped an iced chai and sat in the dappled sunshine on the patio of a funky little vegetarian café. Flat sandstone slabs created an uneven surface and the tables and chairs rocked with movement. A koi pond gurgled behind her and busy black scavenger birds perched on chair backs awaiting the slightest ebb in vigilance when they'd swoop in and steal crumbs from tables and plates.

Nora gazed out at the red cliffs to the west that created one side of the deep canyon that housed Moab. The fresh morning air brightened the patio that overflowed with white tea roses, fragrant honeysuckle, bright purple irises, and brilliant blue cornflowers.

Most of the customers seemed to be regulars—not the old-time cowboy contingent but the rock climbers, bike riders, and Earth savers. Lots of rumpled, free trade clothes to go with the free trade coffee and vegetarian entrees. Nora had eaten here several times with Lisa. They could make a mean tempeh BLT and had a pretty tasty quiche of the day. This morning, Nora picked at a soyrizzo breakfast burrito and waited.

The café sat on the highway that ran through Moab and served as one of its main commerce streets. Four lanes and a wide median made the road an ordeal to cross on foot. Cars and SUVs whizzed by, the day heating up with tourist activity. There a big race in town and everyone seemed to buzz with excitement.

A table of what appeared to be affluent retirees chatted over steel-cut organic oatmeal and vegan scones. They looked fit and wore spotless outdoor gear adorned with the labels of the most expensive outfitters. A group of twenty-somethings who looked and smelled as if they'd been living in the desert for a week grabbed a table on the patio.

One of the women from the table of well-dressed couples stood and approached the youngsters. She gave them a sincere, concerned face. "Good morning. Are you here for the bike race?"

One of the young women, her brown hair in a wispy pony tail, smiled up at her. "We've been here all week. It's a great event."

The dark-haired woman nodded. "I'm sure you've noticed some of the unauthorized HOV trails cutting through the fragile landscapes." She sounded like a public service announcement. Two girls and one guy near the end of the table nodded and gave her their attention while the other people in the group carried on with their own animated conversation.

She continued as if lecturing her children. "We're trying to place restrictions on people running all over the place with their ATVs. The locals don't seem to understand the land is delicate. They abuse it as if it is worthless."

The young people looked trapped and uncomfortable. One of the girls shifted away and joined her friends' conversation. The other two looked trapped.

"These old ranchers don't even know about global warming."

The two young people exchanged a look of desperation.

Marlene shot down the sidewalk. She wore a deep red flowing skirt with vibrant embroidery along the hem. Her sleeveless shirt dipped in a low V in front, hid by a filmy turquoise print scarf.

The finely coiffed woman continued her practiced speech. "They over-graze the sparse prairie lands that have no chance to recuperate, thinking the weather patterns of their ancestors will hold today. But they don't realize their forefathers stripped the land and it needs to rejuvenate without the hooves and teeth of cows."

The girl nodded and stood. "Did you want us to sign a petition or something?"

The woman seemed encouraged by the question. She snapped her fingers at the table where her cohorts sat. One of the men jumped up, grabbing a spiral notebook and pen. He hurried over.

The woman snatched it from him and flipped it open. "If you'll give me your e-mail addresses, I'll put you on our action alert list. We'll contact you when we need you to write your lawmakers and advocate for this special place."

Marlene strode to the front door of the café and caught Nora's attention. "I'll order and be right out," she called. The white pickup pulling the stock trailer slowed and parked on the curb across the street as the two well-dressed couples stared. They leaned across the table and began to talk excitedly. Nerves twanged the first bar of *Dueling Banjos* in Nora's chest as she recognized the black cowboy hat.

A raven squawked on the table and Nora jumped for her phone, happy to see Cole's ID. "Hi!" she answered.

After a few seconds of hellos and where are yous, Cole said, "When are you going home?"

"I need to stick around here for a day or two." She kept her eyes on the white pickup.

"Abigail just called. She's worried." He didn't sound happy.

Lee Evans stepped from his pickup. He hurried up the sidewalk and inside a river raft outfitter's office. Why would a cowboy like Lee go into a river raft outfitters? "About what?"

"She said you're not accepting Lisa's death and she's afraid you'll get hurt like Lisa did," Cole explained.

She couldn't tell Cole her suspicions about Lisa's death. "I need to find Lisa's camera. I think she might have hidden it. I'll be careful."

Frustration darkened his voice. "Why would she hide her camera?"

As the conversation continued, Nora noticed a yacht of an SUV pull up and park along the street in front of Lee's pickup. A blond man and woman climbed out, followed by four kids. A little girl of about five, with fine dark ringlets haloing her head, trotted up the street, the lights adorning the bottoms of her sneakers twinkling. The adults wore worried frowns and scanned the street. The mother called to the little girl and herded all the children inside the outfitter's office.

She knew someone wanted to kill her and put information on the camera she hid. She thought I'd know where to look. Nora watered it down for him. "She was scared of something."

He sighed. "You got all that from her voicemail? Please, just come home. Ever since I've met you, trouble finds you. So far I've been around to protect you, but I can't now."

Her jaw hardened. "I don't need you to protect me."

"Hey! No! Wait!" Cole shouted away from the phone. He came back on the line. "We're branding some calves, and I've gotta go. Do me a favor. Just head back to Boulder."

"Is that an order?"

"Damn it, Nora." He'd never taken an angry tone with her, and he sounded as shocked as she felt. He sighed. "Do whatever you want." He must have thought he hung up, but she heard the phone clunk as if dropped on the pickup seat. Cole hollered in the distance. She was about to hang up when a woman spoke into the phone. "Who is this?"

The voice took Nora by surprise. "This is Cole's phone." She thought maybe the woman didn't know.

"Yes. And you are?" The woman definitely sounded annoyed.

"I'm Cole's friend," Nora answered, trying to sound bolder than she felt. "Who are you?"

"His wife."

SIXTEEN

NORA PUNCHED HER PHONE off and stared at it. She couldn't move.

Breathe, she ordered herself and sucked in air.

Married? Cole's wife. Wife! This couldn't be.

"I thought you'd be on your way back to Boulder by now." Marlene sat down at the table with a plate of eggs and soy sausage along with a cup of coffee.

Nora's attention jolted back to the café patio. Sunshine, flowers, people milling around her. Marlene sitting down. She shoved the woman—Cole's wife—to the back of her mind and tried focusing on Marlene. Right now, Lisa took precedence.

Nora waited until Marlene settled in and took a sip of her coffee. "Can you think of where Lisa might have hidden her camera or where she might have stored a copy of the footage?"

Marlene glared at her and slowly speared a piece of sausage and put it in her mouth. She chewed longer than necessary and swallowed. "You asked me that already. Let me repeat: You need to forget this nonsense and leave town." The older activists pushed back from their table, their chairs scraping against the stone patio.

Nora leaned across the table. "You think Lisa was murdered."

Marlene's fork dropped to her plate with a clang. "I didn't say that, but if it's true, it's the best reason I know for you to leave."

Another boat of a vehicle cruised down the road and pulled in front of the outfitter's. "That seems strange," Nora commented.

Marlene twisted in her chair to watch seven people climb from the vehicle and head into the office. "What?"

"First Lee Evans pulled up and went in. Then a family, and now this group."

Marlene whipped back around. "So?" She sounded uninterested, but she frowned anyway.

"So, none of them are dressed in outdoor gear. They're in jeans or slacks. You don't go down a river dressed like that."

Marlene turned and studied the people entering the shop. "They're tourists. Probably didn't plan on a river trip today."

Maybe, but something seemed odd. She dismissed it, turning back to Lisa and her camera. "Aside from the Canyonlands thing, can you think of any other reason someone would want to kill Lisa?"

Marlene picked up her fork with a shaking hand and poked at her scrambled eggs. "Why?"

Argh. Couldn't she simply answer a question without probing for Nora's hidden agenda? "Lisa had all this information about Mormons and women in the church. Maybe a religious fanatic hurt her." The color drained from Marlene's face.

Interesting, Nora thought. "Maybe something to do with Lisa marrying Rachel?" she continued.

Just then, Darrell rounded the corner, scowling at Lee's pickup across the street. He took a few steps toward the street, then looked back at the café. He spotted Nora, pasted on a smile, and started toward her. Several heads turned in his direction and a few people whispered. Darrell stopped at a couple of tables as he headed toward Nora, shaking hands and throwing out greetings. He stepped over to Nora. "Just the person I wanted to see."

He wore Levi's that seemed to fit him perfectly, deliberately faded to look worn and casual without seeming old. His white shirt, the buttons at his throat open and the sleeves rolled gave a Saturday morning feel, giving him a studied, attractive look. His perfection rivaled Abigail's and felt just as contrived.

Darrell smiled too warmly, felt way too familiar. "Since time is limited, I think we ought to get busy putting together a presentation with some of the stills Lisa sent us."

She wanted to get back to her conversation with Marlene. The woman knew something she wasn't telling Nora. "We've already decided the stills won't have the impact of the film," she reminded him.

Something in the road caught Nora's attention. "What the...?" It took her a couple of seconds to understand the looming catastrophe. She jumped up, her chair overturning on the patio, and took off in a run, brushing past Darrell.

The doors of the stock trailer stood wide open. One rangy Hereford cow nosed the back end of the trailer, looking as though she wanted to jump out.

Nora raced to the street, dodging vehicles on her way across the busy road. The cow dropped her two front hooves onto the pavement. Nora yelled to try to scare her back in. If the cow got loose in the road, it would cause trouble and someone—the cow, drivers, pedestrians—could be hurt.

The trailer door swung inward. The cow spooked and backed up. The door closed with the metallic clank of metal banging on metal. Lee threw his weight against it and slammed the latch shut.

Nora panted, hands on her hips. "Thank god. That would have been bad."

Lee towered over her, fury surging from him. "What were you thinking?"

"Wha—?"

He tilted his head down the street toward the older activists, now lurking in the shade of a shop that rented four-wheel drives. "You and your buddies thought it would be funny to turn my cows loose to prove how bad they are? Did you think someone might be hurt? Did you even think about safety of the cows?"

"I didn't—"

Darrell joined them. "Hey, let's calm down. Nora was at the café with me."

Lee turned on Darrell. "You're involved in this?" He took a step toward Darrell and lowered his face so they were nose to nose.

"Now isn't the time," Darrell threatened.

"When then? You're gonna have to answer for all this. For bringing these meddlers here," Lee shot back.

Marlene stood on the far side of the road, watching with full attention. Her focus wasn't on the men by the stock trailer, though. Nora followed her line of sight. The family with the four kids were climbing into their SUV, the doors slamming one by one.

Lee whirled, facing Nora. "Meddlers like you and your friend."

"Leave her alone," Darrell warned.

Lee, full of menace, leaned toward Nora. "Only you lost this round. That film Lisa was making is gone, along with all the money you spent on it."

How did he get his information? It had to be from Rachel. Nora egged him on, defiant. "Lisa told me where she left her camera. I'll finish that film."

He folded his arms. "That so?"

Coupled with the disturbing phone conversation, Nora bristled with stupid bravado. "When we show it to the committee, they'll vote to expand the borders and there's nothing you can do about it."

Lee smirked at her. "Yep. Seems I heard that before."

SEVENTEEN

WARREN STUDIED THE ROCK art panel under the glass and let the hand of the ancients pull at him. His feet nestled in the plush of his carpet as he stood in the climate-controlled comfort of his office, but his mind soared over the high desert outside Moab. He felt the crunch of rough sand under his boots, squinting in the blazing sun.

His strong, young body climbed the twists in the trail, winding through the spires of Fiery Furnace. The weathered rocks formed a forest of jutting hoodoos that created a maze so dense, hikers weren't allowed to enter without a permit and guide. A hawk sailed overhead.

Warren saw it all as if he were actually drawing breath in Utah. Heat radiated from the rocks that baked in the sun, but between the spires, shadows cooled the sand. Orange globemallow and pinkish milkweed bobbed in the constant wind sweeping across the open desert. Warren traveled deeper into the rocks that stood more dense than the towers that lined Wall Street.

He tilted his head back and lifted his gaze to the revelation some twenty-five feet from the sandy floor. Warren remembered the day his destiny was revealed to him.

The ancients wrote it on the rock for him to discover. His uncle had told him about the sacred drawings located here, but only after Warren had already discovered the messages written on the rocks at the ranch. It had taken Warren days of searching Fiery Furnace to find the rock that told him all he needed to know.

He stared up at the rock and drifted between the past and future. The torment of the Third World's end melded with the coming destruction. Warren saw it all, just as the ancients intended. He alone knew what was coming and had prepared for it.

As they'd done that day over thirty years ago, the couple wandered into his view, interrupting his vision. He knew their meeting was not coincidence. The man, only slightly older than Warren, was obviously Native American. He had to be Hopi, sent to instruct Warren. It was no mystery why the ancients brought them together.

Even now, all these years later, Warren's heart still clutched when he thought of the woman. He'd never felt that way about anyone, before or since. He'd been consumed with her at first glance. Surely God had created her for him, and Warren thought she'd been sent to be his helpmate. But time proved God had only sent her to tempt Warren and harden his will while teaching him self-discipline.

Warren's phone rang and he whiplashed back to his weak body. He took a step toward his desk and his feet shrieked in pain, the neuropathy from the chemo plaguing him.

He picked up the phone and dropped into his office chair, his eyes focusing on the rock art panel, hoping to hold on to the power of the ancients.

"I think we've got a problem." His nephew, always full of dire warnings.

"I trust you can manage it."

"It's that Nora Abbott woman. She's nosing around. What if she finds out about Lisa Taylor's death?"

A minor annoyance at this stage, thought Warren.

His nephew sounded distressed. "She was at the pick-up site today."

He clenched his fist. "Did she see anything?"

Warren heard the worry in his nephew's voice. "Don't know. But she threw attention our way and that bookstore owner sure looked interested."

"Can't Rachel get her to leave?" He'd hoped Rachel would join them. She'd had so many opportunities to destroy them, yet she'd kept her own counsel. But now that her friend—Warren couldn't stomach the disgust he felt at the real definition of their relationship—was dead by his nephew's hand, they'd need to keep her much closer. This was a critical time for Rachel. She'd either become one with them or turn against them.

His nephew didn't sound convinced. "I can try."

"I would prefer you don't kill her."

Shock found its way to his nephew's voice. "Rachel?"

"Either of them." They'd all known the far too independent Rachel since she was born and Warren preferred to keep her alive.

The excitability that often led his nephew to bad decisions flowed in the voice on the phone. "I won't if I don't have to."

Warren crossed his leg over his knee and rubbed his foot, barely biting back a moan of pain. His doctors wanted him to take it easy— no travel, no stress. That wasn't going to happen.

"I'll be there tomorrow."

EIGHTEEN

AMID A CLOUD OF dirt and flying pebbles, Nora jammed on her brakes and jumped from the Jeep. Abbey clambered after her.

Married.

She'd tried to ignore the news from Wyoming, to let it sit until she had time to talk to Cole. But it flooded into her head until everything else washed away.

His wife? When did this happen? Not more than a week ago they'd been talking about their future together. He'd told her how lucky he felt to be with her. Nora finally trusted the relationship, trusted him.

Damn it! Were all men pigs or did she have unusually bad luck? First Scott, handsome and mischievous. He'd been faithful for about ten minutes. The only reason she'd been open to loving again was because Cole had been so patient and kind.

She'd pushed him away and yet he'd wormed his way back to her. She'd treated him pretty rotten and still, he'd stayed by her side through some terrible times. He'd taken a bullet for her. He'd risked his life. And in a couple of days, he'd married someone else.

Betrayed. Again.

Abigail and Charlie stood at their Buick with the trunk open. Abigail crossed her arms over her chest and tilted her head, her mouth moving. Charlie bent into the trunk and pulled out a large suitcase, then hefted a different one from the ground. They both spun around at the sound of the Jeep.

"Nora slammed the door closed and ran for the porch steps. She needed to focus on something other than herself. Lisa's murder. If it was a murder.

Of course it was. Rachel, Marlene, and Darrell all warned her to leave town. They lived here and they had suspicions. Add to that, Lee's arrogance and veiled threats and it made him a prime suspect.

"Nora, what's the matter?" Abigail called after her.

The screen door swung open and Rachel stood in the threshold. "I hear you're spreading it all over town that you're going to find Lisa's film." It hadn't taken Lee long to call Rachel. What a surprise—the backward cowboy had a cell phone! Okay, that was snide and unfair and a tired stereotype. Too bad.

Nora detoured to the side of the porch and climbed over the railing, dropping to the sand.

"Hey!" Rachel shouted. "What's wrong with you?"

Nora was obviously too upset to make nice with Rachel.

"Nora! For heaven's sake," Abigail called again.

Nora stomped off around the back of the cabin, Abbey hot on her heels, ignoring everyone. Think about Lisa. The film. A lump the size of Castle Rock lodged in her throat. She closed her eyes and fought for control, clenching her fists and teeth.

"Nora." Abigail caught her and placed a hand on Nora's rock-hard shoulder. "Are you okay?"

Nora opened her eyes. "Yep." She drew a deep breath and focused on relaxing. "Did you call Cole and tell him I was in danger?"

"What's the matter? Did you and Cole have a fight?" Abigail asked. "I wouldn't take it too seriously, dear. We know Cole is a good man. But every man, especially young ones, can be insensitive at times."

"A fight?"

"I assumed he doesn't think you should stay here in Moab. He thinks you should go back with him to Wyoming. And you, being the independent woman you are, said no. I'm solid with that."

Nora had difficulty following Abigail's blather. "'Solid'?"

Abigail straightened her shoulders. "I've been reading the Urban Dictionary. I can Google it on my notebook and they send me a word of the day. You should try it. It would do you good to update your vocabulary and keep up with technology. That phone of yours is pathetic."

Nora rubbed her forehead, stress headache beginning to throb.

Abigail moved behind Nora and reached up to knead her shoulders. "Let Cole cool off and he'll apologize."

"He's not going to apologize." Nora lifted her chin and stepped away from Abigail's massage. She strode back toward the front of the house.

Abigail scurried after her and tucked Nora's hand in her arm. She slowed Nora's gait. "He's just miffed right now. Give him time."

Nora tugged at Abigail's arm. "He's married."

"When he cools off, he'll—" Abigail stopped. "What?"

"His wife talked to me today when I was in Moab."

Abigail stood in the sand, hand on hips. "What did he say? There's got to be an explanation."

"What explanation could there possibly be? We're through."

Abigail studied Nora as if waiting for a punch line. When Nora started walking again, Abigail fell in step with her. "You can't take this lying down."

"I knew when he told me he loved me that something like this would happen."

"You need to fight for him."

124

Fight for a man who'd already made an irrevocable decision? "I'd say the battle was over before I even knew shots were fired."

Abigail sounded exasperated. "Marriage isn't permanent, you know."

That one stopped Nora in her tracks.

Abigail shrugged. "Well, it's not."

Nora strode away, kicking sand, her backbone hardening with each step.

Abigail struggled to keep up. "What are you going to do?"

Did she mean instead of curling into a ball and waiting for the desert sands to bury her? "I'm going to figure out who killed Lisa."

"Killed? What? Now you're being silly."

Nora regretted blurting that out. "Killed as in working too hard on the film and having the accident."

"Of course. You need to be more careful what you say. People can take things the wrong way." Abigail's attention turned toward Charlie. "No. That bag needs to be up front." She hurried away.

Nora stopped in the driveway and tried to shove Cole from her mind. Focus on something else.

Lisa.

Rachel and Lee had a relationship, but just how close were they? Lee didn't want the film made. The locals didn't approve of Rachel marrying Lisa. Just before Lisa died, she'd mentioned petroglyphs and Mormons and that she'd been afraid. It certainly pointed toward Lee. But if Nora was going to get law enforcement to look into anything, she'd need some proof.

Charlie held a small picnic cooler. He spoke to Abigail. "I've packed your water and Diet Coke. There are those little cheeses you like. I didn't have room for the apples."

Abigail considered that. "I hope there's not too much cheese. I don't need the extra pounds."

Charlie patted her still-shapely rear as he ambled to the backseat of the Buick. "Extra pounds just means more of you for me to adore."

Abigail swatted at him. "Oh, you." She turned her focus back to Nora, probably gearing up for a lecture about the difficulties and rewards of a committed relationship. A thought interrupted and she turned back to Charlie. "Did you remember those biscuits I bought yesterday?"

He looked puzzled.

"Biscuits," she repeated. When he still didn't get it, she said, "The cookies with the dark chocolate." Abigail could spend the rest of her life trying to pound Charlie into a pretentious dandy, but she'd never succeed. "We can stop in Monticello and get some coffee for that boring drive across the reservation."

Nora shook her head. "That boring drive is called Monument Valley."

Abigail shrugged. "I've seen it a thousand times."

Nora stepped toward Charlie and gave him a hug. He smelled of pine forest and friendship. "Come visit me in Boulder soon."

Abigail joined them. She put a palm on Nora's cheek just as she'd done when Nora was a little girl. "Go to Wyoming, dear."

A fat tear struggled to escape Nora's eye. She clenched her teeth and inhaled, willing it away. Abigail kissed Nora's forehead. "You need to decide what you want—a career or a life."

Nora pulled away. "Drive safely."

Abigail's lips tightened and she glared at Nora. The stare-down lasted several seconds before Abigail narrowed her eyes. "All right, then."

She swiveled toward Charlie and snatched the cookies from his hand. She stomped up the stairs, pausing at the screen door. Over her shoulder she said, "Charles. Will you bring my suitcases upstairs, please?"

NINETEEN

A HARD RAIN BATTERED the deck outside the opened French doors of Lisa's office. The afternoon faded toward evening. No wonder Lisa loved this office so much. With the open door and windows, it felt like working outside, except she stayed dry. She let her fingertips outline the blue and black inlay on Lisa's box. She snapped on the desk lamp.

Pictures of petroglyphs and pictographs panels covered the desk. Nora lined them up side by side, looking for similarities. Lisa had carefully labeled the backs of the photos she'd shot with the location and date. She'd scribbled the site addresses on those she'd downloaded from the Internet. They showed the various figures Nora had seen all over—humans, animals, mazes, hand prints. The weird sunburst from Nora's dream showed up in most of the photos, along with snakes and birds and even the profile of the person in a boat.

Nora replayed Lisa's message. What was she trying to say? Nora typed Tokpela Ranch into her laptop and was rewarded with a live-stock auction report. Tokpela Ranch sold six cows several days ago. A little more research revealed the location of the ranch to be about twenty miles south of Moab and that it bordered Canyonlands.

Nora's phone vibrated, startling her. She checked the ID—Cole.

Her heart leapt and she smiled automatically. Then her heart plummeted with a bruising punch as she remembered her situation. Her hand was already halfway to the phone and she hesitated.

He was married. She shouldn't answer it. Clean cut. Don't make it worse, she told herself. Against her better judgement, she picked it up and said hello. He was seven hundred miles away. How could talking to him do any harm, she rationalized, even though she knew better.

There was a slight pause and he spoke in a strained voice. "I wasn't sure you'd answer after this morning."

She pictured the blush climbing his neck and burning in his cheeks. She longed to feel his arms around her but he belonged to another woman. What she really needed was a big dose of backbone. She mouthed the words to try to make it more real. He's married. "I spoke to your wife this morning."

He exhaled. "Oh."

"Oh," she repeated.

"Nora." The longing in his voice made her grab the edge of the desk. She held her breath.

"This thing that's going on. This ... marriage."

She swallowed, her skin hot.

"It's ... complicated."

"Complicated? As in, my wife doesn't understand me, but you do, let's have an affair?"

He exhaled again. "No. Amber." It sounded like he choked on the words. "My w-wife. I need to be careful. She's dangerous."

"Dangerous how?"

He hesitated, then the words spewed out in a decidedly un-Cole-like manner. "Please, trust me for now. Don't give up on us. I love you, Nora. I know you love me. I'm going to fix this, but it'll take a little more time. Can you give me that?"

No. She should end it, like she'd already ended it in Moab this morning. Why was she talking to him on the phone anyway? She'd trusted Scott years ago when he said his affair was over. That had been a stupid mistake. She should learn from that. "Yes. I can give you time. But not forever." She smacked her forehead. Stupid, stupid, stupid. But Cole wasn't Scott. She did trust him. "How's your father?"

His tone brightened a bit. "He's holding his own. The tough ol' guy might just make it."

There was that. He asked about Charlie and Abigail and she asked about the ranch, then the conversation stalled out. "Can I call you again?" He sounded sweet and shy. That vulnerability always undid her. Her gut told her it was authentic even as her head argued.

"Yes," she heard the longing in her own voice. She smacked her forehead again. If she didn't start having easier relationships, she'd give herself brain damage.

She sat for a long time after he hung up, listening to the rain patter on the deck.

TWENTY

ANOTHER SUNRISE ON LISA'S front porch. More corn dust tossed in gratitude for another day. Another appeal to the spirits of her father's clan. More silence.

Maybe the kachina only showed up when Nora faced real, physical danger or when he had something he wanted her to do. But she'd like a personal deity to wrap some support around her. She'd probably lost Cole, someone she thought she'd love for a lifetime. Would it be so much to ask she not lose her imaginary spirit as well?

When the kachina first appeared to Nora on her mountain in Flagstaff, she'd been terrified. There are hundreds of Hopi kachinas that represent everything from animals and nature to ancestors. They generally show up for ceremonies and dances or appear in clouds to rain on the desert corn. The kachina that visited Nora was an old Hopi *kikmongwi*, or chief, from the 1880s. Benny said he was her grandfather of many generations past. Benny knew this because the kachina was also his grandfather and they were in regular communication. If Nora hadn't experienced the kachina's visits, she might not believed what Benny said. Choosing to go along with Benny's explanation let her believe she wasn't a complete lunatic.

He appeared to her in Flagstaff so she would stop the manmade snow on the sacred peaks. He'd inexplicably shown up in Boulder last fall, just weeks before the strict Hopi calendar dictated all kachinas return to the three mesas in Arizona. Then he'd had another mission for her. She tried to convince herself he was only a figment of her over-active imagination.

But he'd saved her life in a very tangible way.

Despite Utah's rising sun warming her face, Nora shivered remembering the Rocky Mountain peak last fall. She'd felt the freezing air of Mount Evans in a snowstorm, seconds before dawn.

Trapped on a ledge, her arm useless from a gunshot, a terrorist dead at her feet, Nora had no choice but to step into the rifle sight of a killer. The gunman held his rifle up, sighting into the scope.

Nora caught her breath. She knew the killer's next shot would tear her apart.

But the shot never came.

The kachina appeared behind the killer. He held his hatchet high.

She'd been to the mesas, listened to Benny's stories about the Hopi and their migrations. She'd prayed with him and walked the trails where the Hopi had lived for centuries. But since that morning on Mount Evans, her kachina remained silent.

Maybe she didn't want him popping out at her all the time, but it might be nice if he'd let her know he still watched over her.

She remembered Benny's words: "When Hopi know things are wrong, they look to themselves for personal responsibility."

What had she done to chase the kachina away? She'd planted corn in pots all over her apartment and office as the Hopi instructed. She hadn't been living simply, though—not if that meant growing her own food and not using electricity or any other convenience.

Benny told her that Hopi would reach a point of confusion because the modern world clashed with the traditional one. This world was in its fourth revision. The three previous worlds had ended when the leaders were corrupted by greed and power. Hopi prophesies warned it could happen again. Was Nora too steeped in the modern world?

A cupboard door banged in the kitchen behind Nora and she was suddenly back in the bright morning on the porch. She studied the yellow bloom of the blazing star in the front yard, still looking for the flash of her kachina's blue sash. He'd abandoned her.

The siren scent of bacon called to her nose. Abigail knew Nora loved bacon and she'd be crisping slices in the microwave. The thought of her mother's care lifted her heart a little. But if she wanted the comfort of the bacon, she'd best hurry inside before Abigail pulled her usual trick and blackened it.

The screen squealed open and banged softly behind Nora as she padded on bare feet to the kitchen in time to see Rachel slide a plate of bacon from the microwave.

Rachel's stony face froze, then thawed slightly after a second. She banged the plate on the counter bar in front of Nora. "So, I hear you're single now, too."

It sounded harsh and the bacon wasn't offered with gentleness, but it showed a modicum of sympathy. Nora plopped on a barstool. "Abigail told you."

Rachel nodded.

"Single's not so bad," Nora said.

Rachel reached over and took a slice of bacon. She'd cooked it just the way Nora liked it, crisp enough to hold its shape but not charred.

"I don't like single," Rachel said.

Maybe she and Rachel could call a truce. "After my disaster of a first marriage, I can fully embrace living alone." She tried to grin, but the words tasted bitter. She truly didn't mind being single, but she hated the thought of losing Cole before ever really having him. She grabbed a piece of bacon and bit into it, tasting the salty, fatty goodness. An entire blue-ribbon pig cured and fried wouldn't be enough to take away her pain, but this mouthful wouldn't hurt.

Rachel stuffed a half a slice of bacon into her mouth, slid the last one off the plate and onto the counter in front of Nora, and reloaded the plate with raw slices. She covered it with paper towels and slapped it into the microwave to convert calories to comfort.

"I've never really been on my own," Rachel said. She stared out the window toward Castle Rock.

Nora didn't know much about Rachel. She'd come into Lisa's life a few years ago. "What did you do before you met Lisa?"

Rachel's inhale vibrated in her chest, as if she were fighting tears. She twirled around and checked the bacon through the microwave window. "I was married."

Nora didn't have to ask if Rachel was married to a man. Marlene was right; Rachel had not only stepped outside the lines, she'd leapt clear to another coloring book. Though if Rachel had been married before, it showed she had relationships with men in the past. Would it be such a stretch to think she might have another? And if so, why not an affair with Lee?

Nora tried to keep the suspicion from gaining a foothold. She needed to trust Lisa and Lisa had loved Rachel. "Will you stay here?" Nora asked.

The microwave dinged and Rachel reached in for the plate. "Where else would I go?" She didn't sound defensive, and it appeared to be a legitimate question.

After the events in Flagstaff and she'd lost her husband, her business, and her entire direction in life, Nora fled to Boulder, where she'd grown up. She'd needed to back up before she could move forward. But Rachel had nowhere to back up to. And even though Nora had pushed him away, Cole had been there for her. Who did Rachel have?

Lee's image popped into Nora's head again.

Abigail's footfalls sounded from the stairs. "What decadence do I smell?" She rounded the corner, coming to stand with her hands on her hips, surveying Nora and Rachel as though they'd broken into a bank. Abigail had sent a forlorn Charlie back to Flagstaff, insisting that she stay until Nora came to her senses.

Nora reached for the plate Rachel set on the counter and helped herself to another slice. "Ambrosia from the pork gods."

Abigail lunged for Nora's hand, but she quickly stuffed the bacon into her mouth. Abigail frowned at her. "You'll never get Cole back if you let yourself get fat."

"A few pieces of bacon aren't going to ruin me. Cole doesn't matter anyway."

Abigail leaned toward the plate. "I suppose a little bacon won't hurt." She snagged a piece and savored a bite. "But you're wrong about Cole. There's an explanation for this alleged marriage, and when we find out, you'll be sorry you were so hard on him."

"Hard on him?" Nora choked out, wanting to start a tirade but realizing the futility and letting it drop. "So, you stayed in Moab to help me cope with my broken heart?"

Abigail made her way to the kitchen and reached for the coffee. "Absolutely not. There will be no feeling sorry for yourself. I'm here to make sure you don't give up on Cole."

"Do you have a plan?"

Rachel leaned back on the counter and watched their interplay.

Abigail measured coffee into a French press. She tapped the tea kettle on the stove, found the temperature acceptable, and poured the water on top of the grounds. "Frankly, I don't know."

Nora hopped off the stool. "Good. I've got a plan, then."

"And what, pray tell, would that be?"

"You can take me to some of the places you and my father visited."

"Why would you want to do that?"

"I don't know. Maybe it will make me feel closer to him. Maybe I can learn something about him." *Maybe a trip to Arches can take us to Fiery Furnace and I can figure out what Lisa wanted to tell me.*

"Well, that's just more of your woo-woo mystic lunacy."

Rachel's eyes twinkled as though she watched a comedy.

She wouldn't admit that her mother might be right. So far, Nora didn't feel any real connection to her father and her Hopi ties felt shaky. If she didn't find Lisa's camera, she might lose her job. Cole was most likely a lost cause. Right now, the only things that felt solid were her connections to Abigail and the land. And her commitment to finding Lisa's killer.

"Okay, then let's just go to Arches and sightsee," she told Abigail.

Abigail depressed the plunger on her coffee. "Can't we go shopping instead?"

Nora turned to Rachel. "Where were some of the last places Lisa filmed?"

Rachel pushed against the counter. Her eyes turned hard. "I don't know. Why?"

"Maybe we could hit a few of the sites. Get some idea what Lisa was thinking."

Rachel picked up the empty plate and banged it into the sink. Luckily, it didn't break. "Lisa was thinking she wanted to change the world to better suit her own whims. The world had a different notion."

Abigail opened a cupboard and plucked out a coffee cup. "It was an accident. It would have happened whether she'd been filming or picnicking."

Rachel stared into the sink, her shoulders rigid. She didn't reply. Perhaps because she knew Lisa's death wasn't an accident?

"Let's go to Fiery Furnace. It was a special place to Lisa." Nora studied Rachel's back. Rachel gripped the edge of the sink, but didn't turn.

Abigail laced her coffee with hazelnut creamer. "I don't suppose there's a mall in Moab," she said, trying to diffuse the tension.

Rachel turned slowly and glared at Nora. "Leave it alone."

"What is there you don't want me to find?" Nora said.

Abigail scoffed. "Rachel's only concerned you don't torture yourself like this, Nora. Going to Lisa's favorite places will only rub salt in the wound."

Rachel and Nora didn't move or acknowledge Abigail. Silence ticked in the kitchen. A mourning dove hoo-hoo-hooted outside.

Abigail set her cup on the counter. "Fine. If you're so set on wallowing in death and pain, we'll visit some of the spots your father and I went to. Now quit harassing Rachel."

TWENTY-ONE

An hour later Nora held the Jeep door open for Abbey to jump in the back.

Abigail walked onto the porch and called back inside through the closed screen door. "I've got my phone, dear. Text me if you decide you need anything from town." She hefted a wicker tote bag onto her shoulder and stepped down the porch. She wore khaki capris and walking shoes. Her cardigan sweater matched the pink T-shirt underneath as well as the trim on her socks and she looked like a catalogue image for tasteful outdoor-wear for older women.

"Ready?" Nora was more than anxious to get moving.

Abigail slid into the passenger seat of the Jeep and twisted around, settling her tote bag on the floor behind Nora's seat. "I've brought sunscreen, snacks, water, an extra jacket, and a first aid kit. Anything else?"

Nora flung her arm over the seat back to look behind her. She backed down the dirt driveway, concentrating on the narrow passage. "I've got most of that stuff in here. I filled my water bottles at the house."

Abigail raised her eyebrows. "I'm sure you've got all sorts of things in this vehicle. How you ever find anything is beyond me—looks like you haven't cleaned it out in years."

Nora pulled onto the road and slid the Jeep in gear. "Abbey and I spend a lot of time in the mountains. I have extra coats and gear in here for that."

"Too bad they didn't wash and detail your Jeep while it was at the shop."

Just another verse of the old "Clean Your Room" ballad. "Where would you like to go first?"

Abigail reached around and dug into her tote bag, pulling out a granola bar. She unwrapped it. "I don't care."

They turned on the highway and headed toward Moab. "Let's start at the windows arches. You and Dan hiked there, didn't you?"

"You can call him your father. You don't have to say his name."

"It's just weird for me. All my life he was this guy that abandoned us, so I didn't want to feel any affection for him. Now I know he died, that he didn't leave us voluntarily. I'd like to know him, even a little."

Abigail chewed her granola bar and watched the tamarisk and willows on the river. Finally she spoke. "It was a long time ago." She finished her granola bar and fidgeted, drumming her fingers on the seat belt buckle. If she felt as nonchalant as she claimed, she wouldn't be eating compulsively and squirming like a five-year-old at church.

"Okay, so Arches it is," Nora decided.

On the half hour drive to the park just north of Moab, Abigail talked nonstop. She commented on the rafters floating the Colorado River and complained about the loud Harleys that zoomed up behind them and passed in a roar. She remarked about the new paved bike trail running alongside the highway. She chattered about her service club in Flagstaff and how it contributed to scholarships for struggling women. Nora heard more about Abigail's efforts to reform Charlie's diet and exercise habits than she cared to know. Obviously, Abigail wanted to avoid talking about Dan Sepakuku.

Abigail's reluctance to share details about this man puzzled Nora. What could Abigail want to hide?

They approached the park entrance—a long, sloping valley dotted with cactus, scrub, and rocks. An RV had pulled off to the right into the parking lot of the visitors' center. Several yards ahead, a kiosk squatted between the outgoing lane and the lane entering the park. The sun wasn't serious yet and the morning felt fresh.

Nora showed her National Park pass and collected the maps and park pamphlet. "Anywhere specific you and my father visited here?"

"Just the regular places. The window arches and Delicate Arch." Abigail dug out another granola bar and tore off the wrapper.

Nora drove up the long incline and maneuvered a few switchbacks. This early in the morning, they had the road to themselves.

The sky opened in an infinity of blue. No clouds marred its perfection. Nora rolled down her window and her lungs enlarged as she let the cool desert air fill her. Abbey poked his head over her shoulder and lifted his nose to the rushing wind.

The red sand and boulders of the hills popped against the sunshine and crisp air. Yellow blazing star and bright orange globemallow dotted the sparse ground along with the pinks and purples of the milkweed and Utah daisy. Sage, Mormon tea, and clump grass accented the sand, still damp from yesterday's afternoon showers.

"So many wildflowers this year. Has it been a wet spring?" Abigail seemed lost in her thoughts, so it surprised Nora she'd be so observant.

Always eager to encourage Abigail's curiosity of the natural world, Nora answered, "Unusually wet here. The ground is pretty well saturated. We'll probably be seeing some flash floods in places that haven't been flooded in years." She'd never understood how anyone could describe the desert as barren. The land sang an aria of beauty, bringing tears to Nora's eyes.

This place cradled Lisa's soul.

Spires rose in majesty like a fantastical army of aliens marching across the desert. The unbelievable power of wind and water formed these gigantic castles of stone. Awesome, in the most basic sense.

They didn't speak as Nora drove past Balanced Rock. They wound up to the parking lot and climbed out of the Jeep to view North and South Windows and Double Arch. Nora let Abbey jump down and clipped a leash to his collar. They climbed a quarter mile on smooth stone along a rock-lined trail in the red sand. Abigail stopped in the shade created from the elongated stone arch. She stared across the desert valley toward the La Sal Mountains in the distance.

Nora sat in a sunny spot and soaked up the scene. Abbey plopped down next to her and she trailed her fingers through his soft fur. The warmth of the stone radiated into her skin. The valley swept before her, an endless ocean dotted with deep green scrub against the amber ground. The soft summer felt like kisses on her bare arms and the tang of sage teased her nose.

Abigail's shoulders hitched. Nora wondered if she was sobbing. She scrambled to her feet and jogged over to Abigail, Abbey following.

Instead of tears, Abigail's face was bright with humor. She chuckled as Nora got close. "See that?" She pointed to a cluster of stunted trees on the valley floor. "We camped there the first night we arrived."

Nora waited, hoping there was more to the story.

Abigail giggled. "We'd brought a bottle of wine and some chips. I was nervous because I'd never been camping and this was the first time I'd been alone with a man. Even though I was sure Dan was The One, I'd only known him for a few weeks."

Nora fought against wanting to know more about her parents and not wanting to know too much. This could slip into the too much zone quickly.

"Sometime in the middle of the night, I woke up with a terrible stomachache. I should have scurried out of the tent to, well, do what you might have to do."

Tilting to the dark side. "You had gas?"

Abigail stared at the old camp site. "But the night was dark and the outside seemed so big and frightening. I stayed where I was and, well, let it go." She blushed and giggled in embarrassment, not noticing Nora at all.

"Oh my. It even brought tears to my eyes. But Dan's breathing never altered so I assumed he slept through it and with us being outside, I figured the tent air would be pure by the time he woke up."

Nora didn't want to think about her mother farting. Ever.

"The next morning, I was making coffee by the fire and Dan was frying bacon. He didn't look at me as he said, 'A bear came by our camp last night.' Well, you can imagine how that upset me. I dropped the coffee pot and almost couldn't speak. 'A bear? When?'" Now Abigail laughed out loud. She caught Nora's eye. "He shrugged and said, 'Well, I didn't actually see him. But I sure smelled him.'"

Abigail laughed again. "I nearly died of embarrassment. 'I thought you were asleep!' I said. He tilted his head and said, 'I *was*.'" She shook her head. "I can still see that mischievous twinkle in his eye."

Nora's father had a sense of humor. Clearly he had an honest streak that was mixed with kindness. Was this too much to glean from one little story?

Abigail relaxed a little. She didn't mention Dan again, but she no longer prattled with nervous energy. They drove to a few more overlooks, commenting on the beauty of the landscapes and sharing bits and pieces of their day-to-day lives.

The sun reached its zenith. They'd eaten the balance of the granola bars and shared water with Abbey. "Do you feel like taking a short hike?" Nora asked.

Abigail shrugged. "If you promise it will be a short one. I don't want to get stuck on a forced march. And it better be on a level path."

"I'd like to walk in Fiery Furnace. Then we can head back to town and I'll buy you lunch."

Nora pulled into the parking lot at the site. They climbed out and Nora waited for Abigail to slather herself with sweet-smelling sunscreen. The desert sun hit Nora's skin and she could almost hear it sizzle. She reached into the back of the Jeep for her own unscented sunscreen spray. It didn't help the heat, but it'd keep her from crisping.

A wood fence blocked the trailhead that led to a one-track path a short distance across a flat plane and wound into an impenetrable stand of fins and spires. Heat waves warped the view across the valley in the opposite direction. A sign at the trailhead warned hikers that they couldn't enter the maze of stone without a permit and a guide. Nora slipped around it and onto the trail.

"We aren't permitted in here," Abigail said, standing her ground.

Nora cast around for witnesses, saw they were alone, and waved her mother in. "If we hurry, we can get behind the stones before someone sees us."

Abigail glanced behind her. "This isn't a good idea," she protested, but hurried after Nora.

They followed the path threading through the fins of stone. The close formations caused them to squeeze between the narrow passages. Could she dislodge another anecdote from Abigail? Nora felt a greedy need for more of her father, but maybe she'd have to be content with one story, albeit one indelicate and incredibly crude by her mother's usual standards, but so telling.

They walked on, breathing in hot air, conserving their water with small sips. She unclipped Abbey from his leash and followed his plodding pace. An unusual change in rock color caught Nora's attention and she veered off the trail to wind through a few fins, hoping to find the petroglyphs Lisa had told her about. The rocks were warm under her hands as she maneuvered through tight places.

"Where are you taking us?" Abigail didn't sound pleased.

"I thought there might be a rock art panel here, but it's just weathered rock."

"Shouldn't we go back to the trail?" Abigail asked.

Nora tried to get her bearings and looked for a trail. "I'm not sure where it is."

Abigail put her hands on her hips. "I knew we shouldn't have come in here without a guide!"

Nora waved her hand. "No big deal. We'll head back toward the trailhead and get there eventually."

Abigail held up her bottle. "I hope that's not a long time. I'm nearly out of water and this heat is withering me."

"We've only been out here for a half hour or so. I'm sure you won't dehydrate."

"I'm glad you have confidence." She glared at Nora. "You take the lead. This place is a maze."

Nora sidled around Abigail in the narrow passage and Abbey struggled to get ahead of them. Nora studied the scenery, trying to put herself in Lisa's head. Where would she hike that she accidently ran into petroglyphs?

She studied the rock around her, peering into crevices as they walked. She followed Abbey's red flag of a tail, already rounding another sharp turn, and nearly smacked into a wall of stone.

Abbey disappeared into a tight passage but Nora stopped in the shade to wait for Abigail. She uncapped her water bottle and tilted her head to take a gulp of warm water, halting as something grabbed her attention.

She gasped and stepped back to get the whole impression. An amazing assortment of images were etched in the rock above her head. The panel measured about six feet wide and four feet tall and started twenty feet above the ground. Either erosion had dug a path or the artists had stood on some sort of bench. The faint designs scratched in the rock could easily be missed if a hiker wasn't paying close attention.

Nora leaned in, a sense of awe she always felt when viewing something so ancient washing over her. A person had stood here a thousand years ago or more. A real someone who loved and struggled and laughed, worried about survival or wondering about God. That person had taken the time to chisel this rock, and the images must have been filled with meaning because carving on rock deep enough to last for millennia was no idle undertaking.

This artist, or artists, had created a hodgepodge of images. Human shapes with large, almost triangular bodies and tiny stick arms and legs shared space with unmistakable images of birds and snakes. Other figures weren't as easy to place. Some looked like they might be turtles or big bugs. Goats or deer ran alongside a boxlike creature that looked sort of like ET. There was even a boat shape, like a half moon on its side, with a figure sitting inside. Big circles, like giant ears, stuck out from the head of the boatman.

Panting behind her that didn't sound like Abbey. She glanced over her shoulder to see Abigail leaning against a spire. Her eyes looked panicked in her pale face.

"What is it?" Nora put a hand to Abigail's forehead to check her temperature. It didn't seem warm enough outside for heat exhaustion. Abigail was nearing sixty but in good shape. Was it a heart attack?

Abigail waved Nora's hand off her face. "Fine. I'm fine. Let's get out of here."

Nora understood. It wasn't heat stroke or heart attack. Fear. It radiated off Abigail's skin. She followed Abigail's gaze to the rock art panel. "What scares you?"

Abigail chuckled, but it sounded more like choking. "Don't be silly. I'm not afraid."

Nora studied the rock. Humans, other animal shapes, a few strange lines. Toward the bottom of the panel she noticed something familiar. The weird sunburst shape. The same design on the graffiti at the Read Rock and in her dream. Her heart stammered, too. "Did you come here with my father?"

Abigail shifted from foot to foot. "Yes. No. Oh, how do I know? Red rocks, sand, arches. It's all the same. Here or in Canyonlands or anywhere else."

Nora stared at the rock again. "Is this what Lisa wanted me to see?" she wondered out loud.

"What?" Abigail sounded irritated.

Nora pointed. "That symbol with the lines. It keeps popping up."

Abigail squinted at the panel. "Dan liked that. After he saw it here, he used to doodle it."

"Do you know what it means?"

Abigail waved her hand. "Who knows? Whatever you want, I suppose."

"My father never said?"

"I never asked. Let's just go."

Nora lowered her gaze to meet her mother's. "Why are you so upset?"

"I'm not upset. Rachel's right. You need to leave things alone. There are enough wilderness places around here to satisfy everyone. Come on. I'm hungry and want to get out of this heat."

Something about the rock art crawled under Abigail's skin. Nora needed to coax it out. They squeezed through the tight passage behind the fins and intersected a worn path.

Abigail tore down the trail. She seemed to have developed a whole new level of fitness, winding in and out of the rock towers and pushing Abbey to keep ahead of her. Nora thought about the symbols on the rock panel. It had something to do with her father. She was sure of it. That's the only connection Abigail would have with Native American history. Her father, the rock art, and Lisa's murder. They couldn't all be coincidence, she thought.

Abigail practically ran the last quarter mile to the Jeep. She stood by the passenger door, her arms crossed and her face tight with tension. "Where should we eat?"

Nora unlocked the door. She pulled Abbey's collapsible dish out of the back seat and filled it with the last of her water. He lapped it up. "Doesn't matter to me."

When Abbey finished his water and jumped in back, they loaded up and headed across the mesa and the switchbacks that led to the park exit.

"How many days did you and Dan spend in Arches?" Nora probed as carefully as she could.

"I don't know, three or four days," her mother responded curtly.

"Did you like it here?" Nora rolled down her window. She inhaled the new growth and sunshine on the breeze. It smelled green and blue and yellow, alive with the unusually wet season.

Abigail's shoulders hiked up with tension. "I was in love. It wouldn't have mattered if we had toured the moon."

"What about Dan? There must have been a reason he brought you here." She steered around the gentle slopes, tapping the brakes in order to keep an easy speed.

"I guess. I don't know. He said it is an important place and he seemed interested in the rock art." Abigail slapped her palms on her leg. "Can we please drop it? Bringing me here makes me sad. He was a good man and he never got a chance to grow old. Like Lisa. We need to let them rest in peace."

A meadowlark's song swirled into the window and around Nora's head. She rounded a curve and headed down the mountainside. The park maintained the road and it was nothing like the narrow, twisting ribbon on the side of Mount Evans outside of Denver. Thinking about that piece of highway leading up to a fourteen thousand-foot peak made Nora break into a sweat.

She gripped the wheel. She was driving too fast. She'd miss a curve. This road descending toward the visitors' center didn't have the hairpin turns of the Mount Evans route, but there were switchbacks and Nora was going too fast to navigate around them.

"Nora, why are you pumping the brakes?" Abigail's voice cut into Nora's concentration.

"What? Oh. I'm … " *Get a grip, Nora.*

"You're driving like a bat out of Hell." Abigail raised her voice. It brought back memories of the one time she'd taken Nora out to teach her to drive. No surprise—Nora had a heavy foot and didn't stop at the stop sign long enough and nearly got them killed in traffic. Berle had taken over driver training after that.

"I'm fine. This is a good road." Nora agreed that she should slow down, too, but reacted automatically to Abigail's complaint.

"You're scaring me!"

Nora tapped the brakes, but instead, the Jeep gained a little more speed. Nora stepped harder on the brakes, but didn't feel any resistance. The hillside out her window blurred. The speedometer needle inched further to the right.

Nora slammed on the brakes.

Nothing.

"What's going on?" Abigail clutched the dash in a panic.

Nora pumped her foot, but she met no pressure from the pedal. "The brakes aren't working!" Sweat lined her face, yet she felt cold all over.

The wind roared. The wheels sounded like a train in Nora's head. Her vision narrowed, seeing only the strip of pavement in front of her.

She tried to remember the road when they'd driven up earlier. How many turns? How sharp? She hadn't paid attention and now couldn't conjure it up.

A yellow diamond sign warned of a curve ahead. Nora automatically hit the brakes again and the action unleashed jolts of panic. She held her breath and gripped the wheel, terrified by the upcoming bend. A boulder the size of the USS *Arizona* sat on the outside of the road. If they didn't make the turn, they'd smash into the side, creating their own gruesome rock art of blood and bone.

They'd never stay upright if Nora stuck to her own lane. The narrow wheelbase of the Jeep would cause it to flip at this speed. If she crossed the center line and someone came uphill on the curve, Nora would smash into them.

She strained to see past where the road swerved. Was another vehicle coming? What should she do? The pavement started to turn. She concentrated on the double yellow line in the middle of the road. Her shoulders felt like steel with her hands welded to the steering wheel. As the curve tightened, she edged to the outside, venturing into the opposite lane.

The wind, the squeal of the tires, and Abigail's screams all combined in a mind hurricane, blocking out everything but automatic action. They rounded the corner with the grill of an ocean liner of an SUV looming a few feet ahead of them.

A screaming horn penetrated Nora's brain. Her hands jerked the wheel to the right before she could form a thought. They swerved out of the SUV's path, the protesting horn following their flight. The Jeep's right tires dropped off the pavement. Abigail screamed again.

The raw cliff face loomed inches from the passenger window. The outside mirror exploded as it tore away from the door. Nora yanked the wheel to the left. The Jeep swung back onto the road. But she'd overcorrected and now they headed for the steep shoulder drop off. Nora swung the wheel back. The Jeep lurched to the right, the tires stuttering. In that instant, she knew they were going to flip.

She twisted the wheel one way, then the next, without any conscious thought. Muscle memory or luck or possibly even her kachina guided her, though he didn't show himself. In seconds or minutes or perhaps years, the Jeep settled into a straight line race down the road.

With no curves in her immediate sight, Nora took a second to gather her bearings. The high rev engine shrieked. The valley stretched before them with one long slope to the visitor's center and a gradual flattening of the road as it swept toward the highway. They still careened down the hill, going way too fast for safety. If they passed the fee kiosk at this speed, they could hit a pedestrian or crash into another vehicle.

Nora considered ramming the Jeep into first or second gear, but if she disengaged the clutch now she might not be able to force it into another gear and they'd be free-wheeling.

A line of cars inched through the fee station on the left. A Cruise America RV with a cheery vacationing family painted on the rear loomed in front of them, making its way through the exit.

"We're going to hit them!" Abigail shrieked. She braced her arms on the dash.

The Jeep lost some momentum as the road leveled, but they still barreled out of control. The back end of the RV grew in the windshield.

Nora laid on the horn.

The brake lights of the RV lit up. No! She needed them to speed up, not stop! Nora held her breath and gripped the wheel. They would collide with the RV at the kiosk. The pavement widened to accommodate the traffic at the fee station.

Please stay inside the RV, she prayed. If someone stepped out from the either the RV or the kiosk, she'd plow into them.

Amid Abigail's screams and the shrieking engine, Nora yanked the wheel. They shot to the right side of the RV, wheels balancing on the edge of the pavement.

Whack. They guillotined the driver's side mirror.

Nora sucked in air. They'd made it! Only a long, flat road ahead, with plenty of time for the Jeep the slow to a stop.

Then she saw it.

A group of motorcycles pulled out in front of her, leaving the visitors' center. Between the group of six or eight, they covered both lanes. They didn't know Nora couldn't slow down. She laid on her horn, but they didn't have enough time to react. She jerked the wheel to the right and the Jeep flew off the road into the sand.

It only took fifty feet or so for the Jeep to come to a complete halt. They banged across shrubs and rocks, their seat belts biting into them as they crossed the brain-rattling, rough terrain. Abbey slammed into the back of Nora's seat and yelped.

They finally stopped and Nora cut the engine.

"My god! We could have been killed!" Abigail panted and clutched her chest. Nora tried to draw in a breath, but struggled. She couldn't let go of the steering wheel.

"I told you two years ago to get a new car. But no, you didn't listen. You aren't happy unless you've got the oldest car on the road."

Oxygen finally seeped into Nora's lungs. She hoped her heart didn't split her chest.

"You're lucky this didn't happen in the mountains. I'd have had to bear the loss of my only daughter."

Nora wanted to close her eyes, but they were stuck wide open in panic mode.

"It is irresponsible of you to have held on to this antique this long. At least now you'll have to get a new car."

Nora popped her seat belt loose, flung her door open, and jumped out. Abbey hopped out after her, no worse for the terror.

Feet on solid ground, Nora leaned her hands against the hot hood and dropped her head. The shaking commenced and when her knees buckled, she sank to a squat.

TWENTY-TWO

ABIGAIL'S RANTING SOUNDED LIKE The Chipmunks on speed. When the shaking subsided and her bones felt solid, Nora stood up. She found her phone in her backpack and called Marlene.

Marlene's voice boomed through the phone. Maybe her annoyance wasn't directed at Nora, but she sounded like she wanted to punch something. "You're at the visitors' center? The brakes? Are you okay?"

"Just hurry. Abigail's lecture is about to drill a hole in my brain."

"Wait." Marlene spoke to someone. After a minute she came back on the line. "Bill Hardy is here. He said he'd come along with me."

"Bill Hardy?"

Marlene spoke to the phantom Bill. "I'll lock up and meet you at the garage." The bell above the door tinkled and Marlene spoke into the phone. "Bill owns the repair shop down the street from me."

That must be the shop Darrell warned her against. "The Conoco? How do you know Bill?"

"He's a friend." Marlene sounded distracted, probably closing up the Read Rock.

"And you think he's a good mechanic? Fair?"

"What are you talking about? I just told you he's a friend. So yeah, he's fair. Would you like to call the Better Business Bureau?" The bell dinged again and a door bang closed.

Nora closed her eyes against the glare. "No, sorry. I'm not thinking."

"Of course not. We're on the way."

Marlene and Bill Hardy arrived in less than a half hour, long enough for Abigail to calm down. She had pulled out some moistened towelettes and done some sort of magical repair to her face and hair that made her look as though she'd just stepped out of the salon. The sweat drying from her shirt and a quick wipe of one of Abigail's towlettes constituted enough freshening up for Nora.

Park rangers and a few curious tourists ventured out, hoping to get the story. Nora explained the brake failure and that help was on the way. Since no one was injured and the damage was limited to the Jeep's mirrors, the authorities seemed willing to let the incident drop.

Abigail sat in the Jeep with the doors opened to catch the slight breeze. Abbey stretched out in the shade under the Jeep. Nora paced, going from a three-foot Mormon tea shrub, around two rocks the size of picnic tables, and back again, her boots crunching on a crust of gravel and grit.

Marlene and Bill arrived in a tow truck that had faded to a colorless gray. Tool boxes lined the heavy truck and an assortment of tools and equipment filled the bed. Marlene spilled out of the passenger side, her red-and-yellow-striped skirt billowing in the breeze. She strode over to Nora and Abigail and stopped to inspect them. "You seem okay."

"Barely," Abigail spewed in a breathless fury. "That Jeep is done for and it nearly took us out with it."

Bill Hardy sauntered over. He might have been fifty or eighty, with deep lines etched in his face. He reached out to shake Nora's hand, his grease-stained paw bearing black half moons under his fingernails. He wore dark blue Oshkosh overalls and a stretched and faded T-shirt. "How do."

Nora accepted his quick and crushing handshake. "The brakes went out."

"Hmm." He stepped to the Jeep and popped the hood. He hummed while he surveyed the engine. Nora turned to Marlene. "Thank you so much for coming out here," she said.

Abigail gazed up at Marlene, whose Amazonian elegance seemed fitting to the red stone and sand. "You're an angel. I just don't know what we would have done without you."

Still humming, Bill pulled back from the engine and squatted down to look under the Jeep.

Marlene watched the mechanic as he got on his hands and knees and reached behind the passenger side front wheel. "You were lucky Bill was in the shop when you called. He's a big mystery fan and comes in once a month for all the new paperbacks."

Bill came out from under the Jeep and put a hand on the fender to help himself up. "Found your problem. It's an easy fix and you'll be on your way." He ambled toward his truck.

"What happened?" Nora asked.

He rummaged in the bed of his truck and pulled out a plastic gallon container and held it up. "Out of brake fluid."

Abigail crept up behind him. "That's all?"

He walked back to the Jeep and addressed Nora. "Have you noticed the brakes getting spongy lately?"

She nodded.

"Fluid's probably been leaking out for a couple of days. When you hit the brakes coming down that slope, it squeezed the last of the fluid out and then you were done. Nice work getting her slowed down and stopped, though." He picked up his humming again.

"I've never heard of the brakes losing fluid," Abigail said.

He interrupted his humming. "I haven't seen it myself. Not like this."

"What do you mean?" Nora asked.

He twisted the cap of the brake fluid container. "Looked like the bleeder valve somehow worked loose. Then the drive sort of wiggled it even more loose. It leaked out a little at a time, until you hit them hard, then it blew the rest of the fluid out." He unscrewed a cap in the engine and poured the fluid. "I tightened the bleeder valve and I'll get this filled up. You'll be good to go."

"How would this have happened?" Nora asked.

He put the cap back on the jug and puckered his lips in consideration. "I don't know."

Abigail crossed her arms. "It happened because this Jeep is so old it's literally falling apart. I say we drive it right onto a lot in Moab and get you something decent."

Bill sauntered back to his tow truck. "Oh, this beauty has lots of life in her. I wouldn't go trading her off just yet. Especially now that she's all fixed up."

Nora braced herself. "What do I owe you?"

He placed the jug into the mess of his truck bed. He squinted his eyes and gazed down the road, calculating. "Let's see. Mileage out here both ways, plus filling the fluid." He winked at Nora. "And a little something for my expertise." Here it comes. Darrell said this guy gouged tourists. "How about twenty bucks?"

Nora waited. The first twenty for the drive one way, then another twenty for the drive back. Add a hundred or so for his expertise.

He waited. Frowned. "You think that's too much?"

Marlene hit Nora on the arm. "Twenty? For the whole thing?" she stammered.

He hardened his face. "Any lower and I'd lose money on the gas alone."

"No, no. Of course." Nora trotted back to her Jeep. She dug in her pack for her wallet, extracted a twenty and a ten. Then put the ten back and took another twenty. She hurried to Bill and handed him the cash.

He took it, then held out one of the bills. "You got a couple of them stuck together."

"That's for you. For your trouble. Buy yourself a few new paperbacks." He shrugged as though he couldn't understand her and didn't really care to. He climbed back into the truck.

Marlene and Abigail stood chatting by the passenger door to the truck. Nora hurried over. "I hate that you closed the bookstore for this. If I'd been thinking, I would have called the shop where I had it fixed earlier. But I'm really glad I didn't. Bill's great."

Marlene glanced into the cab and grinned. "And more well-read than you'd expect. Where did you have it worked on before?"

"A shop Darrell suggested."

Marlene tilted her head. "What's the name of it?"

Nora tried to remember the logo on the letterhead. "A star or planet or something."

Marlene's eyebrows drew together. "Polaris?"

That didn't sound good. "What's the matter?"

"Nothing." Marlene's worried eyes didn't look like it was nothing.

Abigail put her hand on Marlene's arm. "You need to tell us."

Marlene gazed up at the spires in the distance. She inhaled and looked at Nora. "Polaris is owned by one of the oldest Mormon families in Moab. They kind of keep to themselves and mostly service their own and relatives' vehicles."

"So?" Abigail was clearly running out of patience.

"Ranching around here is a hard way to make a living. Most ranchers need to supplement their income."

"And?" Abigail urged.

"Lee works for them sometimes."

If that hadn't knocked the air out of Nora, the next words out of Marlene's mouth would have.

"They serviced Lisa's truck." Marlene paused. "Right before her brakes went out."

TWENTY-THREE

WARREN EVANS DENIED THE pain in his bones. The meds his physician prescribed were becoming less effective. He sat upright and plastered an enthusiastic grin on his face. All he needed to do was pull himself together for an hour, then he could return to his house and collapse, alone. He had the strength for that.

He lowered his head to pray, resisting the urge to rest his forehead on the steering wheel. He wanted to sleep, to lie back in his four-poster bed, surrounded by his children and grandchildren who would weep at the thought of his passing.

He would promise to see them again in the afterlife, when he, like his brother Jesus, would command his own planet, populated by his sons and daughters.

But he didn't have his own sons and daughters. God had withheld that blessing from him.

Christine's sharp voice cut through the silence in the Cadillac. "I don't know why you insist on putting yourself through this. You obviously don't feel up to it."

Warren pushed himself from the steering wheel to sit oak-tree tall. "We need to help Darrell. It's our duty."

Christine flipped the visor down and studied her face in the mirror. She pulled a tube of lipstick from her purse and twisted it. The red color emerged like the disgusting penis of a dog. Before she applied it, she addressed him. "Why? Because he's Mormon and you have to stick together?"

He wanted to slap the lipstick from her hand. God made her the way He wanted her. And yet, never satisfied with His blessings, she'd pulled and tucked, dyed and plucked until she resembled a cartoon of the beauty he'd married so long ago. Maybe there had been the need for subterfuge while they courted investors and built Bourne Enterprises, but his fortune was made. He needed her to be his wife now, his helpmate—not just a cosigner on some of his bank accounts.

He unbuckled his seat belt. "I want to help him."

She ran the lipstick over her mouth, smacked her lips, and puckered for the mirror, then fluffed her raven hair. "You've earned your rest. Why would you drag us both to this godforsaken dust bin to campaign for Darrell when we could have stayed in Manhattan so you could recover from chemo?"

She didn't fool him. Christine didn't care if this trip made Warren uncomfortable. She hated Moab, always had. She preferred expensive restaurants and shopping and her work on her charitable committees. She disdained anything that reminded her of Warren's roots. He'd watched her cringe every time he'd mentioned his Utah upbringing to prospective business associates. Maybe he should have left her in New York.

But she was his wife, married before God. Not a Temple wedding, because he'd been headstrong and hadn't chosen in the faith. For that, God had punished him. Maybe she didn't comfort him and he couldn't count on her to walk hand in hand with him to the threshold, but she hadn't shirked her public responsibilities. As far as he knew, she'd been faithful to him. When her time came, he'd call her through the veil. He owed her that much.

"This is important." He opened the car door and pulled himself to stand. He'd lost weight, as well as his hair, during the chemo. The well-made toupee camouflaged his bald pate and only the most observant would detect anything out of the ordinary. His tailor had made him a few new suits. He hoped he didn't look anything worse than tired.

Warren crossed in front of the Caddy and opened the passenger door for Christine. She climbed from the car with as much grace as an actress stepping onto the red carpet. She smiled up at him, habit from years of playing generous and supportive spouse to a rich man. She never let her cover slip. He should be grateful.

They walked across the dirt parking lot and up the wooden board-walk. He held the heavy log door open for her and she entered the restaurant. He followed and let the door close behind him.

He'd always liked this restaurant. The adobe walls, slick and white-washed, made him feel clean and cool. The umber tones and the rustic log furniture felt far removed from the pretensions of New York and high finance. He missed this country, his roots. He wouldn't go back to New York. He had no need to acquire more on this side of the veil. Surely God would grant him peace now.

But not just yet. He still needed to decide who would carry the banner when he was called home.

The tables had been moved to the perimeter of the large dining room. Smells of roasting meat and the grease from French fries and onion rings permeated the building. The room buzzed with energy and conversation, knots of people congregating throughout the dining room.

He spotted Darrell at the far end of the room. Rage squeezed into him, but he banished it in a heartbeat. Not even Christine noticed. He kept his face relaxed as he watched Darrell raise a frosty glass of amber liquid to his mouth.

Beer! Darrell knew better than to indulge in sin like this. It showed a weakness that troubled Warren deeply.

Warren and Christine weren't in the room more than three seconds before Todd Grayson, a local sporting goods store owner, noticed them.

Todd hurried over, all grins and outstretched hand. "Warren! So good to see you. Darrell didn't say you'd be here." Warren returned a firm grip, followed by several more hearty handshakes with others. People swarmed around him as they usually did. Some wanted to bask in his celebrity, some hoped to get close enough he'd do them a favor down the road, some genuinely liked him. He didn't waste energy trying to figure out which category they landed in. He shook hands, accepted hearty pats on the back, chatted and joked. A crush of admirers swept Christine away. Hers or his fans, he didn't care.

The crowd around Warren parted and Darrell stood in front of him, an ear-to-ear grin playing on his face. The boy was good. Even Warren couldn't discern the authenticity of his smile. He grabbed Warren's hand and gave it a warm squeeze. "What a great surprise. When did you get to town?"

"Christine and I got in around two this afternoon."

"Good flight?"

Inane conversation. He had more on his mind than the endlessly uncomfortable flight in his private jet. "Not bad. Looks like you've got a great crowd here." At two hundred dollars a plate, he'd better. Of course, Moab never brought in many campaign dollars. But a vote was a vote and Darrell needed them all.

Darrell surveyed the room with satisfaction. "We've got a lot of good friends here. Thanks to you."

Warren kept up his warm tone but lowered his voice a bit. "The polls have you slipping a few points."

Darrell's expression didn't falter but the light hardened in his eyes. "Nothing to worry about. We have a slump in cash flow right now so we're holding off for a media push in a couple of weeks."

Meaning, if only Warren ponied up cash, all would be well. Darrell so cleverly blamed his declining numbers on Warren.

A waitress wearing jeans and a too-small T-shirt appeared with two beading glasses of lemonade on a tray. The shirt stretched too tight across her breasts and the jeans rode too low on her hips. Sinful, thought Warren. Darrell took the glasses from her and held one out for Warren. "Thought you might be thirsty."

Warren accepted it and watched as Darrell drank nearly half of his glass. He probably hoped the lemon would mask the smell of the beer. His religion allowed no caffeine and definitely no alcohol. These might seem harsh and arbitrary rules, but the kosher restrictions of the Jews were equally as obtuse. God asked; man must comply. "We'll talk later," he said to Darrell. "You need to circulate."

Warren turned to an aging dowager, who wanted to discuss environmental issues. He did his best to focus on the woman, but nausea threatened and he felt weak. He caught a passing waitress, handed her the lemonade, and asked for ice water instead.

When he looked up, he caught sight of a black cowboy hat. The hat dangled in Lee's hands as he stood awkwardly in the back corner of the dining room. His mood brightened. Lee looked so much like Warren's dear sister Lydia, right down to the perpetually worried expression. It made them appear stern when Warren knew the opposite was true.

He disregarded the pain in his bones and strode over to Lee, hand extended. The corner of Lee's mouth ticked up. "Uncle Warren. Thought you might be here."

"It's good to see you supporting Darrell like this."

Lee chuckled. "I'm here to see you, not that blowhard."

Warren refrained from smiling. "The Lord uses everyone according to their talents."

The worry line appeared again in Lee's forehead. "I know you've been called to do great things. And I know the sacrifices you've made. Me and mine, we're grateful."

The toupee, the new suits, and the effort to appear energetic hadn't done the trick. Lee had detected his illness. Darrell probably had, too. He took the opportunity to drop into a chair next to a table that had been shoved against the wall. Lee sat down across from him.

Warren tried to lighten the boy's mood. "I wasn't fishing for compliments. And before you start in with your humility and all the proof of God's plan for you to be a steward of the land, I'm not going to lay any more burdens on you. Today." Lee looked at him in the same grateful, trusting way he used to when Warren took him fishing or hunting or they worked cattle. "But you said you came here to see me. What about?"

Lee hesitated. "A lot of people are arriving daily."

Warren glanced up to make sure they wouldn't be overheard. "Is there a problem?"

Lee positioned his chair so his back was to the room, trusting Warren to keep watch. "Lisa Taylor was close, Uncle Warren. She figured out what we're doing. If she hadn't died, we'd have been exposed."

Warren nodded. He couldn't let anyone know how shaken the incident made him feel.

Lee focused on Warren's face. "Rachel said that Trust woman thinks Lisa was murdered."

"That's why I'm here."

Lee exhaled in relief. "I hoped you'd handle it this time. With you here, it won't be as much a problem as it was with Lisa."

There. That's what Warren looked for. "You're a faithful servant, Lee."

The lines in Lee's forehead deepened. "I'm here to defend God's plan from the people who wouldn't understand."

Warren offered a gentle smile. "I'll let you know if I need you. And until then keep doing what you're doing—living a righteous life, keeping God's principles, and protecting the lands he gave us."

Lee pushed his chair back and stood. He made room for Warren to rise. Despite his effort to appear strong, Warren leaned heavily on the table. He stumbled and Lee grabbed Warren's elbows. With the strength that told of his days of physical labor, he righted Warren. As soon as Warren felt solid, Lee stepped back, deftly turning them so Warren faced away from the room and Lee looked into the room.

Warren took a moment to regain his balance and wipe the strain from his face. Lee pretended not to notice. "No doubt you and Christine will want to stay here for a while. I'll send Tessa around with some fresh eggs and produce." He paused to see if Warren felt up to answering and then continued. "I know Christine has a fond spot for Tessa. And Tessa thinks the world of Christine." As he spoke, Lee's eyes traveled the room as though searching for anyone who would dare harm Warren here.

Warren willed his legs to be like thick pine branches. He demanded his queasy stomach to calm. He only needed to stay a few more minutes, then he could make excuses that Christine was tired after traveling and he could retreat home to his bed. He looked up, ready to get the ordeal over with.

Lee's face reminded Warren of the cow dog he'd had as a youngster. His eyes shone with purpose as he zeroed in on his prey. The rest of his body seemed ready to strike. Warren swiveled around to see what caught Lee's attention.

A young woman with coppery hair that swung around her face spoke with Darrell. She smiled briefly but seemed to be concerned with the business at hand. Instead of a dress or slacks, she wore khaki shorts and hiking boots. By the dust on her well-worn hiking shirt, it seemed she'd just stepped off the trail.

Lee's voice sounded like a growl. "That's her. Nora Abbott. The woman from the Trust." It did seem like the red-head had a feisty edge to her. "We've got to deal with her before she causes us trouble."

"I don't like what happened to Lisa and I'd hate for it to happen again. Let's see if I can't send Ms. Abbott on her way."

Lee's mouth clamped shut. He'd never been one to argue. Not that he gave in. Words never meant a lot to Lee.

Warren approached Darrell and Nora Abbott. She seemed agitated. "Did you know he worked there? Would he tamper with my brakes?"

Lee's mouth clamped shut. He'd never been one to argue. Darrell leaned closer, his face wreathed in concern. "Do you have any proof? The sheriff in this county is—"

"Mormon and won't help me. I know. Someone messed with Lisa's brakes, too."

Darrell's frown of distress pleased Warren. "We can't talk here. Meet me tonight."

She obviously didn't like the brush-off, but she nodded briskly and turned. She smacked into Warren. "Excuse me."

He put out a hand as if to steady her, but it was more to keep himself from toppling. Her eyes flew open in recognition. Immediately she snapped her head to the right, then left, then over his shoulder as though looking for someone. People often wanted their friends to witness their brush with celebrity. She frowned briefly and returned her attention to him. "Mr. Evans."

He gave her his easy grin, the one investors trusted. "And you're Nora Abbott from Living Earth Trust. Darrell has told me about the accident involving that young woman making a film."

Before she had a chance to respond, Warren continued. "I'm a great supporter of expanding Canyonlands boundaries." She looked skeptical. "I've looked into Living Earth Trust and am impressed with your organization's stellar reputation. I'd like to make a sizable contribution."

Her eyes lit up. "We're always looking for additional funding."

"I've got some Hollywood connections. We'll get a top-notch videographer, writers, and a director. Let me see what I can do," he said.

She sighed. "That would be great, except we need the film before Congress votes in two weeks."

Warren made sure to look disappointed and concerned. "That's not good. However, they'll vote again. This subject comes up often. Having spent a lifetime following political dog fights, my advice is that you present your strongest testimonial and not dilute it with a less than professional film. Then channel your resources on a spectacular film. I do have an in with Robert Redford." For added impact, he acted as if he'd just thought of it. "Or even Ken Burns."

She seemed to consider his pitch. Most people would have been salivating over an offer like that. He didn't need unbridled enthusiasm. He just needed her to back off—and by the time she received any word from him, it would all be over.

Darrell's grin flashed with charm. "Wow! Ken Burns. That would be perfect. Do you think you could do that?"

"But it wouldn't come up for vote again for a year at the soonest, probably later," Nora said.

"That's unfortunate. But we don't have much choice, do we? Perhaps you and Darrell can make a compelling enough statement to bring in the vote now. Just in case, let's start the ball rolling for the next round and come back swinging." Money, celebrity, promises of future success—he'd given her a golden triangle of reasons to leave town.

Darrell continued to cheerlead. "This is the best news we've had since ..." His face contorted in sorrow before he went on. "Lisa would have been thrilled."

Time to close the sale. "Do you have a card? Never mind. I know I can contact you at Living Earth Trust. That's in Boulder, correct? I'll make some calls and get back to you early next week."

TWENTY-FOUR

Warren stepped from the noisy, cool restaurant onto the wooden boardwalk. He let the heavy log door bump closed behind him. He'd put in his appearance, made his generous offer to Nora Abbott, and said his goodbyes.

Christine had been right behind him, but one of her fans must have sidetracked her. Christine loved her admiring public, but probably enjoyed making him wait. She knew he wanted to get back to their spacious home by the creek.

He leaned against the side of the restaurant and watched as cars and RVs zipped past on the highway. Across the valley the cliffs rose in familiar splendor. It wasn't in his destiny to lead his people to the new land but here, this harsh and rugged place, was his promised land. He thanked God for letting him come home.

He pushed himself upright and stepped across the boardwalk and down into the gravel. He held his head high, his shoulders erect. Not long ago, that posture wouldn't have required conscious thought. Careful steps carried him across a rutted parking lot. With daily monsoon showers, the dirt lot stayed damp with muddy puddles.

His eye caught sight of a petite woman with blonde hair standing beside a beat-up Jeep. His breath caught as it always did when he saw someone like this. The reaction had been his personal torture for the last thirty years. He never forgot her. Every blonde woman with that height and build shot him back in time for a split second and his heart cracked every time.

Of course, none of those women ever turned out to be her.

This woman stood with her back to him. It wasn't her, either, but seeing someone so similar in this place stole another beat of his heart. He didn't have many to spare, but he'd willingly give one to her. He started to look away just as she moved her head to give him a view of her profile.

The world stopped.

A swell of blood rose through him, rushed to his arms and legs, and surged through every cell. It couldn't be. It was impossible. And yet, she stood in front of him.

Unconsciously, he moved until he found himself by her side. He heard his own choked voice before he realized he spoke. "Abigail."

She squeaked and jerked around, her hand at her throat. Blood rushed to her face and her eyes, still crystal blue, flew open. She stepped back and flattened herself against the side of the Jeep.

Warren reached for her hand, but she pulled it away. "You are still so beautiful," he told her.

She swallowed hard. "Get away from me."

He understood her shock. They hadn't seen one another for at least thirty years. No doubt he'd aged beyond her imagination, especially as a result of the cancer. She'd probably aged as well. She had to be almost sixty. Yet to his eyes, she looked the same as she did almost every night in his dreams. "Abigail, I … "

Christine's voice chirped from behind him. "There you are. I'm ready to go."

He couldn't turn away from Abigail, even though he knew he had to. If he closed his eyes or looked away, she might disappear forever. He'd learned to live without her for so long. But now that she stood close, now that God had put her back in his life, he couldn't let her go again.

"Warren?" Christine said.

Abigail brushed past him and hurried to the passenger side of the Jeep. She climbed inside, locked the door, and stared straight ahead.

Christine put a hand on his arm and shifted her gaze from him to Abigail and back. "Ready?"

A trickle of air leaked into his lungs and he blinked, fighting to appear normal. "Of course." He forced himself not to glance back at the woman in the Jeep as he followed Christine's elegant stride to the Caddy.

They opened their respective doors and slid inside. Christine let out a relieved breath. "Thank God you cut it short. All these people want to talk about is environmental issues and Darrell Burke's future."

Warren backed out of the parking space, his breath still ragged, his head a muddle of memories and desire.

He put the Caddy in gear.

The door of the restaurant opened and Nora Abbott walked out. She scanned the lot, then headed in the direction of the Jeep. Warren couldn't help but follow her with his eyes. She gave him an excuse to look in Abigail's direction and maybe catch sight of her again.

He expected Nora Abbott to climb into the sedan parked next to the Jeep. But she didn't. She pulled open the driver's door and plopped inside, her lips moving in conversation.

Nora Abbott and his Abigail. What was the connection?

TWENTY-FIVE

Nora jumped into the driver's seat. Abigail sat in the passenger seat, her head held at an angle, staring ahead, ramrod straight like a steel statue. Abbey sat up in back, greeted Nora with a cold nose to her cheek, and turned his attention to the windshield to help Nora watch the road.

"What's the matter?" Nora asked.

Abigail appeared every bit as frightened as when the Jeep caromed down the mesa. "Nothing."

Nora exhaled in frustration. "Mother."

Abigail spied her from the corner of her eye without turning her head. "I can't stand that man."

"Which man?"

"Warren Evans. He's a scoundrel and a cheat."

Knowing how Abigail admired wealth, this news surprised her. "That sounds personal."

"It is."

"You know Warren Evans?"

Abigail folded her arms and stared straight ahead.

"Okay, cough it up. How do you know him and why didn't you tell me about it?"

Abigail spoke through tight lips. "Did Darrell tell you anything about Polaris or Lee Evans?"

Nora started the engine. "Don't evade the question. What about Warren Evans?"

Abigail's jaw twitched with her clenched teeth. Without turning from the windshield, she said, "We knew him in college."

"We, as in you and my father? Evans went to CU?" She didn't remember that from the bios of the tycoon she'd read while in business school. What she knew was that he was from southern Utah, had grown up poor, built a windshield repair business that he leveraged to buy another company, and had kept adding and building businesses. He eventually became a corporate raider, had more money than anyone could count, and freely donated to charities.

"Only for a year or so, then he transferred to Yale."

"And you were friends?"

Abigail reddened in agitation. "I wouldn't call it that."

Nora grinned. "You had a thing, didn't you?"

"Stop it!" Abigail shouted the words. They echoed in the quiet Jeep, swallowed by Nora's shock. Abigail still hadn't turned from the windshield. "Just drop it. Tell me what Darrell had to say."

Nora backed out of the parking spot, wrenched the steering wheel, and edged around the lot toward the exit. She strained to the right to make sure no one was driving through the alley.

Wait!

Her eye caught the white of Lee's pickup. She slammed on the brakes as Abbey scrambled to stay on the backseat.

"What in heaven's name?" Abigail gasped.

Nora gestured to the white pickup parked by the restaurant's back door. "Lee's pickup."

Abigail eyed the vehicle, then Nora.

"For a man that makes his living off the land, he sure spends a lot of time in town."

"Was Lee Evans at the bookstore after Lisa's funeral? Is he the sour-faced man with the black hat?" Abigail's forehead wrinkled.

"That's him," Nora affirmed.

Abigail settled back into the seat. "He seems to have anger issues. You remember Margie Bowen. Her husband went through a behavior modification course to learn to control his temper. Might do Lee Evans some good."

Nora drummed her fingers on the wheel, thinking. "Lee works part time for Polaris. Lisa's brakes went out recently, then our brakes went out. Plus, Lee ran me off the road after the funeral."

Abigail inhaled and looked at the pickup. "You think he's trying to scare you away from finding the film?"

"Or something worse."

"Why would he do that?"

Did Abigail not pay attention to anything? "Maybe to keep Canyonlands' borders from expanding. Maybe because he's old school Mormon and hates that Rachel married Lisa."

Abigail huffed. "You're being ridiculous." Nora pushed the gearshift into first and rolled forward. "Where are we going?"

Nora gunned the Jeep and popped out on the highway heading south into Moab. "To try to find some answers."

Nora threaded her way through heavy traffic. Banners and signs celebrated the bike race and Moab buzzed with activity. She found a shady spot in the packed parking lot behind the Read Rock.

"Why are we here?" Abigail asked.

Nora opened her window for Abbey and scratched his ear. He loved napping in the Jeep and with a slight breeze and the shade, it didn't feel too warm. "Marlene knows more than she's telling me."

They climbed from the Jeep and walked through the alley. "About what?" her mother wondered.

"Not sure."

The bell above the door jingled as they walked in. Marlene stood at the display of local books with an elderly couple. Her gaze acknowledged them but she kept talking to her customers: "This is the best map for day hikes. Some of them are challenging, but there are some nice ones on level ground."

The man flipped through the guidebook Marlene handed him. "We liked the rim trail at the Grand Canyon. Is there something like that in Canyonlands?" Marlene pulled another book off the shelf and handed it to the woman as they continued discussing the best hiking options.

Nora and Abigail browsed the shelves, waiting for Marlene. Nora settled herself by the paperback mysteries located close to the back room. Whispers and a nervous giggle filtered through the curtain. Someone was in the back of the store.

The floor creaked as Marlene led the couple to the cash register with three books. "How long will you be in Moab?"

Marlene was busy with the customers and ringing up the sale. With only a moment of hesitation and a deep inhale to control her nerves, Nora slipped behind the curtain and into the back room.

She waited several seconds for her eyes to adjust to the darkness. Shelves and boxes cluttered the small space, which was little more than a wide corridor leading to a door that must open out into the parking lot. A secretary desk heaped with invoices, catalogues, and books was shoved against a wall.

A gasp brought her attention to the corner next to an open doorway. It must be a bathroom because a sink was visible. Two figures stood in the doorway.

Abigail practically shouted from the bookstore. "I'm not sure where she went. Maybe to the coffee shop down the street."

The curtain was whisked back and light flooded the back room. Two teen-aged girls in ill-fitting pastel dresses huddled together.

"What are you doing back here?" Marlene lunged toward Nora, her big hand clamping on Nora's arm. Marlene yanked her into the store and stood guard in front of the curtain.

Abigail pushed in front of Nora. "She had to use the restroom so I suggested she look back there."

Temper pushed around the edges of Marlene's eyes. "You said she went for coffee. I think she got nosy and went snooping where she doesn't belong."

Nora tried to put it together. "Are those girls hiding?"

Marlene lowered her eyebrows. "Not very well." She whirled around and disappeared behind the curtain. Her muffled voice sounded stern. "I told you to stay quiet and keep this door locked. What if it had been the church people?"

The girls whispered. Marlene lowered her voice. A door closed and seconds later, Marlene appeared. "Sit down." She indicated the reading nook in the corner.

When they'd settled, Abigail started in. "What girls?"

Marlene considered them a moment. "Those are runaways. They're from Colorado City."

Abigail gasped and put a hand to her mouth. "Polygamists. I saw this on *60 Minutes*. They lock these girls away in their compounds, don't let them go to school past the sixth grade, and keep them brainwashed. When they turn fourteen or so, they marry them off to middle-aged men as second and third wives and they start having babies every year."

Nora's stomach turned. "Those girls?"

Marlene nodded. "It's criminal, but the local cops around there are all part of the church."

Abigail's face burned. "Why would a man want so many wives and children?"

Marlene's eyes hardened. "The mainstream LDS church has some strange ideas and one of them involves descendants and what happens when men die."

Nora and Abigail waited for Marlene to continue.

"Basically, if a man is righteous, when he dies he'll get his own planet. That planet will be populated with his wives and children and all their children. So the more he has here on Earth, the bigger planet and more powerful he'll be in the afterlife."

"That's nuts," Abigail said.

"That's bad enough, but there are pockets of the Mormon Church—cults—that have their own notions. The LDS church doesn't condone polygamists, but other Mormons practice it. And even among polygamists, there are decent families and then there are the Taliban types that make women slaves, like the Colorado City bunch."

Frustration and helplessness pooled in Nora.

Marlene sighed. "So we help when we can."

"We?" Nora asked.

Marlene frowned. "Look. This is dangerous for these girls and for us. Secrecy is vital. I can't tell you who else is involved. The girls are here today, and tonight they'll be gone. We'll move them to someplace safe and give them what help we can."

Nora couldn't imagine the terror of being so young and running from everything you've ever known. "What happens if they're found by the church?"

Marlene's hands clenched on the table. "They'll go back and be under so much control they'll never be able to break out again."

Abigail placed a hand on Marlene's. "What a brave and admirable thing you're doing."

Tears threatened in Marlene's eyes. "I have to help. I can't let them to go through what I did."

Nora braced herself. "You were raised in that?"

Marlene closed her eyes. "I ran when I was sixteen and pregnant. It was ugly and I won't talk about how I survived. When my baby was born, I gave it up. I don't even know if was a boy or a girl, but I do know it has a better life than I could have given it, either on the compound or away."

Abigail patted Marlene's hand. At least she had comforting words—Nora couldn't make her mouth work. "You did the right thing. And now you're helping those girls."

They sat quietly for a few minutes. Finally, Nora thought she ought to speak. "Lisa helped, too."

Marlene nodded.

That explained all the articles on Lisa's desk about women in the Mormon Church. Maybe Lisa's last message dealt with the underground railroad and not Canyonlands. "That's what she meant when she said the Tokpela Ranch. Is that one of the places you take the girls?"

Marlene's eyes opened wide. "When did Lisa say anything about that place?"

"Right before she died."

"It's got nothing to do with helping these girls."

Maybe, but it upset Marlene. "Why would she mention it?"

Marlene stood up and walked toward the center of the room. "I wouldn't know. But whatever it is, you need to leave it alone."

Nora followed Marlene. "The Tokpela Ranch? Why?"

Abigail made a beeline for the back room, but Marlene intercepted her. "Don't go back there."

"I only wanted to give them a hug."

Marlene stood firm. "No."

Abigail looked like she might argue, and instead, reached inside her purse. She brought out her wallet and pulled out several bills, handing them to Marlene. "Then give them this. And if you won't do that, buy them some clothes or a nice dinner."

Marlene took the money. "Thank you," she whispered.

Abigail nodded and strode toward Nora. She threaded her arm through Nora's and they walked out the door, leaving the bell tinkling behind them.

TWENTY-SIX

AFTER GIVING ABBEY A chance to stretch, water a tire, and get a drink, they settled back into the Jeep.

Abigail clicked her seat belt. "Those poor girls. I'm glad Marlene is helping them."

Nora vowed to get involved when she got back to Boulder. Right now she had to figure out what had spooked Lisa and if it was related to the reason someone tampered with her brakes, if all of it led to Lisa's death and why.

Nora squinted out the windshield.

Abigail scrutinized her. "What are you thinking?"

She started the Jeep and backed out of the parking place. "Want to take a drive?"

"No."

Nora grinned. "Okay."

"Where are we going?"

Nora pulled onto the street, working her way west out of town. "We're going to the Tokpela Ranch."

Abigail shook her head. "Marlene said to leave it alone."

Nora nodded. "That's a good enough reason to go."

Abigail's voice was tight. "Bad idea."

"We'll just look around, see if we find any reason it would have concerned Lisa." Her heart picked up its pace.

Abigail sounded tense. "What could you possibly find?"

Nora shrugged. "Won't know if we don't try."

Abigail put a hand on the wheel in protest. "Turn this around. We are not going snooping at someone's ranch. Especially if you suspect it might be dangerous."

"We'll pretend we're tourists that got lost. What's the harm in looking around?"

"Do you even know where it is?"

"Actually, I do."

"Oh, for heaven's sake." Abigail pursed her lips and folded her arms.

They rode in silence for a while, nothing but Abbey's panting and the knocking rhythm of the wheels on the highway to keep them company.

Finally Abigail spoke. "I'm sorry I never told you about Warren. It was a long time ago. I never liked him and he's still creepy."

Nora needed to tread gently, but to say she was curious would be to call Mount Everest a bunny hill. "What was he like in school?"

Abigail's shoulders crept toward her ears with tension. "We actually met him here. He took a real liking to Dan."

Nora held her breath and waited. Abigail didn't continue. "Did a lot of people like Dan?" She corrected, "My father."

Abigail considered the question. "Not really. You have to remember in those days, being a Native American wasn't like it is now."

"What do you mean?"

Abigail considered. "That was the seventies. A time of transition and we were living in Boulder, the epicenter of change."

For Abigail, wherever she existed was the epicenter. But Boulder was probably an interesting place to experience that decade.

"The hippies and 'enlightened' people embraced the Indians and thought everything they did was superior to white people. The others, the older people and establishment types, thought of Indians as inferior and lazy. They believed the stereotypes of all Indians being drunks or on welfare."

Nora tried to study Abigail out of the corner of her eye. She couldn't imagine her mother in bell bottoms with a bandana tied around her head, John Lennon sunglasses perched on her nose. She always pictured Abigail wearing a pink empire-waist mini dress with a white sash, carrying a white patent leather purse with matching go-go boots. Her hair would be teased in a *That Girl* flip.

But Abigail had fallen for Dan, a Native American. They'd backpacked and, even though it seemed more like science fiction than truth, probably slept together before marriage. Reconciling her lifelong image of young Abigail with the facts might be more than Nora could assimilate in a few days.

Nora tiptoed. "Which camp did Warren fall into?"

Abigail's mouth twisted with distaste. "Warren honed his persuasive skills early. He didn't seem to belong to either category. He showed up on campus right after we'd met him in Moab. He acted like he accidently bumped into us and then sort of weaseled his way into being Dan's friend."

"What do you mean?"

Abigail paused as if remembering. "Dan kept to himself a lot. He didn't trust many people and he was serious about his classes."

Nora interrupted. "What was he studying?"

A smile of pride crept onto Abigail's face. "Physics. He wanted to go into the space program."

This bit of new information shifted her mental image of her father. That was one thing she didn't share with him. Nora's science aptitude ranked even lower than her interest in the subject. And where she inherited her accounting acumen was anyone's guess because Abigail couldn't even balance her checkbook.

Abigail readjusted herself. "Warren wanted to hang out with us and hike and drink coffee, you know, just young people things."

"So what changed?"

Nora could almost see the ice form along Abigail's spine. "He wasn't a friend to Dan. Or to me."

"What happened?"

Abigail snapped her head toward Nora. "Can we drop it, please? It doesn't matter. Warren is and was an opportunist and takes what doesn't belong to him."

"He stole from Dan?"

Abigail's eyes shot a ray of anger mixed with a hint of something else. Revulsion? "I don't want to talk about it."

Nora turned off the highway. According to directions she'd looked up, getting to Tokpela Ranch meant driving south about twenty miles along questionable roads. The route outside of Moab twisted around what looked like industrial sites, complete with large Dumpsters overflowing with debris, broken blacktop parking lots, and giant Quonset garages with their gaping doors open and all manner of equipment and trash visible inside. Electrical wires with bright red balls crisscrossed the skyline as far as Nora could see. Despite its earth-loving, outdoors-enthusiast reputation, the area around Moab hosted pockets of environmental neglect.

The road turned south and after a few miles, the pavement gave way to gravel that pinged against the underside of the Jeep.

Abigail's voice sounded pinched. "We should not be going there."

Nora didn't answer. She was more and more convinced Lee had something to do with Lisa's death and maybe she'd find some proof at Tokpela Ranch.

The road wound along a creek in a narrow valley with oaks and elms and cottonwood trees shading sandy clearings and entrances to slot canyons. A monsoon rain could make the canyons deadly. A big storm upstream might send water flash flooding downstream where the weather was clear. With no way to climb the slick sides to safety and water roaring through them, the canyons could claim people caught unaware.

The road deteriorated even further. Washboards nearly rattled their teeth loose and grass grew thicker down here. They rumbled across a cattle guard and a wide valley spread before them. In dry weather, the valley would be a lush pasture. But in this unusually wet spring, a small lake had puddled in the low ground with tall reeds forming a circle, giving way to spongy ground.

Across the valley, a collection of buildings marked the headquarters of Tokpela Ranch. The narrow dirt road wound around the edge of the meadow, leading directly to headquarters. Nora followed the bumpy trail, closing in on the buildings. The traditionally shaped barn sat like a sentinel at the side of the road. The enormous wooden structure looked like it had been built over a hundred years ago and hadn't been painted since. It blocked the view of the rest of the compound. A pit of anxiety formed in Nora's stomach. What would they find at the Tokpela Ranch?

Nora's foot was light on the gas pedal as they crawled past the barn. Weathered wood corrals opened off the barn and a gray workhorse stood dozing in the sun. He didn't stir as they idled past. Another corral held a large, bony cow. Its white and black markings copied onto a rambunctious calf that kicked and sprinted across the enclosure. A fat, spotted pig lay on its side in the dirt of another corral.

An acre of fresh plowed ground showed evidence of soft green plants breaking through the rich, dark soil in neat rows, along with rows of bushy greens. A garden this size would feed a small village and take that many to tend it. The road curved into the center of the ranch compound, its area about a quarter of the size of a football field and the packed dirt spotted with patches of worn prairie grass.

A giant structure faced the aging barn across the center yard. Only two small windows graced the ground floor of the plain two-story building. A smattering of tiny windows lined the second story, evenly spaced, making it look like a barracks.

Off to the side of the barn, a cozy-looking stone house filled the gap between the barn and the looming building. It must have been the original homestead. A front porch faced the east and the sunrise. The chinking appeared to be falling out between the colored stones and the roof sagged with age. A lean-to jutted off to the south and a cellar door took up space to the north of the house, with a small building, no doubt an outhouse, off to the back. A kitchen garden added a bright spot of green to the front yard and a hitching post marked the transition from the rugged grass to the dirt.

Nora pulled the Jeep in front of the hitching post and shut it off.

Two young blonde girls and a dark-haired girl with a purple ribbon around her ponytail squatted in the grass of the front yard. The blondes each held a small tennis shoe and were banging them on the ground to watch them light up. The blondes' pale eyes widened in their faces when they saw Nora and Abigail climb from the Jeep.

"Hello!"

Nora turned to the greeting from a woman coming from the barn.

"Are you lost?" The solidly built blonde woman wore jeans and a faded blue T-shirt, smeared with dirt or mud or maybe something even earthier. Her round, flat face gave off a friendliness mixed with a good dose of wariness. She looked sturdy enough to dispatch Nora and Abigail with one solid swat. Nora's chest tightened.

The woman strode across the dirt carrying a red plastic bucket. When she stopped in front of them, Nora saw the bucket contained a dozen or so brown eggs. She glanced behind the woman to a shack with a low roof in the shade of the barn. The door stood open and white hens pecked at the ground.

The woman held a hand up to shield the sun. "That curve to the highway can be easy to miss. You aren't the first one to keep going straight and end up here instead of turning back toward the highway."

A stooped slip of a woman stepped onto the porch of the stone house. She wore a housedress covered by a full apron in a pastel print. Wrinkles as deep as the slot canyons ran along her face. She descended the porch steps quicker than Nora would have thought possible. She tottered over to them in a rushed gait that rocked from one foot to another. The top of her balding head barely reached Abigail's shoulder.

Abigail smiled at her. "Good afternoon. This is a lovely place." She indicated the stone house behind the woman. "When was it built?"

The little woman's face soured, as if detecting some sort of falseness in Abigail's compliment. "It's old. Like me. If you go back up the road a piece, you'll see where you turned wrong. Won't take but an extra fifteen minutes."

What was Nora going to say to the woman? Should she tell them they weren't lost tourists? What good would that do? While she debated her next move, she watched the blonde woman. Something about her looked familiar. Then it clicked.

Rachel. She looked like an older version—she had the same thin blonde hair, same blue eyes, round face, and guarded expression. She supposed that wasn't unusual. The gene pool around here might be pretty shallow and the families large. Rachel had to be related to many of them.

Abigail stepped closer to the house. "The colors of the stone are really striking, especially in the sunlight. It looks like the house was built first and all the others sort of came along as money and need dictated."

The old woman's distaste showed in her beady eyes. "You from Salt Lake City? LDS?"

Abigail was undaunted. "How many generations have lived here? I'll bet you are descended from the first homesteaders."

The wizened woman frowned outright. "We mostly like it out here because no one bothers us."

The younger woman, who was probably ten years or so older than Nora, maybe in her mid-forties, forced a smile. "Lydia doesn't mean to be rude, but she's right—we're busy."

Nora thought the old woman did, indeed, mean to be rude.

"Cassie and me got a lot to get done this time of year. Like I said, follow the road back out and you won't get lost."

The front door of the big house opened and another blonde woman emerged. From where Nora stood, about thirty yards away, she appeared much younger than the egg woman, Cassie. She resembled Rachel as well, and looked to be in the home stretch of pregnancy. A tow-headed toddler tumbled out the door after the her.

Abigail appeared not to notice. She addressed Cassie. "Your garden is very impressive. I like to think of myself as an amateur horticulturist, but even if I had the space, I couldn't possibly raise a garden like that without a crew to help with the work or people to eat the produce. Do you raise other livestock, too?"

Abigail sounded too nosy for a random tourist and Cassie's expression hardened by the second. "We make organic cheese and sell it at farmer's markets."

The pregnant woman stepped off the concrete slab that served as a front porch. She held the hand of the child as he, or she, tottered into the grass. Nora looked for the little girls sitting in the old woman's yard. Sometime during the conversation they had sneaked off.

Abigail suddenly strode out, heading across the dirt toward the barn. "Was that chard I saw growing in your garden? Is it a particularly hardy hybrid to stand the cold nights this time of year? You know, I love the early vegetables. The peas and lettuces and broccoli."

Cassie took off after her. Lydia scowled at Nora. "That's a chattery old fool."

The pregnant woman stretched and rubbed her lower back. She glanced over to where Nora and Lydia stood. Her head jerked to the Jeep. She bent over, scooped up the toddler, and hurried into the house.

Abigail succeeded in getting to the garden, Cassie in tow. Her perky chatter carried across the yard. Annoying at her best of times, when she put an effort into it, Abigail could make Mother Teresa snap. Although Cassie seemed nice enough, she was no saint. "We don't allow tourists in our garden."

"Oh, look at these carrots. How do you keep your rows so straight?" Abigail was doing her best to distract Cassie.

A lot of good it did Nora, with Lydia eyeing her like a hawk sizes up a mouse.

Nora struggled for something to say while trying to take in everything in the compound. "You should have seen her at the Hopi reservation. She kept looking in people's houses."

Lydia perked up, her eyes becoming lasers. "Hopi? Not LDS?"

Lydia's reaction seemed strange but then, nothing about this place was normal. Nora understood why she kept asking if they were LDS since the mainstream church didn't approve of polygamists and this place could be one of those cults Marlene spoke of. But why would mentioning Hopi set her off? "I've got friends on Second Mesa."

Lydia flicked her hands in a "scat" motion. "It's time for you to leave. Pick up that fool and get gone."

There wouldn't be any finessing this woman. Abigail crossed the yard toward Nora and Cassie stormed behind her with a stony face.

They heard the rumble of an engine. Whoever was coming might mean trouble for Nora and Abigail. They should leave now. "Come on, Mother. We should go." Nora tried not to appear panicked as she hurried back to the Jeep.

Abigail slowed her pace even though Cassie seemed determined to keep her moving. "I'd love to see the inside of the barn. I'll bet it has some history. When did the Mormons settle this part of the country?"

Wheels rattled on a cattle guard, warning of an approaching vehicle. Nora tried to sound casual. "Mother? I think we've bothered these people enough. We really should be heading back."

"Perhaps we could come back another day," Abigail said, not making a move toward the Jeep.

The hood, then cab, then bed of a white pickup popped around the barn, taking the curve of the road into the yard. The silhouette of a black hat hung in its rear window. Lee.

Was the Tokpela Ranch his? If so, that doubled Nora's suspicions.

Abigail finally noticed it. She spun around and skipped to the Jeep. "Thank you much for the tour. You have a lovely spread here."

Spread?

They both jumped into the Jeep and slammed the doors. Nora turned the key and shifted into reverse.

She twisted to look behind her, aware that a couple of children could be anywhere.

The white pickup loomed in her rearview mirror like a shark with open jaws.

Nora spun around, jammed the gear into first, and eased off the clutch to crawl forward. She might have to run across the yard a little, but she'd just be able to squeeze around the hitching post.

Before she moved more than an inch, though, Lee jumped in front of the Jeep and banged his fists on the hood. The clang made Abigail scream.

Nora squeezed her brakes.

He slapped the hood of the Jeep again and glared at her.

Abbey barked. The noise gnawed through her control. She disengaged the gear lever.

Cassie joined Lee in front of the Jeep. Her fierce expression was even more frightening than Lee's. Lydia, probably the scariest of all, hobbled in that see-saw way toward them.

Nora grabbed the door handle and Abigail clutched at her. "Don't go out there. This is an evil cult and they'll take you into the barn for human sacrifice."

While that jibed with Nora's imaginative scenario, it seemed an exaggerated response, even in Nora-world.

She jumped out of the Jeep, slamming the door before Abbey could join her. With way more courage than she felt, Nora demanded, "Get out of the way."

Lee strode over to her. She fought the wise urge to run. He stopped within inches of her, breathing hard. "What do you want?"

Nora countered with, "Did you mess with my brakes?"

He let out air as though she'd punched his stomach. His face clouded. "Did I what?"

Nora felt a little momentum shift her way. "Like you tampered with Lisa's brakes."

He narrowed his eyes. "You're crazy, aren't you?"

Nora imagined him slipping his hands around her throat and squeezing her like a chicken. A smart woman would bolt, run for the hills. But even if Nora could leave Abigail to fend for herself, locked in the Jeep, she wouldn't get far with Cassie standing a few feet behind her. Her only weapon was her wits.

They were screwed.

"It wouldn't be a good idea to hurt us. Everyone knows we came out here. If we don't show up in town, they'll come after you." Sweat beaded on her lip and pooled under her arms.

He smirked. "Everyone? Rachel?" He chuckled.

She didn't see the little girls so she wouldn't have to worry about flattening them with the Jeep in a quick getaway. If she jumped in and gunned it, they could probably make it out of here. Lee didn't have a gun in his hand, so he'd have to get to his pickup to chase them down.

"She's not the only one who knows we're here. We told Marlene. She already suspects you killed Lisa." How would he react to an accusation of murder?

He laughed. "Half the town of Moab thinks I killed Lisa. They're convinced I swallow hikers whole. They suspect I kill cyclists and sell their mountain bikes on the black market. They can't prove it any more than you can prove I messed with your Jeep."

His ridicule brought out her anger. "Did you hate Lisa because she was a lesbian or because of her work to expand the park? Or maybe it was something else." *Like her helping rescue girls from polygamist cults like yours?*

Cassie let out a huff of annoyance.

He spoke slowly. "I wasn't the one trying to change her way of life. She—and all you people—are working pretty darned hard to destroy mine."

So you killed her. She didn't say the words out loud but they must have been plain on her face.

His face looked like black thunder. "Lisa was someplace she shouldn't have been and she had an accident."

Cassie put a hand on her hip. "You don't belong here, sister."

The air felt like lead as Nora tried to steady her breath. Was this where they'd drag Nora and Abigail away and bludgeon them?

Lee's hateful eyes bored into her. "You'd best get while you can. You're too scrawny to do much good, but we can always use some bones for soup."

Cassie lunged forward, as if to attack, and laughed.

Nora marched to her Jeep with as much dignity as she could muster. She pulled open the door and pushed Abbey into the back seat.

Abigail's voice squeaked. "Could we please get out of here?"

Nora turned at the anxiety in her mother's tone. Abigail sat straight, staring ahead, all blood drained from her face. Her hands trembled.

Lydia stood outside Abigail's rolled-up window. Her creepy dried apple face hovered only inches away, a malevolent and toothless grin aimed at Abigail. The nightmares from that image would stay with Nora for a very long time.

Nora eased forward, the vehicle nearly brushing the hitching post. As soon as she straightened the wheel, she surveyed the area for any stray children, saw none, and gunned the engine. They sped around the curve by the garden and down the road.

Nora's insides felt as solid as the marshy lake in the meadow. Her hands shook on the wheel. "That was straight out of a horror movie. I expected an army of zombies to come out of the barn with scythes and torches."

Abigail reached for her handbag and rummaged inside. Her hands shook every bit as much as Nora's. She pulled a lipstick case out and opened it, taking out the tube. She held the case open for the mirror and started to apply the lipstick. She shook too hard for precision and dropped both hands to her lap. "They lacked basic social graces."

That was the worst Abigail could come up with? "Can you imagine tea and cookies with Granny Evil?"

Abigail shook her head. "The woman should have started a good skin regimen about eighty years ago."

They laughed and it eased some of the strain.

Nora didn't start breathing regularly until they found the road to the highway and headed safely toward civilization. "Marlene knows they're dangerous. That's why she told me to stay away."

Abigail finished a successful attempt at her lipstick and slid the kit into her bag. Her voice shook and she clutched her hands together. "Who knew farmer's markets could be so lucrative?"

"What do you mean?"

"I assumed they'd have a couple of old tractors in that big barn. But they had three SUVs back there. One of them was an Escalade."

What?

Recognition slipped into place. The dark-haired little girl sitting on the grass reminded Nora of the little girl outside the outfitters in Moab yesterday. She wore the same purple T-shirt and light-up shoes. Wasn't she getting into an Escalade?

"Something else," Abigail said.

"There's more?"

"You know those images on the petroglyphs? The symbols you were so fascinated with?"

"The symbols you said my father doodled?"

"Yes. Well, that was painted on the barn."

TWENTY-SEVEN

CRICKETS CHIRPED SOMEWHERE IN the desert beyond Lisa's front porch as night closed around the cabin. The glow from a citronella candle gave the only light. Abbey stretched on the porch floor, twitching in the rabbit hunt of his dreams.

The boards on the north end of the porch squeaked again as Nora pivoted and paced back to the south. She was convinced Lee had tampered with her breaks and tried to kill her and Abigail. He'd murdered Lisa. Did he really think he could eliminate everyone advocating park expansion? He'd eventually run out of clever ways to arrange accidents and the environmentalists would keep coming. Sort of like the Indians trying to staunch the flow of white immigrants two hundred years ago. Right or wrong, Lee would lose.

But Nora didn't care about the park issues right now. Runaway girls, religious cults, and attempted murder seemed more important. Abigail had gone to ground. Actually, to her room. When they'd returned from the excursion to Tokpela, she'd marched upstairs and closed her door. She'd done her share of pacing, too, but Nora hadn't heard movement since the sun set several hours ago. Maybe she'd finally gone to sleep.

Rachel wasn't home when Nora and Abigail reached the cabin and still hadn't returned.

Aside from the crickets, the night had the volume set on mute. The perfume of the sand, sage, and other scents from the typical afternoon shower didn't do much to ease Nora's concerns. A sliver of moon barely restrained the darkness. Nora wore Lisa's old hoodie to ward off the chill.

Did whatever Lisa left on the camera reveal Lee's threats to her or the runaway girls? Where would Lisa hide it so that Nora would find it? And what about the symbol? It was in Nora's dreams, on Rachel's pictures, and now on Lee's barn.

Headlights swung from the dirt road to shine along the rutted driveway lane. Rachel must be coming home. Nora steeled herself. Rachel might be on a war path and want to engage Nora in combat. Or their truce from breakfast might hold and she'd want company.

The soft purr of an engine approached, sounding nothing like the rumble of Nora's old Jeep. When it got closer, Nora let out a breath. It wasn't Rachel's Passat. The Toyota 4Runner belonged to Darrell. He shut the engine off and climbed out.

"I'm glad you're still up," he said. "I was afraid it's too late. I got hung up in a meeting with some constituents, but I wanted to check on you and your mother."

He plodded up the steps and leaned on the porch railing. Somewhere along the day, he'd pulled his tie off, leaving the collar open on his wrinkled blue shirt. Dark whiskers dusted his chin and cheeks.

"You didn't need to come all the way out here. We're fine."

"You seemed pretty upset at the fundraiser this afternoon and I felt bad about not being able to help you." He stood and held out his arms. "So here I am, even though it's nearly midnight, at your disposal."

His easy grin teased one of her own in response. "Can I get you something? A beer? Iced tea?"

He plopped into one of the Adirondack chairs and slumped down. "Mormons have some strict rules about alcohol and caffeine."

She should have known better. "Let me see what Rachel has in the kitchen."

He laughed. "I'd love a beer. But if you tell anyone, I'll call you a liar."

"I have to warn you, I crack under torture."

"I'll take my chances and hope the Mormon deacons don't get a hold of you."

She slipped into the house for the beers. The light from the refrigerator splashed across the dark kitchen. She was trying to flirt with Darrell, but it didn't feel right.

It should be Cole on the front porch. They'd sit together on the steps, laugh and tease and share a kiss or two. Maybe even stroll into the soft night hand in hand. She pictured his lanky frame in his jeans and hiking boots, goofy grin on his face, pointing out the columbines on the hillside next to the trail. "I'd pick you a bouquet but I know you'd rather I let them live," he'd say.

In the short time they'd been together, Cole seemed to understand her and know her from the inside out.

"Did you get lost?" Darrell's voice floated in from the porch.

She reached inside and grabbed two bottles of beer, then shut the door. While she opened the bottles in the scant light from the window, she reminded herself that Cole was married and though she clung to some hope he'd work it out, she had to be prepared that he wouldn't.

By the time she got back to the porch and handed Darrell his bottle, she'd found a smidgeon of equilibrium.

"Did you raise a lot of campaign money today?" She sank into a chair.

He took a long pull and sighed. "It wasn't really about the money. We've got a lot of work to do with getting the locals on board."

"It didn't look like many ranchers or native Moab folks were there today." Except Lee.

"That's the problem. The activists and environmentalists that have retired here or moved here in the last few years have more money than the old timers. But votes are votes. We need to find a way to talk to the traditionalists and get them to understand how important it is to protect Canyonlands."

"As much as I'd like the locals on board,"—*if for no other reason than to keep them from trying to kill us*—"the decision is really out of their hands. It's up to Congress."

He gulped his beer. "Right. Did you make any progress on finding Lisa's camera?"

The beer tasted bitter and she set it aside and stood. "Since the cops won't help, I went out to Lee's ranch this afternoon."

He sat up at full attention. "You shouldn't have done that. He's dangerous."

"I didn't know he owned the Tokpela Ranch. Lisa seemed interested in it so I wanted to check it out."

He set his empty bottle on the porch floor. "What did Lisa … ?"

She interrupted him. "He's a polygamist."

Darrell stared at her. "How do you know?"

She waved him off. "There were a couple of wives and a ton of children and this creepy old lady. It's obvious. But there's something else."

He leaned back and studied her. "What?"

"I can't figure it out, but it has something to do with this symbol I saw on petroglyphs today. It's three concentric circles, like a target. Then lines run outward, like rays. Or kind of like the state symbol for New Mexico, but instead of several lines coming out from one circle in four directions, two lines shoot out in six directions. "

He laughed. "What are you talking about?"

She sounded like Abigail chattering away and realized she'd probably inherited that tendency.

"This symbol that I saw on the rock is the same one painted on the side of Lee's barn."

He tilted his head as if waiting for more. "Uh-huh?"

"It means something." She pointed out the obvious.

"What does it mean?" He stood up and walked to where she'd planted herself by the rail.

She paced away. "I don't know. That's the problem."

"Maybe he likes the symbol. You know, like the coil symbol you see everywhere or the hand or kokopelli. People tack them up on their houses or jewelry because they like the design, not necessarily because of their meaning."

The coil he talked about was a Hopi symbol telling the story of their ancient migrations. After they'd climbed from the Third World into the new and improved Fourth World, they wandered for years, probably centuries, until they settled on the garden spot of the three mesas in barren, sun-scorched Northern Arizona. The more time she spent on the mesas, the more she appreciated the hidden beauty. The Hopi might have settled in the desert but they'd figured out a way to survive and knew how to grow corn and other food. Benny had taken her to spots of lush green hidden from the casual visitor.

"Everything on the Hopi reservation has a meaning. Those symbols represent something."

"Maybe they aren't Hopi." He followed her to where she'd retreated across the porch.

"They might not be. But they're ancient. The Hopi traveled all over this area centuries ago. They claim to be descendants of the Anasazi." She hesitated. "My cousin on the rez will know."

"You've talked to him?" Darrell asked.

She swallowed a gulp of beer. "He's not answering his phone. He probably let the battery die. He's got a generator for electricity, but he doesn't use it all the time."

"Why not?"

Good question. "I haven't figured out how he decides which modern conveniences to use and when. He grows most of his own food, but then also had prepackaged stuff. He has a cell phone but only uses it sometimes."

Darrell seemed to consider that. "Interesting."

It normally fascinated Nora, but not tonight. "I need to figure out what the symbol means."

Darrell seemed to have lost interest in the conversation. He studied her face. "Can I ask you a personal question?"

No. She didn't want any personal questions. She shrugged. "Sure."

"Are you in a relationship?"

Yes. Cole and I should be together. We were together. Until we weren't. "Yes. No. Not anymore. I mean, it's complicated."

He waited a moment. "I'm sorry. It must be a recent breakup?"

"Very recent." She didn't want to talk about it. And she didn't want Darrell standing quite as close to her as he was.

"I'm sorry." His voice softened like melting ice cream.

She stepped back. "I'm sorting through Lisa's desk drawers. I'll bet she left some clue for me about where the camera is hidden."

A small smile played on his face as if acknowledging her not-so-subtle topic change. "I'm a good politician. I can mediate disputes and persuade. I can talk to people who don't agree with me and negotiate different positions. But I'm a disaster in my personal life. As you can see from me being thirty-five and still single."

"Single is not a bad thing." Single is fine.

His confidence evaporated in an uncertain smile. "Even strong people need a partner."

Time to change the subject. "What do you know about Lee? You grew up around here, right? Did you know each other when you were younger?"

He dropped his shoulders, the long day falling on him. "I left this place when I was young. My mother and I moved to Salt Lake City. I didn't come back until I had finished law school. Don't tell anyone, but I really came back to establish residency so I could run for office here."

Nora pulled her hoodie closer to ward off the night's chill. "Lee's lived here all his life; do people like him?"

"He's kind of anti-social, don't you think? If you're right and he is a polygamist, he probably doesn't want to call attention to himself. Polygamy is still against the law, even if it is tolerated."

Nora eyed Darrell, weighing whether to tell him her suspicions. Maybe he could help. "I'm sure he messed with my brakes. And," she inhaled, "I think he killed Lisa."

Darrell grabbed her hand, startling her. "Leave him alone. Go back to Boulder, send your mother back to Flagstaff. I'll do what needs to be done here. I want you safe, Nora."

"You believe me?" Part of her hoped he'd convince her it was all coincidence.

Darrell stared into the darkness. "Lee's afraid of losing his way of life. He's desperate."

"I just need undeniable proof, then I can go to the FBI or tell someone not connected to this place."

"I won't allow it!" he hissed. It sounded like a shout in the quiet night.

The words fell to the porch floor like a bucket of cold water. They faced each other and it was hard to tell who was more surprised.

"You won't allow it?"

He rubbed his eyes. "I'm sorry. I didn't mean that. I'm beat and the thought of you getting hurt upsets me."

He may act charming and steady, but a crack here and there gave Nora the uneasy feeling he might not be so perfect.

He pulled his phone from his pocket. "Don't do anything right now. Let me make a phone call and see what I can get going."

"Now?"

He gave her a tired grin. "I know people who never sleep."

She watched him plod down the porch steps, murmuring into his phone. The screen door squealed and Nora jumped.

"What was that about?" Abigail stepped onto the darkened porch wearing her pink bathrobe and slippers. She smelled of expensive face cream and her skin sparkled in the glow of the candle. Darrell stood with his back to the porch, his voice vibrating quietly.

"He's calling someone to help prove Lee is guilty of Lisa's murder."

Abigail frowned at Darrell but she didn't argue. She must be starting to accept the possibility.

"I thought you'd gone to bed," Nora said.

"I can't sleep. I came down for some warm milk. Where do you suppose Rachel's gone?"

Nora shrugged. Abigail folded her arms. "You need to call Cole. His pride won't let him call you."

Abigail had her priorities. Murder and white slavery took second place to romance. "Pride? I'd say it's more like his wife that won't let him call."

"So 'it's your party and you'll cry if you want to.'"

Nora lowered herself to sit on the front step. Abbey got to his feet and ambled over to sit next to her. He put a paw into her lap. She trailed her fingers through his fur. "This hardly seems like the time to discuss my love life."

Abigail leaned against the porch rail. "Or lack thereof."

Irritated, Nora stood, disturbing Abbey. He trotted down the porch steps. "I need to go to the rez."

Abigail furrowed her brow. "In Arizona? That seems a bit out of the blue."

"Benny's not answering his phone and I need to know what that symbol means."

"You think Benny can help?"

Nora moved close to Abigail to give her some warmth. "I don't know, but he's the best source I can think of."

Abigail wrapped an arm around Nora.

Nora studied the dark circles under her mother's eyes. "What upset you so much today?"

Abigail waved her arm in the air. "Oh, I don't know." Her voice rang with sarcasm. "Your antique car fell apart and nearly killed us, and if that wasn't enough, you drove us out to a hostile enemy camp to be harassed by polygamists. And then there's the possibility Lee Evans is a murderer."

"You got spooked when you saw the rock art, then seeing Warren Evans at the restaurant pushed you to the edge, and the symbols on the barn just about did you in. What's going on?"

Abigail swiveled and swung the screen door open. Her slippers scuffed across the wood floor toward the kitchen.

Nora followed. "Does all this remind you too much of Dan?"

The glow from the refrigerator light glistened on Abigail's greased cheeks. "Don't be ridiculous."

"Then what?" Nora tucked one leg under herself and perched on the edge of a stool.

Abigail snatched the milk carton and slammed the door closed, shutting off the light. "Then nothing."

"Lisa's brakes went out about a week ago."

Abigail thumped the milk carton on the counter. Her face paled.

"Lee Evans is dangerous."

Abigail gasped as if discovering a new horror. Her fist flew to her mouth. "No."

Nora jumped up.

"Evans. It has to be." Abigail slumped against the counter and gripped the edge.

Afraid her mother might be having a stroke, Nora rounded the counter to Abigail. "What is it?"

Abigail trembled. "Evans is a common name so I didn't put it together, but it has to be."

Glad her mother hadn't fallen to the floor clutching her head, Nora said, "What?"

"Lee Evans is related to Warren."

Warren had no children. Nora remembered that from business school when she and her friends joked about getting him to adopt them. Lee must be a nephew or cousin or something.

Tears glistened in Abigail's eyes. She trembled. "I didn't see it before."

Nora led Abigail to the couch and sat her down. She clicked on a lamp, glad for the soft glow of the stained glass shade. "Didn't see what? Tell me."

Abigail's cloudy eyes cleared and she collected herself. "It's Warren Evans."

"What does Warren Evans have to do with this?"

Nora waited for Abigail to explain, fighting the urge to squirm, shake her mother, or simply crawl up the side of the wall to expel tension.

Finally, Abigail started. "I thought your father's car crash was an accident. It didn't occur to me that Warren killed him."

Whatever Nora expected, it wasn't this.

Abigail's voice shook. "His car flipped going around a curve. At the bottom of a steep hill. The brakes went out because there was no fluid in the brake line."

"What?" Nora couldn't believe what she was hearing.

Abigail swallowed, hardening her tone. "It had to be Warren."

"Why do you say that?"

Abigail inhaled. "Dan and I met Warren here, in Moab. In fact, at that place where we were today. The rock art panel."

"And that's why you got upset?" Nora asked.

Abigail seemed to float back to that time. "Warren was sitting there studying the panel when we hiked out there. He had all this wild, dark hair and even wilder eyes. He was so suntanned he looked like he could have been related to your father.

"He didn't say anything at first, just watched. We'd been laughing and chatting on the hike up there, but as soon as Dan saw the petro-glyphs, he became serious. It made me nervous the way he stared at them for so long."

Nora tried to picture a young Abigail holding hands and flirting with a Hopi man.

"After a time, Warren stood up and introduced himself. He started asking Dan questions about the symbols. I could tell Dan didn't want to answer." Abigail considered Nora. "Well, you know how secretive Hopi are. And the symbols seemed important to your father.

"Warren was polite and friendly. He dropped his questioning right away. See, even back then, he knew how to work people. He offered to

203

show us around the area. Dan was reluctant but I thought Warren was fun and nice and he knew where the great hiking and camping and swimming places were. We told him all about CU and exchanged phone numbers.

"The week after we returned to Boulder, Warren showed up. He got a job and earned money so he could go to school the next semester."

None of this explained why he would kill Nora's father. She waited for Abigail to continue.

"He seemed to always be around. I thought he was one of those woo-woo types who wanted to understand the relationship Indians have with the earth and sky and all of that."

Abigail's hands wound round and round each other in her lap. "Dan didn't like to talk about his beliefs. But he was always polite and sometimes he just couldn't avoid telling Warren things."

"Warren Evans, the guy who amassed a fortune, was a Hopi wannabe?"

Abigail fluttered her hands. "I don't know what he was. Maybe it was his excuse."

"Excuse for what?"

Abigail fidgeted. Her voice sounded like someone had stretched her vocal chords. "I should have put a stop to him coming over. It seemed like he was always there. Even when Dan was at class."

Abigail rocked slightly. "I didn't think too much about it. And, I'm sorry to say, I enjoyed the company because Dan was studying so hard and not home a lot and I got lonely. And Warren was so charming."

Her rocking accelerated and her voice broke. "I probably did something to encourage him. I don't know what. I didn't mean to, I know. We just became good friends because he was there so often. At least for me, it was only friendship."

Nora put a hand on Abigail's back and her mother startled. "What happened?"

Abigail jumped up and paced to the window. "I should never have let him be there when Dan wasn't home. It gave him ideas. It must have suggested I liked him. Liked him in that way."

Nora didn't want to hear the rest, but knew not to stop Abigail from purging a secret buried so long.

"He." A sob escaped. "Warren. He. He." She covered her face with her hands. "He … took me. Right there. In our apartment. On the floor in front of our broken sofa."

A wave of ice crashed around Nora's head. She held her breath against the shock. Her paralysis broke and Nora rushed to Abigail. She pulled her close and held her while Abigail sobbed. When the worst had subsided, she led her mother to the couch and lowered her to sit.

Abigail found a tissue in her robe pocket. "I never told Dan."

"And you think Warren killed my father? Why? Jealousy?"

Abigail closed her eyes. "I never considered it, honestly. But now I see the coincidence of the brakes and I add it to the … incident. And then the fight Dan and Warren had the day before the accident. It all makes sense."

"They had a fight?"

Abigail blew her nose and got up to dispose of the tissue and pluck another from the box on the kitchen counter. "I came home from class and heard shouting from our apartment. Dan never raised his voice. Dan was Hopi and believed in peace. But something had him more upset than I'd ever seen him. I opened the door and he was calling Warren stupid. Stupid! I'd never heard Dan say anything so mean.

"When they saw me, Warren ran out. Dan refused to tell me anything. And the next day, he died."

Nora pictured the scene. Dan, dark skinned, black hair cut in a bowl, his eyes sharp. Actually, she pictured him looking like her cousin Benny. Warren, shoulder-length hippie hair, faded bell bottoms, calculating expression. And Abigail. Nora still fought to see her in jeans, maybe a bandana, a peasant blouse...

Peasant blouse. Over a pregnant belly? If Dan died the next day, Abigail would have been pregnant with Nora when Warren raped her. According to Abigail, Nora had been born after her father died. Nine months after? Or six? It made a difference.

Nora's heart thudded. "How long after Dan's accident was I born?"

Abigail's eyes flew open.

Nora squeezed Abigail's thigh. "How long, Mother?"

"It's not what you think," Abigail said. "Dan is your father!"

"Could it have been Warren Evans? Is it possible?"

"You were born eight months after Dan died. You were not premature. I know Dan is your father."

"You don't know!" Nora's chest constricted. She struggled for the words. "Warren Evans could be my father."

Abigail shook her head, tears streaming from her eyes.

A floorboard on the porch creaked.

Nora swung her head around. She'd forgotten Darrell.

He sounded normal and raised his hand in a wave. "I got the ball rolling looking into Lee. It's late so I'm going to head home."

Abigail buried her face in her hands.

Nora strode to the front door to say thanks and goodbye. She returned to a sobbing Abigail.

"He heard me, I know he did."

Nora patted her back and reassured Abigail, even if she had her own doubts. "He was on the phone in the yard. He didn't hear anything."

TWENTY-EIGHT

Coarse yellow sand crunched under Nora's hiking boots and echoed in the deserted dawn atop the mesa. Abbey padded next to her, probably enjoying his freedom after the five-hour drive from Moab to the mesa. As soon as Abigail had calmed down, she'd returned to bed and Nora had taken off for the rez. The sun danced suddenly from the edge of the world beyond the valley floor accompanied by the low, soft rhythm of Benny's singing.

She lifted her head and abandoned herself to the feeling of floating. At the edge of a mesa that rose from the valley, she felt like she stood on the deck of a mythical god's clipper ship as they circumnavigated the globe.

She tried to shed the heaviness she'd carried from Moab at the thought of what Abigail had endured so many years ago—rape, her husband dead, having a baby on her own. Growing up, Nora had always thought of her mother as a vapid social climber. It now made sense that Abigail clung to a wealthy husband and security. The new insight also revealed how far Abigail had come when she'd let go of the financial stability to marry Charlie.

Nora rubbed at the fatigue behind her eyes. After Abigail's confession, the only thing Nora could think to do was run to the reservation. Even this seemed like a bad idea. It didn't matter how much her mother protested and claimed Nora resembled Dan in gestures and "that look in your eyes," Nora could be Warren Evans's daughter. If the Evans family had red hair in their lineage, it would explain a lot.

Instead of joining Benny with her own morning tribute of cornmeal, Nora stayed back and listened. If she had no Hopi ties, it didn't seem right to barge into his ceremony. Still, she didn't deny the warmth of the new sun felt welcoming and hopeful.

Lisa could no longer laugh in that deep, freeing way. Cole probably greeted the new day with a kiss for his bride. Two runaway girls huddled together in uncertainty, and Nora's future seemed iffy. But the sun still climbed its cheery path across the sky—keep it all in perspective, her Hopi training would tell her.

The Hopi way of life still had value, even if the tribal blood didn't pump through her veins.

Right?

Benny finished his song. When he backed from the edge of the mesa and turned to Nora, he already grinned, as if he knew she'd been standing there. He probably did. Not much surprised him, even someone showing up unannounced on the isolated mesa at dawn.

"It is good to see you."

Though not much of a hugger herself, she didn't let Benny off with that formal of a greeting. She threw her arms around him and welcomed his returning embrace. "I need to talk to you." Her throat crept dangerously close to shutting, but she managed those few words before tears filled her eyes.

He plodded away from the precipice down a worn path in the yellow dust. Nora fell into step beside him and they walked the fifty yards to the squalid village in silence. The sound of their feet crunching on the sand echoed through the collection of several dozen dwellings that sprawled along the mesa. They spoked from a plaza formed by four two-story structures. Their construction showed desert rock, cinder blocks, and various cheap building supplies.

Benny lived in a section of one of the buildings that made up the plaza. In a modern city, it might be an apartment or condo. Here, it was his part of the pueblo. He led her toward the far side of the plaza. "I'll make coffee and you can tell me."

Benny never told her his age but she guessed he was somewhere between forty and sixty. He spoke as if each word formed from the sands of time and baked in the sun. It would take Nora several days to acclimate to his pace before she lost the urge to dangle him by his feet and shake the words out quicker.

This morning he wore his usual dark blue jeans that hung loose on his narrow hips, plaid cotton shirt, and dusty cowboy boots. His black hair lay thick and short on his head. He stood a few inches shorter than Nora but carried an air of confidence and strength she rarely saw in others.

The yellow powder of the path trod by countless generations puffed around her boots and the silence felt like gauze around her. Not many people lived in Benny's ancient village, and if they'd been out greeting the sun in the traditional way, they'd picked their own private place on the mesa.

The first time Nora had been on the Hopi rez, about an hour's drive north of Winslow, she'd gone to a dance on another of the three mesas that made up Hopiland. She'd been disappointed by the poverty and dirt and general third-world feel. As in Benny's village, the houses were an odd collection of ancient stone and every cheap kind of repair imaginable meant to shore up dwellings that were originally built a thousand years ago. Four pueblo-like structures outlined a central plaza used for dances and ceremonies. These buildings rose two stories and lacked all but the tiniest of windows. The plaza stretched about half the length of a soccer field and had a stone floor.

After spending time up here with Benny a few months ago, Nora accepted what she'd once thought sad and desperate was a free choice to live the traditional life they cherished.

Nora enjoyed her dishwasher and microwave too much to embrace this Spartan lifestyle, but she now understood Benny's priorities didn't mirror hers.

No breeze disturbed the peace, just a gentle sun and soft air. They made their way across the plaza to Benny's house and he held the screen open for her and Abbey to enter.

The same dilapidated couch with a yellow sheet serving as a slip cover, the folding table with a couple of woven-seated camp chairs, the bare bulb dangled from the ceiling—she'd have been shocked if it had changed.

Benny stood in the kitchen and filled a coffee pot with water from a four-gallon jug. He set it on a propane stove, struck a match to the burner, and turned to Nora. "Let's sit outside."

They sat on a low wooden bench perched along the side of his house. "Tell me what is bothering you."

"He won't come to see me anymore." She blurted it out without premeditation. This wasn't what she was here to talk about.

Since Benny didn't answer—though he might be formulating words that would take another lifetime to crawl from his mouth—she rattled on. "I know it's not like he's a genie I can call on demand and I know that I haven't been all that welcoming when he's shown up in the past. But I really feel like I need him to put in a cameo appearance. Even a walk-on in a dream or something."

Benny displayed his usual poker face. "Nakwaiyamtewa?"

Slow down, inhale. Remember to think in Hopi time. "Yes. I've been in Moab and there's all this rock art that has something to do with Hopi and I can't figure it out. If I can understand what these symbols mean, I know I can figure out who killed my friend Lisa and why."

Benny's gaze drifted to the plaza as if in thought. "You are making no more sense than your mother did."

"My mother?"

He still focused into the plaza. "Yes. She sent me a long text that said you were upset about your friend's death and that you questioned your place in Hopi."

"Wait a minute. Abigail texted you that I'd be coming to see you?"

He nodded.

"So you'll text with Abigail, but you won't talk to me on the phone? I've been trying to call you all night."

"I didn't say I texted Abigail back. Besides, why talk to you on the phone when I knew you'd be here?" A twinkle sparked in his eyes.

"Did Abigail tell you I might not be Hopi after all?"

"Why do you say this?"

"Have you heard of Warren Evans?"

His mouth turned up and he actually chuckled. "Every three moons I ride my pony into the white man's town, scalp a few settlers, and steal their cattle. I then take the opportunity to catch up on my investments and read the *Wall Street Journal*."

"Okay, fine. Sorry. But I have no idea what you keep up on and what you don't. You don't answer your phone and you hardly ever turn on your generator. What do I know?" Benny could use his cell phone when it suited him. Nora's phone never had a signal on the mesas, but Benny didn't seem to have any trouble. Nora chose not to question that fact.

He patted her hand. "Yes, Nora, I know who Warren Evans is."

"He's probably my father."

One of his eyebrows arched, a sign she'd shocked him.

211

"He raped my mother. Nice Mormon family guy. All those years my mother lied about my father abandoning us and finally she told me about Dan Sepakuku. Now I find out the father she wasn't telling me about was really Warren Evans."

Benny let that settle. "You didn't know you were Hopi until a few months ago. Now you find out it's possible you are not Hopi and you feel betrayed?"

"Why would I have this red hair? Hopi don't have red hair."

"Warren Evans does not have red hair."

"When I found out about Dan Sepakuku, for the first time in my life I felt like I belonged."

"To Hopi?"

She felt a burn in her cheeks. "Well, maybe not really, yet. I was excited to learn everything Hopi. I felt kind of special that Nakwaiyamtewa visited me. He chose me to save the sacred mountain."

Pause. "As I remember, you were not that excited at the time. 'I'm not Enviro Girl' is what you said to me."

"Okay. Yes. At the time, it seemed scary and dangerous and weird that this chief from the 1880s was visiting me with mystic messages. But why isn't he coming to see me now?"

"It could be that he's busy. We are in the summer season and the kachinas are performing their ancient duties."

The fatigue of the five-hour drive pounded in her temples. "You're right. I didn't really come here to whine."

Again, the shocked, raised eyebrow.

The smell of coffee perking wafted from Benny's house. "I came here to ask you about all these weird petroglyphs in southern Utah. I think they mean something."

"Of course they mean something."

"If I show you, can you tell me what it is?"

He shrugged. "How would I know? The people who made those images lived over a thousand years ago. I'm a modern guy, growing my corn, trying to ignore my cell phone when it rings."

"Maybe, but you have a daily coffee klatch with a guy who's been dead for over a hundred years."

"Not every day. And he doesn't know everything, either. Maybe he likes my coffee."

They filed back into Benny's house. He found a used envelope to write on and scrounged around for a pencil. While he poured the coffee, she sketched the sunburst symbol from the rock and the barn.

He handed her a chipped mug and took the envelope. They stood in the kitchen while he sipped his coffee and studied the drawing. The *Jeopardy!* theme song dinged away in the back of Nora's brain while she waited for his comment.

He set the envelope on the table and took another swig of his coffee. "These lines are a special message from the Sky People."

"What Sky People?"

"The people who come from beyond."

Beyond. Great.

He placed his cup on the table. "You might call them aliens. They visit Hopi. Always have. They bring messages. These lines, they indicate places where the Sky People are welcome."

"You believe in aliens? As in, people from other planets who visit here. Flying saucers?"

"I've never met them. They come to certain people—elders, mostly."

Nora picked up Benny's cup and poured them both more coffee. He opened a cracked wood cupboard and pulled out two granola bars, his version of breakfast. It looked like a feast to Nora.

The nighttime chill evaporated as the little house absorbed the heat from the rising sun.

"You saw this on a panel? What other signs were there?"

She drew the animals and the person in a boat. "These lines are also on a barn on Tokpela Ranch."

"Tokpela?"

She nodded. "It's close to Canyonlands Park."

He gave her a puzzled look. "A white man's barn?"

"Warren Evans's nephew's barn. What do you make of that?"

"Tokpela is a Hopi word."

Of course he wouldn't simply say. "What does it mean?"

He tilted his head in consideration. "Sky."

"Is that significant? Sky Ranch. With the space alien symbols?"

"Hmm." She wouldn't get much more out of him on that.

"Do you know what the rest of this stuff means?"

"Not much. I can tell you this," he pointed to the drawing of the person in a boat, "is a Hopi maiden in a Sky Person's ship. You see the circles on the sides of her head? That is the traditional squash blossom hair worn by Hopi maidens. The rest?" He shrugged.

She lowered herself to one of the chairs. "So here's what I know. Lisa was murdered, maybe after she filmed the panel with this on it. Abigail freaked out when she saw the line symbols on the wall. She said Warren Evans was all into the Hopi stuff and that's why he hooked up with her and my father, or rather, Dan Sepakuku."

Benny munched on his granola bar and didn't seem to have heard anything she'd said.

"Oh, and here's the other thing my mother thinks. She thinks Warren killed Dan. Because he died in a car crash when his brakes went out and the brakes in my Jeep went out the other day."

Benny leaned back. "Do you think Warren Evans tried to kill you?"

She shook her head. "No. I think his nephew did."

He considered that. "And you wonder if the Sky People have something to do with Warren Evans and his nephew and your friend?"

Sure, when he put it like that it seemed far-fetched. "Yes."

Benny threw his granola bar wrapper in the trash. He took a half dozen steps to cross the room and open the one door leading off the living room. "First you must sleep. Then we will investigate this mystery."

"I'm not tired. Let's figure it out now."

Benny held the door to the bedroom open for her and she knew arguing would do no good. She trudged into the dark room, sparsely furnished with a chipped dresser and sagging double bed. The blanket was tidy and clean. Benny picked up a blanket that had been folded at the foot of a neatly made bed. The faint smells of damp dirt, soap, and coffee lingered in the dark bedroom.

Nora took it and sat on the edge of the bed to remove her boots. Abbey plopped on the floor next to the bed, apparently agreeing with Benny. A short nap wouldn't do her any harm.

Benny stood in the doorway. "You worry that because Nakwaiyamtewa has not been to see you that you are not Hopi. Think of who you are in your heart. How many signs do you need to make you believe?"

Nora curled up on the bed, certain Benny's words would swirl in her head and prevent any sleep. But not Benny's coffee, worry, or thoughts about her identity kept her from falling into a deep sleep.

TWENTY-NINE

WARREN COULDN'T EVER REMEMBER feeling this much hope. Not even when his first IPO exceeded everyone's expectations. This time, God had given him his heart's desire.

The soft purr of the Caddy carried him down the highway to his long-awaited dream. He'd given up on this so many years ago. Like Job, he hadn't cursed God, but the pain of loss burned in his bones throughout his life. Again, like Job, God rewarded him at the end.

The early evening light on Castle Rock glowed with promise. He rolled down the window just to let the soft air blow across his face, its touch feeling like a kiss from heaven. He hadn't felt this strong in months. The desert floor bloomed with orange, purple, yellow, and green. Air perfumed with sweet clover and fresh cut hay from lush bottom land filled his lungs. He'd lived long enough to see the summer in its fullness, to smell the new life, and to know that his legacy would survive.

It had taken one phone call and less than an hour before his sources confirmed what he'd hoped. Nora Abbott, the only daughter of Abigail Podanski, was born thirty-two years ago. As soon as he was certain, he'd rushed to Castle Valley.

The driveway leading to Rachel's house needed new gravel, but his Caddy navigated it handily. He hummed in anticipation as he eased to a stop. The bright warble of a meadowlark greeted him as he opened the door and planted his foot on the sand. He marched toward the rustic cabin, alive with the sensation of a circle closing, the perfection of God's plan flowering as surely as the wild sweet pea blooming by the porch.

The screen door squeaked opened and Rachel stepped out on the porch, her arms folded across her breast. The warm breeze lifted her thin hair and sent single strands dancing around the eyes she squinted at him. "What are you doing here?"

"I haven't come to see you." A few days ago he could barely stagger across his Manhattan office. Now he knew he'd charge through Rachel if she didn't get out of his way.

She crossed the porch to stand guard at the top of the stairs. "You're not welcome here."

He didn't need to lean on the rail as he climbed. "You were always one of my favorites, Rachel. You were smart and courageous. You had a spark your sisters lacked. I'm truly sickened by what you've become."

"My own person, you mean? Not ruled by the church or men?"

He reached the top stair without slowing. He could tell she didn't know what to do. At the last minute, she stepped back instead of shoving him from the stairs.

"God intended for men and women to be together. What you're doing is unnatural."

Her thin lips turned into a hard sneer. "You're the expert on natural? How natural is it for one man to have two wives, or three, or even more?"

"There is an order to the world. Tell me you can't feel God's disapproval."

He stepped toward the screen but this time, Rachel didn't move. He bumped against her, taking a step as if she weren't there. She thrust her chest, poking her folded arms against him. "Go away."

"I'll pray you find your true path, but I'm afraid it's too late. You know the time is short. Who will call your name and draw you through the veil if you don't give up your sinful ways and ask forgiveness?"

"Screw you." The bright blue of her eyes, the same eyes of her mother and sisters, clouded with hatred. He grieved for her lost soul.

He put a hand out to shove her aside. He'd done his best to save her. Now he would do what he'd come for.

She shoved back. "Get out of here."

He stumbled and a wave hit him again, the affliction more insidious than the cancer that ate his insides. He'd thought, with God's help, he'd conquered that black rage that rose up and flooded his mind. He gritted his teeth against the urge to fling Rachel from the porch...

"Warren!" Small hands grabbed his arm and yanked him backwards.

Rachel sprawled on the porch in front of him, her eyes wide, hatred splashed in red slashes on her cheeks. He'd shoved her yet couldn't remember doing so.

Warren's eyes traveled from the delicate hands on his arm to the woman standing beside him. He'd imagined a moment like this a billion times. He'd turn in a crowd and there she would be. Her golden beauty radiated toward him. She would have thought of him over the years, missing him, imaging what their lives would have been like together.

But this was no dream.

His Abigail, standing close enough that his senses filled with her sweet scent, her touch, the life in her eyes. He saw a woman in her twenties, firm skin and muscles strong from mountain hikes. He saw the sprinkle of freckles across her nose, the swinging gold of her long ponytail. It had only been one time but he still felt her beneath him, her longing matching his own. Why had he ever let her go?

"Warren, stop it. Go away." Her words pummeled him like stones. He focused on her now. Still beautiful. Still full of life.

"Abigail. You've come back."

He hadn't meant to say that. She flinched and disgust stole the shine from her eyes. She hurried over to help Rachel to her feet. Together they faced him. Abigail laced her arm through Rachel's.

"I need to talk to you, Abigail."

"I hoped I'd never have to set eyes on you again."

He knew how she felt. Throughout his life he'd been tempted to find her. It would have been easy, given all his resources. But he knew if he did, they'd never be able to resist each other. Maybe he and Christine didn't have a loving marriage, but he'd promised her and God he'd be faithful. No other woman except Abigail would make him break that vow.

"It doesn't matter now. All the pain, all the longing. It's over and our reward is here."

"You're as deranged as you were then. The difference is that I'm not afraid of you now."

"Afraid? You have never needed to be afraid. I love you, Abigail." What a relief it was to say those words, so often resisted and never spoken out loud. He laughed like a young buck after his first kiss. "Do you hear that? I love you. I've always loved you."

Her revulsion was obvious. "What are you talking about?"

Rachel's eyes opened even wider. "You know each other?"

Abigail's nose turned up as though she smelled rotten garbage. "Knew. Briefly."

The warmth of the memory filled him, loosening the tightness cancer had clamped on him. "We never had the time together we should have. That's my fault. I'm sorry I left you. But I felt God called me to a mission. Sometimes, the signs are clear and sometimes they seem murky. Now that we're together again, I know that road, no matter how hard and lonely, was the right one."

Abigail pulled herself up. "Go away."

He loved her fire. He loved the bright flash of her eyes. Everything about her stirred him in a way Christine never had. "I don't understand why you're so resistant. This is our chance, after all these years, to grab our small piece of happiness. Is it because you're married?"

She advanced on him, dropping her arm from Rachel. "It's because you raped me and you killed my husband!"

The words sat between them for several seconds. She didn't pry her eyes from his face while he studied her and tried to find a response.

"I could never hurt you. Never. How can you call what we had together rape?"

He watched the struggle for composure play across her face. Her eyes filled with tears and her voice sounded like sandpaper on rough wood. "I trusted you. I let you into our home. And you forced yourself on me."

Warren shook his head. "No. No. That's not the way it was. We loved each other. I know you felt it, too."

She spit at him like a feral cat. "I only felt sorry for a kid who seemed so lost and eager to know about Hopi."

She must have justified her infidelity over the years. Thirty years of convincing herself she'd never loved him might have turned her heart. She'd remember. "Isn't there something you need to tell me?"

"The only thing I need to tell you is to leave us alone!"

"What about our daughter?" Saying it filled him with a pounding strength.

She paled. "What?"

"Nora. The evidence of our love."

A flush of fury rose quickly to her face. "Nora is *not* your daughter. She's Dan's."

"There's no way God would allow Dan to be her father. He needs me to have an heir. Someone to lead the faithful."

Rachel watched the exchange of words with her mouth open in shock.

Why did Abigail fight against him?

She set her face in hard lines. "I have proof she's Dan's daughter. Something a Hopi-lover like you will appreciate."

His confidence never wavered. "You can't prove what isn't true."

"I know she's Dan's daughter because she's had Hopi signs and visitations."

He knew God had chosen him and his heirs for glory. "Tell me. What do you mean, visitations?"

She waved her hand in the air. "She won't tell me everything. I've had to piece it together from conversations between her and her cousin. Her real cousin. Benny Sepakuku, from the Hopi reservation." She pointed at him. "An old chief that talks to her. I know it's true because Benny knows everyone and everything and he is her Hopi spiritual guide because they're related."

If God had revealed all of this to him when he was younger, he might not have understood the great gift he'd received. His childhood of disgrace and rejection all made sense now. The sad pieces of his journey fit together to create a life lived for God. Now, he had an heir to complete the task.

He smiled. "You never knew about my family."

She folded her arms. "I read the 'Man of the Year' article about you. You were raised on a farm in southern Utah by hard-working Americans. You lived the American Dream, rose from poverty, made a fortune, and now you just want to protect America for future generations, blah, blah, blah."

He wished he could draw her inside his mind to share his memories so that she could know his heart. "It's true. I was raised in southern Utah by hard workers. It's just that four of those hard workers were my mothers and one was my father. My biological mother wasn't a favored wife, though. And I wasn't like the rest of my siblings. When I got old enough to be interested in girls or maybe just because he didn't like me, my father sent me away. I was fourteen and my mother came with me. She couldn't get a job so I supported us. And then I made a fortune."

Abigail pretended to be bored. "Good for you. Now go."

Hope surged through him as he went on. "Here's why I know Nora is my daughter. The reason my mother was least favorite and the reason I was so different is that she wasn't born and raised a good Mormon girl. She grew up on the reservation, a full-blooded Hopi."

He'd succeeded in shocking Abigail. Her eyes widened. "If you're Hopi, why did you need Dan to tell you about the history and prophesies?"

He itched to take her hand, to set his lips lightly against hers. "The people on the mesas happily welcomed me. They invited me to several ceremonies. But they wouldn't trust me enough to tell me what I needed to know. It would have taken me decades to learn."

"What did you need to know so badly?"

Such relief to tell her. "It's the signs. I first saw them on the ranch. My father drove me away, but he didn't know God put me there to see the signs."

"Your Mormon God? How does that mesh with Hopi?"

"You're like the others. You think religions are mutually exclusive. But it's all one. God showed me that. I needed Dan to teach me about the Sky People."

She laughed in a cruel way he didn't remember from her youth. "You're absolutely insane. Completely fruit loops."

"All great leaders were considered crazy. Many thought Jesus was a lunatic."

She smirked at him. "What are these Sky People going to do?"

Her skepticism bit at him. "They're coming for the faithful. We'll be taken away and given planets of our own. This is written in the Book of Mormon as well. It all fits together."

"And you're the chosen one?"

Instead of the sorrow and frustration, a surge of joy lifted him. "God has provided an heir."

"She's not your heir, but even if she were, she's a woman. You can't believe your God would hand over the keys to a female."

"It's God's plan. Maybe she'll give birth to a great leader."

Abigail's eyebrows drew down in concern.

Warren spun around. He scanned the porch and didn't see anything. "Where's Rachel?"

Abigail widened her eyes in feigned innocence. "I didn't notice she'd gone."

Warren strode across the porch and into the house.

Abigail ran after him. "Leave her alone!"

Rachel stood in the kitchen with a phone to her ear. When she saw him, she set it down.

Warren's heart jumped to his throat. "Who was that? What did you say? Did you tell him?"

Rachel didn't answer.

Warren couldn't waste time. He rushed across the room and grabbed Abigail by the arms. "Where is she? Where's Nora?"

Abigail clamped her mouth closed and glared at him.

He shook her and a strand of hair stuck to the corner of her mouth. Her eyes glittered with fear but she still didn't speak. "Tell me!"

Tears threatened and her lips quivered but stayed locked.

"Rachel just told my nephew about Nora. He expects to be the leader. Now that he knows I have a true heir, he'll kill her!"

THIRTY

Nora woke, disoriented. It took several moments of that frantic, lost feeling to place the rickety furniture in the dim light of Benny's bedroom. Abbey stretched and wagged his tail. It only took Nora a few seconds to lace up her boots and shoot from the bedroom.

Benny stood at the front door gazing into the plaza. "Are you ready to go?"

"Where?"

"I have something to show you."

They walked into the quiet village in the blinding sunshine of early afternoon. Across the plaza a woman stepped from a door, probably from a home similar to Benny's. She didn't wave and offer a hello as you might expect in suburban America. Hopi respected each other and seemed to have genuine affection for their neighbors, but they didn't jump into each other's lives. Nora had been surprised to learn they didn't have a word for hello.

Late morning sun blazed in the plaza, bringing out the red of the adobe buildings. Dust settled across the stone surface. The doors of the other dwellings remained closed against the gathering heat of the day.

She followed Benny around the edge of the plaza and through winding alleys to his aging pickup. Rust covered it so completely that it reminded Nora of tie-dye. She held the door open for Abbey and he hefted himself onto the floor, then up to the bench seat to sit and eagerly stare out the windshield. Nora and Benny climbed inside and he coaxed the engine into a rough rattle.

At the speed of a dozing snail, they made their way down the steep switchbacks of the mesa and bottomed out onto the highway. Benny didn't speak so Nora spent the ten-minute drive following wormholes in her brain.

After five miles, Benny pulled off the highway onto an obscure two-track trail heading across the desert. Another six or seven miles north of the highway, they bumped down a steep arroyo and Benny followed the dry creek bed, winding around stones and the sandy banks.

After a time he idled to a stop and cut the engine. He climbed out and Nora followed.

"Where are we going?" she finally asked.

"I told you about the prophesies given to us by the one who brought us here."

"Yes." Ever logical, Nora felt uncomfortable with thousand-year-old prophesies that foretold the coming of the white men, the political splits of the tribe, the decline of Hopi. They warned about taking things from the moon and had even described the atom bomb.

He gave her one of his rare smiles. "And we talked about the instructions."

She matched his steady pace as he climbed from the creek bed and hiked toward a stand of three rocks that stood like eight-foot-high sentinels. "Live simply. Take no more than you need. Plant seeds. Recognize the creator is within us."

Benny kept walking without looking at her. "Are you living according to the instructions?"

Guilt bit at her. "I could do better."

"Hopi need to immerse ourselves in Mother Earth and blend with her to celebrate life. As we join together, a new attitude will take hold and the world will be gently transformed."

Nora thought about that while they trudged along. "I think what you're saying is that I'm focusing on what I want to happen, like having the kachina come to me, instead of focusing on what I should do for the world."

He chuckled. "Always looking for the answers."

Benny made it to the rock formation and rounded a corner to stand in the enclosure created by them. He gazed up the smooth surface of the towering rock.

Nora followed his line of sight. Before her, a series of images etched in the stone told a story. Of course, it was in a language she couldn't understand. She recognized the Hopi maiden in the space ship and the weird sunburst symbol. She turned to Benny. "Do you know what it means?"

He shrugged. "No."

She gave him an exasperated glare.

That little grin slipped onto his face. "I can tell you what I think."

"Please do."

He picked up a stick and pointed at a long, diagonal line that ran from the bottom left corner to the top right corner of the scene. "This is the journey of Hopi." He sketched along vertical lines. "These three that intersect show where the people have made choices, some for good and some not so good. These three circles are world wars. You see, this last one is on the other side of the third decision."

"Does that mean if the people make a good decision we won't have another war?"

"Maybe."

Gotta love those definitive messages.

"This maiden, who represents the Sky People." Benny pointed to the image. "You see she is next to the symbol that interests you?"

"Yes."

"And it all sits above the third decision and the circle of war."

"But what does it mean?"

"The Sky People have been visiting the Hopi for many years. Our elders know of them. Many of them have gone with the Sky People."

"Gone with them?"

"The prophesies tell us that Sky People will come gather the true Hopi at the end of the Fourth World and take them to the other planets."

"You never told me anything about Sky People."

"Hopi is an old tribe. There is much you don't know. This symbol," he outlined the image. "It is a sign for the Sky People. It tells them where they are welcome."

Nora's phone vibrated in her shorts pocket. She hadn't been aware she carried it on her. Habit. She pulled it out, not recognizing the number. "How is it there's a signal this far out?"

Benny's eyes twinkled. "How many times have I told you that Hopi is the center of the world?"

She rolled her eyes and answered her phone.

Darrell's words tumbled out. "He's got your mother."

"What?" Alarms jangled through her. "Who? Where?"

He was breathless. "Warren Evans. I came out to the cabin and she was gone. Rachel said Warren took her."

"Oh, God." Panic shot through her veins. "I'm calling the cops."

"No!"

"Why not?"

"No telling what Warren will do." He paused. "I'm sorry. I heard Abigail tell you about him last night. He might want to shut Abigail up. Or maybe he wants to claim you're his daughter."

"But he doesn't know for sure."

Darrell hesitated. "He thinks he knows. He came out here and confronted Abigail. Rachel isn't your friend. She found out about Abigail and Warren and went straight to Lee."

Nora struggled to restart her brain. "Why would she go to Lee?"

Darrell hesitated. "They're in it together."

"Wait. I don't understand. In *what* together?"

"Lee is set to inherit Warren's estate. Warren's tried to keep it secret, but he's dying. If Warren thinks you're his heir and decides to leave his wealth to you, Lee is cut out."

She turned from the rocks. "I'm coming to Moab. I've got to find Abigail."

"Where are you?"

Her heart thundered in her chest. "I'm at the rez."

"Stay there and let me handle it. Lee is dangerous."

Nora was already running to Benny's pickup. "I'm coming."

Darrell sighed as if resigning himself. "Rachel is somewhere with Lee, so meet me at the cabin and we can go after Abigail together."

THIRTY-ONE

DARK CLOUDS, HEAVY WITH rain, blocked the sun. Thunder rumbled and occasionally cracked. A few drops, fat as bumblebees, splatted on her windshield. She slapped on her wipers and sped down the highway. She'd been driving for hours across empty Navajo land.

What kind of danger was Abigail in? Nora had to find her and get her back to Flagstaff. She'd hand Abigail over to Charlie and make him promise to never let her mother out of his sight.

Abbey resettled himself in the passenger seat, yawned, and closed his eyes again. He obviously didn't feel empathy with her anxiety.

The raven cawed. She checked the phone's caller ID. Cole. A dose of his calm would do her good. But he was married. "Don't answer," she instructed Abbey.

Her phone squawked again and she punched it on.

"It's over." Cole sounded jubilant—definitely not his usual tone.

"Huh?" She'd thought those words might refer to his father, but Cole sounded happy.

"It all worked out as I'd hoped and my marriage has been annulled. When are you coming home so we can celebrate?"

Pop, pop, pop, swish. Pop, pop, pop, swish. The rain and wipers filled the silence.

"I don't understand," she finally said.

"Sorry. Here's what happened. When I was eighteen, I thought I was in love with Amber. She was sixteen. We ran off and got married. But, of course, we headed home after a couple of days and she went back to her parents and I went to college and I figured since she was under age it wasn't a legal thing anyway. Years later, she and my brother got married."

"Your girlfriend married your brother?"

He paused. "Yeah. It caused some bad blood. Still does, I guess. I thought we'd gotten past that."

"How did it end up you were still married?"

"It was a real mess. Derek divorced Amber last year. He didn't have much, since the ranch is in my father's name. So Amber makes her living waitressing in Sheridan." She pictured his frown. "But when Dad had his stroke and it looked like he might not make it, Amber figured she could get a piece of that inheritance."

"How is your father?"

Cole rushed on. "He's starting to talk again. He's confused, but I think he's coming back."

Nora welcomed that good news. "That's great. So what happened with Amber?"

"She dragged out this license. It looks legal since her parents' signature is on it, but I know she forged it."

"Why didn't you deny it and call her a liar?"

"I didn't want it to come to a big public battle. So I sent it off to a lawyer and had him draw up a legal letter. It only took a couple of days—she's backed down and it's all over."

"You don't want to be married to her?"

He laughed. "Of course not. I want to be married to you."

She caught her breath and managed to squeak. "You do?"

"Yes." It sounded strong and definite. "Whenever you're ready. As far as I'm concerned, we could head up to the courthouse as soon as you get back to Boulder."

She blinked back a tear. "I thought you didn't want me."

He sounded exasperated. "Nora. How many signs do you need before you have some faith?"

Wham. Talk about a brick upside the head. Benny said the same thing to her. Both Lisa and Abigail told her to figure out who she was and what she wanted. In that magical confluence that almost never happens, Nora felt the truth of something she'd always believed but never completely understood: She got one life. Her life. No genetics, no expectations, no doubts or fears could define her. She could make it her own.

Great insight. It might take her the rest of her life to believe it, but she had a start. She grinned. "I'll be home soon. Then we'll take that trip to the courthouse."

"I love you, Nora."

"I love you, too." Much as she hated to, she severed the connection. Almost immediately, her rosy glow disappeared. Lee wanted her dead. Warren had Abigail. If Nora wanted to keep that date at the courthouse, she needed to find proof to lock Lee away and get Abigail from Warren's clutches.

No problem.

The pavement darkened, then shone in her headlights as the rain continued to smash against the windshield. Nora topped a hill and the smattering of lights from Moab glowed below.

"Where is your camera?" she spoke to Lisa.

Lisa probably suspected Rachel and Lee were plotting together. At the very least, Lisa was fighting with Rachel due to the film and maybe even her involvment with the underground railroad. So obviously Lisa wouldn't hide the film at home.

Think! The camera had to be someplace that had specific ties to Nora.

Nora always stayed at the cabin when she visited Moab. They hiked trails all over the area. It would take her months to check out all those places. Lisa would pick a place special to the both of them.

Almost immediately, as if Lisa's ghost had whispered the answer in her ear, Nora knew. She blinked and her mouth opened and closed. "How could I be so stupid?" She might be talking to Abbey. Probably she just talked to herself.

They popped into Moab from the south, racing along the highway. Nora gunned the Jeep and turned left in front of an oncoming Cruise America RV. It honked as she sped down the residential lane. Such an obvious hiding place and yet, Nora hadn't thought about it.

She wound through town and out west, racing through the curves and bends. Her back tires slipped on some of the sharper curves. The Jeep wouldn't go fast enough and Nora rocked in her seat with impatience.

Rain smacked the windshield between the swish of the wipers and the squeak of the dry glass. The sky hadn't opened up and dumped here, yet, and Nora hoped it would wait until she had the camera. Finally, she spotted the turnout at the trailhead and whipped off the road. She slammed on the brakes and slid ten feet on the loose dirt at Moonflower campground.

In the gathering darkness, the canyon walls loomed, creating shadows amid the cottonwoods and shrubs. Beyond her headlights, the trail wound into a void. The rain pocked the sand and dotted the rock faces as Nora climbed from the Jeep. "Stay here," she said to Abbey.

It did no good to try to avoid seeing the rock art panel and the crevice containing the ladder at the opening to the canyon. The ancient tree trunks notched to create a vertical path to safety. Nora struggled not to picture Lisa laying there, her sightless eyes staring at the sky, dark waves falling across her cheeks, her neck twisted at an impossible angle. They found her here, but that's not where she died.

Nora concentrated on the path, dodging rocks and willing herself to move quickly without stumbling. She gulped air, her lungs protesting the long and difficult run. She passed the clearing by the creek where people had gathered for Lisa's funeral.

Hiking this trail with Lisa could take a couple of hours as she'd bend to take in the tiniest rare flower or contemplate the clouds. In the looming darkness and gathering storm, Nora cut the time to twenty minutes.

The canyon narrowed so the trail climbed a steep ridge and traversed twenty feet above the creek. It wound along a ledge then opened onto a wide expanse of slick rock. She crossed the open stretch of wet rock and managed to arrive at the worn trail on the other side without slipping to the creek below.

She made it to where the trail ended at the swimming hole with its natural rock slide. If Nora and Lisa had a special place, this was it. Of course she would have hidden the camera here. But where, exactly? The swimming hole filled the bottom of a small valley roughly fifty feet in diameter.

The walls of the box canyon were made up of stone pillars and cliffs raising high in the air, hiding the area and making it feel secret. Bubbles rose in her gut and she clenched her teeth. Panic wouldn't help. She slowed her panting, exhaling long and inhaling deeply.

What would Benny do? Benny would still be on the rez thinking about getting into his pickup. She needed to act. But not irrationally. Calm down.

She studied two rocks separated by a narrow crevice, letting her eyes travel up the mystic columns. A video camera case could be wedged in any of the crags and niches along the phallic structures. Suddenly, Nora knew exactly where Lisa would hide it. She remembered that afternoon right after Lisa had moved to Moab.

> *They'd climbed from the pool after one last slide down the slick rock. Lisa spread her towel in a shaft of sunlight. Nora wrapped herself in her towel and chose a shady spot to protect her fair skin from sunburn.*
>
> *"This is a beautiful place," Nora said.*
>
> *Lisa leaned back and sighed in contentment. "I love it here." She eyed the two columns close together. "Except I'm not fond of those rocks."*
>
> *Nora twisted around to inspect them. "Why?"*
>
> *Lisa laughed. "Look at them! They look like two penises."*
>
> *"They do not. They look more like a woman the way they line up." Nora blushed a little at the thought.*
>
> *Lisa grinned at them. "You're right. I'm claiming them in the name of all lesbians."*

That had to be the spot.

Nora scrambled to the rock. A swollen raindrop splashed on her nose and dripped down her chin. Thunder cracked overhead.

Nora wedged herself between the two rocks and started to climb. She managed inches at a time, her back to the cold face of one rock, her knees scraping the other and her feet pushing while she searched for each hand hold to pull her up.

Rain fell in a steady patter now, chilling the top of her head and dribbling down her neck. She cursed Lisa for her natural rock climbing ability. Nora always followed Lisa on the more difficult climbs. Nora would struggle to find hand holds and have to concentrate to distribute her weight just right. It often felt counterintuitive to lean away from the rock instead of into it or to understand the three-point of contact rule. With Lisa to lead her, Nora placed her hands in the same holds.

Tonight, Nora was on her own, trying to imagine Lisa shimmying in the crevice between the rocks, somehow managing a camera case, desperation driving her on.

Nora propped her foot against the rock in front of her and pressed her back into the other. With her legs more or less parallel to the ground and her knees bent, she wedged between the two stone pillars. She paused to snatch a breath before tilting her head back and surveying the rock above her. She was nearly to the top and she imagined the corner of a black vinyl case peeking over the ledge.

Only ten more feet. She pushed with her legs and slid her back up the rock. Her T-shirt caught on a sharp nipple of rock and ripped. Nora inched her feet up and repeated the motion several more times.

There. It wasn't her imagination. The camera case barely showed over the lip of the summit. Nora stretched, pushing her feet into the rock and arching her back. Her fingers brushed the case and pushed it further away from her.

She shimmied up the crevice once again. Reached and tapped at the side of the case, shoving it at an angle away from her but closer to the edge of the rock. She lunged and knocked it with her fingers, finally sending it tumbling into her lap.

Rain tapped the vinyl lid. Balancing the case on her legs and steadying it with each movement as her grip allowed, Nora scraped and slid down the crevice until she finally stood at the base.

She gripped the case and scrambled into one of the narrow, cave-like arches next to the swimming hole to escape the increasing rain. Her legs trembled. With shaking hands, she snapped open the latches and pulled the camera out of the dense padding. It took a minute to make out the labels on the dials in the fading light.

She finally gave up and through trial and error and a fair amount of cursing, found the right command to play the video.

Lisa's face came on the screen in a good imitation of a scene from *The Blair Witch Project*. "I knew you'd find this, Nora. I'm sorry it's not the film project you expected. I'm afraid all copies of that are gone. Or will be by the time you see this. Unless Rachel doesn't find the one in the bookcase. You've got to tell someone. I don't know who. The cops around here are all in on it. It's a Mormon thing. Only, not the official Mormon Church. This is a cult. And Warren Evans is their leader."

The background of the video showed hazy light and the trailhead where Nora's Jeep sat now. Lisa must have propped the camera on her old Toyota pickup. The sun was setting behind her. Lisa's face looked drawn and pale and her eyes kept darting where the road would be.

Nora wanted to reach into the camera and throw her arms around her friend. Why hadn't she taken Lisa's call that afternoon?

"I know you. You'll want to go all mother hen and take responsibility for everyone. This is not your fault. And it's not Rachel's fault, either. She was raised a certain way and it was pounded into her over and over. She tried to get away from it. But it's too deep inside her. Don't blame her."

The hitch in Nora's chest forced her breath into a tight wheeze. It sounded like Lisa knew Rachel had turned against her. Did she suspect Rachel and Lee were together? Had Rachel helped Lee murder Lisa?

"It's the rock art, Nor. The signs and the lines on Tokpela's barn are the same. They think the Sky People are coming for them. It's happening soon. I think at summer solstice. The lines tell them where to go. Marlene knows some of this. If I can't call her, tell Marlene…" Her head jerked up and she gasped. "Damn. Nora, I've got to go. Protect Rachel. She needs your help."

Nora watched as Lisa jumped up and grabbed the camera but didn't turn it off as she swung it around. The view showed a sickening mishmash of sage, scrub, red dirt, gray sky, and the white of the evening primrose. Lisa grunted and the black of the camera case flitted in and out of the screen as she struggled to load the camera. A heartbeat before the screen went black and the sound died, Nora saw something, just a snatch of an image caught as Lisa swung the camera on its final arc to the case.

Nora's stomach clenched and she held her breath.

She hit rewind, then play.

Oh my God.

Rewind. Play. Pause.

Her ears rang as she stared at the image. A white pickup straddled the center line of the road, heading up the last stretch to the trailhead.

She had her proof.

THIRTY-TWO

THE RAIN FELL JUST enough to make the trail slick and in her rush to reach the trailhead, Nora tripped and scraped her knee. Heart thundering, she sprinted past the clearing. Muddy and wet, Nora made it back to the Jeep. She wrenched open the door and jumped in. Abbey licked her face and sat in the passenger seat.

Warren had Abigail. The Evanses were all killers, and now that Nora had proof Lee had murdered Lisa, she might be able to use it to save Abigail.

Somehow.

Nora started the Jeep and backed onto the highway. She grabbed her phone and dialed Marlene.

"I found Lisa's camera," she said when Marlene answered. "She said to ask you what's going on."

Marlene hesitated. "The less you know, the better."

Nora barely restrained herself from yelling into the phone. "Warren kidnapped Abigail. I need to know everything!"

"What's he doing with Abigail?"

Nora clamped the phone to her ear using her shoulder and shifted gears. Still breathless from her run from the swimming hole, she said, "I don't have time to explain. Lisa said Warren Evans is leader of a cult. Did he have Lee kill Lisa? It's got nothing to do with Canyonlands, does it?"

"You think Lee killed Lisa?" She sounded disbelieving.

Nora concentrated on the black road in front of her. "Is it the Underground Railroad? Did she help one of his wives escape?"

Marlene whispered. "Slow down. Lee didn't kill Lisa because of the railroad. He was helping those girls."

"Maybe he's just acting like he's helping. He's dangerous. I know it."

"Okay, maybe there is something else going on," Marlene stammered. "It's not what you think. But we learned about it through the girls."

"About what?" Nora wanted to scream.

"You know all those people you saw with Lee the day the cows almost got loose?"

"Yes."

"They're immigrants to Warren's colony. They came from Germany."

"How do you know this?"

"A few months ago one of the girls we helped said her mother's family had disappeared. Before that, her mother had talked about Sky People coming for them."

Nora hit a flooded dip in the road and splashing water roared.

"They were supposed to immigrate to another planet on the summer solstice."

That was in two days. "Immigrate from where?"

"The mother told her they were going to the Sky Ranch. But we didn't know where that was."

"Tokpela! Tokpela Ranch. Sky in Hopi."

"Yeah. I figured that out today. How did you know?"

"Lisa."

Something crashed as if Marlene had slammed a fist down. "She must have figured it out and they killed her to keep her quiet."

Snakes knotted in Nora's stomach. "Warren? He's got a god syndrome and people think he's leading them to outer space. Crackpots like that come along all the time. Why would he have Lisa killed to keep her from telling anyone?"

"How the hell would I know?" Marlene yelled. She paused and continued, calmer now. "He's a crazy man. This family from Germany arrived at the ranch yesterday. Hans and his wife and kids. Hans's half-brother had immigrated a couple of weeks ago but Hans didn't tell Warren he was related in case there were family quotas. When they got to the Sky Ranch, Hans's half-brother and family weren't in the bunker."

Nora swung the Jeep onto the highway and zoomed north. "A bunker?"

"Apparently there is a massive underground facility that can house a couple of thousand people and they've been gathering in the last week or so to wait for the solstice. Warren had it built at his family ranch. It must have been under constructions for years to complete it without anyone noticing."

As isolated as Tokpela Ranch seemed, building something on the sly would be possible. "This guy's brother from Germany went missing? Maybe he changed his mind and left."

"Yeah, I thought so, too. But Hans picked up clues from the other immigrants. They all give up their assets when they join. He's convinced his brother wanted to leave, but Warren's people didn't want him to spill the beans on their plans and they really didn't want to give him his money back. So they killed him. That's when Hans and his family snuck away."

People hiding underground in the desert waiting for the aliens to take them home—this couldn't be real. "Why did they come to you?"

"Hans tried to get another family to leave, too. They were too frightened, but they knew about the Underground Railroad so they gave him my name."

It sounded too far-fetched. "You believe him about all of this?"

"I don't know." She paused. "Yes, I guess I do. Until he showed up here today, I didn't know about the bunker or Topkela. Lisa did and now she's dead."

"Call the FBI. Tell them all of this and send them out to Lee's ranch."

Steel sounded in Marlene's voice. "I already did it an hour ago."

Nora hung up and swung through Moab, speeding along the highway past the café and outfitter's office. She squealed her brakes to turn on the highway that ran alongside the river. Rain from afternoon monsoon storms upstream had swollen it and it raged muddy in the dusky shadow.

The only plan Nora could concoct was to go to Darrell. He had the resources to find Warren and stop him. She dialed him but it went straight to voicemail.

The rain smacked against the windshield and Nora felt time slipping by as she raced to Castle Valley. Full-on dark dropped before Nora whipped the Jeep from the highway onto the narrow road into the village.

A crack of lightning flared and she automatically counted until the boom of thunder followed. Four seconds. The storm would crash over them soon.

Her back tires skidded as she jerked the wheel to make the hard left into Lisa's lane. She gunned it down the sloshy tracks and slowed before rounding the last curve. A dark shape loomed ahead and she slammed on the brakes.

Darrell's 4Runner was parked along the road. He'd know who to call to help them find Abigail. Abbey jumped to his feet and put his front feet on her lap, ready to escape the Jeep after being cooped up so long.

She killed the engine and slipped from the Jeep. Abbey wanted out, but Nora held her hand up, blocking his exit. She pushed the Jeep door, snicking it closed instead of slamming it, though the roar of the wind would have masked a marching band.

She sprinted for the house but when she ran around the curve, she stopped. Lee's white pickup snugged up behind Rachel's Passat in front of the porch. Where was Darrell? Did he have Rachel and Lee subdued inside? Did they have him?

Hoping to avoid detection if Lee and Rachel were in the kitchen or living room or even on the front porch, Nora snuck around the cabin and came up the back. Maybe she'd be able to get some information about Abigail.

Wind tugged at her hair and whipped it into her face. She fumbled a ponytail elastic from her wrist and gathered her hair, twisting the tie around it while she ran. The rain still fell in fat drops, slapping the dirt and dampening the sage and pinion, letting off their spicy scents.

She slowed her pace as she neared the back deck. The wind continued its camouflaging racket and she sank to her knees. With great care, she moved as slowly as possible, careful not to draw attention to herself. Lying on her belly, she peered through the French doors into Lisa's office.

The office sat dark and empty. But lights in the kitchen shone on Rachel as she perched on a barstool facing the kitchen, her back to Nora.

Lee leaned against the sink, his black hat pushed back on his forehead. He wore his standard scowl and radiated a super-intense attitude. His lips moved and Rachel nodded as he talked, but Nora couldn't hear through the closed doors. She didn't see Darrell.

Nora backed away from the door and off the porch. She crawled along the side of the house, ducking under the open living room windows. The cabin blocked the full force of the wind and when Nora positioned herself directly under the window closest to Lee and Rachel, she could hear the hard notes of Rachel's voice.

"Nora's gone. She knows there's no film. She's not going to cause any more trouble." Yay, Rachel—sticking up for Nora's life.

"Darrell will find her and then it'll be all over." If Lee's voice had fingers, they'd be wrapped around Nora's neck.

Darrell was in on the Warren cult along with Rachel and Lee? That didn't make any sense. He must be playing along until he had the information needed to expose them.

"Darrell's not around, either. Maybe he's finally going to do what Warren ordered him to do and then we don't have anything to worry about." Warren must have ordered Darrell to kill Nora.

"Darrell won't do it." Disgust iced Lee's words. "He's never done Warren's bidding unless there was something in it for him. He won't put himself in danger just to please a dying man."

Of course Darrell wouldn't do it. He wasn't really working for Warren. But where was he?

Nora eased up to peer over the windowsill.

Rachel dropped her head to her folded arms on the counter. "We'll need to get them both."

Lee's mouth twisted as if he chewed on spoiled meat. "We'll take care of them."

Like they'd taken care of Lisa. Like Warren might take care of Abigail?

"Is Uncle Warren still determined to go through with this? It's crazy." Rachel said.

Lee stomped to the end of the kitchen and back, as though his hatred couldn't be contained. "It's not crazy. The Sky People are coming.

Uncle Warren's more determined than ever now that he's got his rightful heir."

Rachel sat up. "Why did she have to come here? Why did she have to know Lisa? If it wasn't for Nora and her precious film, Lisa wouldn't have died."

It sounded like Lee spit darts at Rachel. "Maybe Lisa died because of her unnatural ways. Maybe it's her punishment for leading you to sin."

Rachel let out a sob. "She should still be alive."

Lee leaned on the counter and his eyes drilled into Rachel. "Alive for what? For you to continue this sinful life?"

Rachel glared at him. "What kind of life do you think suits me better?"

Surprisingly, he sounded almost gentle. "You know." He reached out and touched her cheek. "You remember."

Rachel backed away. "I remember two good years."

"It didn't have to end," he said.

She shook her head. "Even back then, you knew I wasn't the right wife for you."

He straightened and the rime of hatred lifted from his face. "That's not true. I loved you. I wanted you."

"That's just it. You wanted me, but I didn't want you in that same way. And you knew it."

"We could have worked it out."

Now her voice rose in near-hysteria. "I didn't want to work it out. And then you brought Tessa into our home. I didn't mind, really. In fact, it gave me a break from the part of our marriage I couldn't stand."

He studied her. "Then why?"

She swiped at tears. "Tessa was the younger sister. She loved me and is so easygoing. But then you brought Cassie. That ruined everything."

"She's your sister. And she was getting too old for anyone else. I thought I owed it to you, to your family. I thought you'd want your sisters with you."

"No woman wants to share her husband with her sisters!"

The rain intensified and Nora leaned closer to hear above the rumbling on the roof.

"You never asked me or even discussed it. You filled up our home with the others. They pushed me out. And when they started having babies, you never even looked at me anymore."

Lee reached out again and she backed up further. "Then I met Lisa. She was smart and wild and so pretty."

He flinched as if she had burned him.

"I finally knew what was wrong with me and Lisa didn't think it was wrong at all."

Lee looked like he wanted to stick his fingers in his ears. "It's wrong. It's against God's law."

"Whose God? A lot of people say what you do is a sin."

"You decided to love a woman because she paid attention to you and made you feel special." He said it as if she were a six-year-old who stole her friend's doll.

"No. I didn't decide. I discovered. One day, I was working at the farmer's market and Lisa was buying cheese. She used to come by the stand every week and we'd talk about everything and anything."

Rachel drew in a shaky breath but smiled at the memory. "A mountain biking team walked by and they were tanned and muscled and nice looking. Lisa said, 'I can appreciate a good-looking man, and those are excellent bodies, but they don't do it for me.'"

Lee let out a sound that might have been a wretch.

"And I thought, 'That's how I feel. It's how I've always felt.' I looked at Lisa and I knew why I always got tongue-tied when she stopped at the stand. I knew why I flushed when I saw her in the crowd and got all flustered when she left."

A whine at the screen made Rachel and Lee jerk their heads to the front door.

"Abbey?" Rachel said.

Lee swung his head to the window. He made eye contact with Nora before she spun around and sprinted from the cabin.

Once away from the protection of the eves, the wind and rain battered her. She swiveled her head to see Lee vault the front porch railing and land in the mud. He slipped in his cowboy boots, but pushed himself up and came after her.

Clay caked on the bottom of her boots and soon she carried what felt like ten extra pounds with each step. She pumped her arms and took off for the Jeep.

Lightning cracked and almost immediately, the thunder hit with a rumbling she felt in her bones. Another flash of lightning followed in rapid succession.

Her legs fought the sucking mud. The rain slashed at her face and her arms ripped through the sharp thorns of the wolfberry bush.

She barely made it out of the yard. The Jeep was a dark hulk camouflaged by rain. Lee grunted behind her. With the slick leather of his cowboy boots, he hadn't gathered the layers of clay to drag him down.

Fear fueled an extra surge of speed.

Something slammed into her back with the force of a freight train, knocking her down to splash in two inches of water and mud. Her cheek slammed into something hard and Lee landed on top of her. He felt like a solid lead skeleton—heavy, hard, and bony, grinding her into the grime and red slurry.

He pushed himself to his knees and grabbed a fistful of her T-shirt, hauling her up as he got to his feet. He didn't speak, just turned toward the house and started dragging her.

She pulled back, struggling and twisting. "Let me go!"

The night closed around them in deep darkness and the rain felt like a curtain. The illumination of the cabin flitted like a strobe light.

Lee slipped in the slick mud and Nora lurched back, ready to make another run. He reached out and closed long fingers around her ankle. He jerked and sent her to the mud bath again. Then Lee yanked her arm and pulled her to her feet. Without stopping, he grabbed her around her waist and hoisted her to his shoulder. With Nora's rear in the air, Lee struggled through the red soup toward the house. She knew her kicking and squirming wouldn't do much good. He had wrestled calves and cows meaner and stronger than Nora.

Rachel met them on the front porch. She held the door open and Lee shoved Nora inside. He followed her and Rachel came after him, shutting the heavy oak door against the rain and wind. Abbey closed in on her, wedging himself so close to her legs he nearly sent her sprawling. He panted and dripped saliva on the floor. Mud and rain slid from his fur. Thunder and lightning scared him and he must have panicked in the Jeep, throwing himself against the loosely latched door until it opened. She put a hand on his head to reassure him and he leaned against her.

Nora straightened and planted her dripping feet on the wood floor. She put her hand on her hips and demanded, "What have you done with my mother?"

"She's with Uncle Warren," Lee growled and took hold of her shoulder, forcing her to sit on a barstool.

Abbey pressed against her.

A gust of wind rattled against the windows, roaring its challenge to the night.

Abigail was alone with the man who'd raped her more than thirty years ago. She'd be terrified, assuming she was still alive. "What does he want with her?"

247

Lee pressed Nora's shoulders down, keeping her in the chair. "My best guess is that he's looking for you."

"Call him, tell him to let Abigail go."

"Why would I do that?"

She glared at him. "If you don't, I'll go to the FBI."

He called over his shoulder to Rachel. "Get me some rope."

Nora jerked her arms but he didn't lose his grip. "I've got proof you killed Lisa. I found her camera and it shows you there."

He frowned. "Where?"

"Let me go and I'll give you the camera."

He ignored her and hollered for Rachel to bring the rope.

Nora struggled against him but made little headway. Any knot Lee tied would hold Nora for decades—or at least as long as it took for Warren to hurt Abigail.

Outside, lightning flashed and thunder sounded like a hungry lion. Abbey whined and put both front paws on Nora's thighs, lifting himself to standing. If she hadn't been propped on the barstool, he'd have crawled into her lap. The rain streamed down the windows in a black cascade.

Rachel appeared behind Lee, a roll of duct tape in her hands. "We don't have any rope. You can use this."

He grabbed it from Rachel with one hand while keeping a vise grip on Nora's shoulder. He held the roll to his mouth and peeled a corner loose with his teeth.

Rachel shifted from foot to foot. "You don't have to tape her up. She'll stay here."

With the end of the tape in his mouth, he jerked the roll away from him, making it squawk. He lifted his hand from her shoulder.

Nora shoved her feet against the rungs of the stool and leaped from the chair. She had barely moved before Lee's fingers clamped around her wrist and yanked her back. Her arm twisted behind her and she cried out.

A German shepherd or Doberman pinscher might have taken her cry of pain as a sign to go for the jugular of her attacker. Abbey just appeared more agitated and frightened than ever.

Lee snapped her other wrist around. The tape roll dangled from his mouth. He used the same motions he'd probably practiced a million times for rodeo calf tying. Within seconds he'd whipped the end of the tape from his mouth, slapped it on her wrist, and wound the roll around both wrists to secure her.

He held her down by her shoulder again and hollered at Rachel. "Tape her ankles to the stool."

"This isn't necessary. We can take care of her without taping her up."

Rachel was right. How much strapping down does it take to hold someone still enough to shoot them? Or slit a throat, or bash in their brains with a rock?

"Besides, she can't go anywhere in this storm," Rachel said.

"It's always this way with you. Always arguing, always questioning, needing to know why."

Maybe they'd strike up a lover's spat and Nora could bolt. But Rachel was right. The ground had been soup when they'd been outside. The rain had continued, driving down in sheets and running along the desert floor. Her Jeep might be stuck.

"We've got to keep her here," Lee said. "What if she gets away and Darrell finds her?"

"Damn it! Listen to me for once. Leave her alone. She's not going anywhere."

"Do you want to take that chance?"

If Darrell was here, he'd have made a move to rescue her by now. Maybe Warren had him. Her last hope of help faded.

Rachel took the roll of tape and bent down to Nora's legs. Abbey licked her face and she gently pushed him aside. He crowded in close to her.

Nora twitched her legs back and forth to keep Rachel from binding them. Lee's face exploded with pent-up temper. He pulled one hand back to strike her. Rachel jumped up and grabbed it before he could swing. "No!"

He stared at Rachel, nostrils flaring.

Rachel's voice dipped low and slow. "As far as I know, you've never hit a woman. Don't start now."

Never hit a woman? She guessed snapping someone's neck and arranging her body to look like an accident didn't count as hitting.

Lee gritted his teeth and said to Nora, "Cooperate. This is for your own good."

Interesting what he thought was good for Nora. Maybe if she didn't fight, he wouldn't need to smack her around before he killed her.

She fought against the duct tape. It gave slightly, and in time, she'd probably be able to work free. But she needed something immediate. *Think!* She had nothing to bargain with. Or so she thought.

Inspiration struck. "I'll go to Warren. Trade me for Abigail."

"You don't want anything to do with Warren," Rachel said. She secured one ankle and moved to the other.

Lightning split the sky. Hairs on Nora's neck tingled. Thunder cawhacked, thrashing the walls and floor. Abbey whined again and jumped, his front paws brushing Nora. He slid to the floor and sat beside her chair, panting and dripping saliva.

Rachel huffed, nearly as frightened as Abbey. She closed her eyes for a second, then finished taping Nora's leg and stood. Lee released his grip on her shoulder, easing the crushing pressure, and plopped on the couch facing her. Seeing the chance to get closer to a human who might make the terrifying storm go away, Abbey trotted over and leaned into Lee, putting his face far up into Lee's lap. Lee put a hand on Abbey's head.

"Tell Warren I'll do whatever he wants," Nora pleaded.

Lee's fingers played in Abbey's fur. Rachel folded her arms on her chest and bit her lip. "You don't understand. We need to keep you here."

"I understand perfectly." If Nora's hands were free, she'd point her finger at Lee. "He needs to kill me so he can inherit everything. I swear I don't want Warren's money. He can have it all."

Bright crimson streaked Rachel's pale cheeks. "It's not just the money. It's the power. He's always craved it. That's why he killed Lisa, to keep her from telling anyone what she knew."

Pop. Sizzle. Ba-whump. Nature's artillery shells bombarded the cabin.

Nora narrowed her eyes at Lee but he stared ahead, deep in thought, stroking Abbey's head. Nora started to call out to him. She never got the words out.

The world erupted in chaos.

A freight train roared outside the cabin. The walls shook and the floor heaved. Rachel screamed.

Nora's heart flew to her throat as lightning flashed.

THIRTY-THREE

LEE SPRANG FROM THE couch. Abbey let out a yelp and barked as if he couldn't decide to run and hide or take the offensive. Lee bounded across the room to the door and wrenched it open. The deafening noise increased. Rachel raced after Lee. They both disappeared into the darkness of the front porch amid the sound of a jet engine firing up.

"What is it?" Nora strained against the duct tape.

The house shook again and the windows rattled in the wind. Abbey lunged at Nora, trying to land in her sloping lap. He dropped to the floor and whined.

Lee and Rachel bolted inside. Together they shoved the door closed. Rachel's blonde hair was dark and hung limp with rain.

Lee swiped an arm across his face to dry it and strode to the window opposite Nora. His movements were jerky, as if he'd been zapped by electricity. He pressed his face to the glass. Rachel leaned against the door, pale and shaking.

"What?" Nora said.

No one answered. Another boom of thunder shook the floor. Rachel ducked her head between her shoulders and Lee drew in a sharp breath. "Dear Lord," he began, his words edged in razors of tension as he jerked his head toward Nora. "Cut her loose," he said to Rachel.

Rachel was too shocked to move.

"What's happening?" Nora said.

Lee shouted at Rachel. "Do it. If this house is swept away, she deserves a fighting chance!"

Icy sweat sprang out on Nora's face. "The house can't get swept away. We're on a flat plain."

Lee's fiery eyes turned on her. "A plain in a valley with mountains on each side. This house sits in a channel—a flash flood wash."

Rachel hadn't moved from the door. Her lips were a white line.

"Just cut her loose!" Lee bellowed.

Rachel sank to the floor, her eyes vacant, as if she'd retreated to some dark place for protection against the storm.

Lee rushed across the room. He reached into his pocket and fished out a knife. It took him only seconds to slice through the tape.

Nora leapt to her feet and sprang for the door. She had to shove Rachel out of the way before she could open it and run onto the porch. Even under the protection of the porch roof, rain pelted her face. The deck vibrated and she slipped on the inch-deep water that seemed to blanket the wooden surface.

Two inches.

Three.

Oh my God. Nora understood the roar, the shaking house, the wet deck. A flash flood raged in the black night just beyond the cabin. They were trapped here amid the swirling, roiling sea of mud and frenzied water.

She fled back inside and slammed the door, dripping with icy rain. How would she get away to help Abigail?

She stared at Lee. His grim expression met hers. Now there was no escape. He'd kill her. Gun, knife, garotte, bare hands—it was dealer's choice.

"Why did you do it?" she asked.

He raised an eyebrow in response.

She pressed him. "Do you really believe space ships are coming to take you away?"

His shoulders drooped. "Is it so impossible to believe in life on other planets? So many things are unexplained. All the ancient religions mention people from the sky, even the Bible. Look at the rock art from thousands of years ago."

A shiver ran over her skin, the rain raising goose bumps on her arms. "Maybe, but how can you be sure they're coming back? And then pinpoint an exact day?"

His perpetual scowl deepened. "That's not for me to say. Uncle Warren has accomplished things that should have been impossible. He started out with nothing. How could he have risen so far without the hand of God interceding?"

"What has God and Mormonism got to do with space people and ancient Hopi prophecy?"

"We are all one," he said softly.

These words she knew. Lee could be reading from Benny's phrase book.

"The truth is there, and people from all nations, all corners of the Earth, know it. Why else would so many pilgrims follow the true prophet and gather in the desert?"

"What about the people in the bunkers who change their minds?"

"Sometimes their doubts overcome them."

"So you kill them to keep their money?"

His mouth opened in shock. "We don't need their money. We simply keep them with us until they calm down again."

"You lock them in so they can't leave?" Nora was horrified.

"They'll leave when the Sky People come for us. They chose freely. They come from all over the world and they'll be the seeds of the Fifth World."

The walls creaked and the din from the raging water made it nearly impossible to hold a conversation. Nora's fingers cramped from clutching the chair and Rachel still huddled on the floor, but when she raised her eyes, Nora could see the focus coming back into them.

Lee strained to see out a window. The wind howled like an air raid siren. Rain blasted against the windows like bullets. The river attacked them, battering the house, rocking and crashing as debris smashed against it.

A deafening explosion erupted at the north wall. Rachel screamed again as the house shuddered. It sounded like cannonballs impacted against the cabin.

Rachel sprung from the floor to the kitchen. She clung to the counter as if it were a lifeboat. "The cabin is going to break apart! We need to get out!"

Lee left the window and hurried to Rachel. He grabbed her hands in a rough grip and pulled her close to him. He focused on her face, meeting her terrified eyes. "It's okay. We're safer in the house than in the water."

Lee was probably right. The raging swirl of mud and freezing water could sweep them away. It might only be a few feet deep, but they'd lose their footing in the swift current. They could get wrapped around a fence, pinned against a building, be bashed by debris, or get sucked under until their lungs burst and they drowned.

Rachel clutched Lee's hands and concentrated on his face. Gradually her jaw unclenched and control seeped into her eyes.

The windows bowed and rattled while the wind roared with fury. Tree branches scratched against the house. The water rampaged as if sent to claim them for its own. Nora inched ever closer to the edge of control. The roar, accented by flashes of lightning and the boom of thunder, shredded her nerves.

Abbey whined and panted, lost in his own hell.

The house jerked and tilted. The lights died with a sizzle and a pop, the smell of ozone heavy in the air. Both women screamed as the scant light from the window limited their vision.

Rachel's face betrayed her battle to stay calm. "At least we'll be able to take care of her." She pointed her chin at Nora, her fingers still gripping Lee's.

"Darrell can't get to her in this flood," Lee agreed.

A shadow fell across the floor and Nora jerked her head toward the stairs.

"Unless he's already here," Darrell said. He stood midway up the stairs.

Thank God! He'd been here the whole time. Why hadn't he intervened earlier as Lee shoved Rachel behind him and leaped toward the stairs.

Darrell pulled his arm up, a gun clutched in his hand. Without hesitating, he fired at Lee. It happened so suddenly Nora hardly had time to register the shot. Lee cried out as he crumpled to the floor, blood blossoming across the shoulder of his plaid shirt.

"No!" Rachel threw herself at Darrell, knocking into him. He dropped the gun as he grappled with her. Nora flew to Lee and bent close to him in the gloom. Color drained from Lee's face as he gripped at his shoulder. Nora jumped up and raced to the kitchen. She grabbed a dish towel and ran back to him. She pulled his hand away from the gushing wound. Behind her, Darrell and Rachel grunted, still struggling. The house lurched and Nora thought she felt it slide a few inches. She pressed the towel to Lee's shoulder.

He opened his eyes. With surprising speed and strength, he gripped her hand. "Darrell…"

A terrible crashing interrupted him. Did Nora scream? Did Rachel? Or was it the chaos of the storm and the shriek of the cabin as it tore from its tenuous mooring? Timbers cracked and popped as dishes shattered. The kitchen window blew open and icy water, mixed with clay and grit in a swirling stew of mud and sticks and weeds, surged from the office into the living room.

Suddenly, Rachel appeared at Nora's side and together they heaved Lee from the water to the couch. The water was rapidly rising as the house jerked again. Nora scanned the room, looking for Darrell. She saw him sprawled out on the stairs. He had either fallen or had been knocked down by Rachel.

The gun rested a few steps above him and he reached for it as he pulled himself up. Rachel shoved Nora out of the way and leaned in close to Lee. He appeared weak and in pain. Nora knew the burning agony of being shot, but had no idea if it was a shallow wound or if it would prove to be fatal. She hoped Lee would survive, but he needed to get to a hospital.

The house convulsed again, coming to rest at a sharp angle. Something upstairs banged and the ceiling sounded like it might cave in. More glass shattered. Nora stood above Lee and Rachel, watching as Darrell pushed himself up another step and reached for the gun.

A hand grabbed her arm, yanking her backward. Rachel tried to tug Nora out the front door, now unhinged and hanging open. They struggled in the mud now blanketing the floor, each step proving to be a slipping struggle. Rachel shouted something at her but the rush of the flood and the rain and thunder masked her words. Nora tugged back, fighting to stay in the house.

With a deafening crash, one of the ceiling beams dislodged. The vibrations rocked the whole house and Rachel used the momentum to throw all of her weight against Nora. The perfect storm of motion knocked Nora off balance and she pitched headfirst to splash in the water on the floor. Rachel pulled on her arm again, dragging her through the front door.

Nora slid on her stomach, her arm wrenched high over her head. Rachel tugged her across the pitching front porch. With one last lunge, Rachel propelled them both off the porch and into the roiling waters. She lost her grip on Nora's arm and disappeared as the black rush of the freezing flood stole her away.

THIRTY-FOUR

THE CONFIDENCE AND POWER that had rushed through Warren earlier seeped away, leaving him frail. He huddled in the passenger seat of his Caddy, coughing and wheezing, fighting for every breath. His body burned with fever and he'd shed his expensive toupee hours ago, even though he hated for Abigail to see him bald.

He longed to give up, let his earthly body finally rest. But Warren knew God expected him to keep going. He had prepared a reward for Warren and he needed to show strength of spirit and mind. God hadn't made Warren's path easy, but He'd always rewarded him. He couldn't succumb to weakness now that the end grew near.

Abigail leaned forward over the steering wheel, peering into the inky night. The wipers slapped at high speed. She squinted. "I can't see anything."

He labored for breath. "Keep a light hand on the wheel. God will guide us."

She tightened her lips. "I've had enough of your God and His ridiculous plans. You're crazy. You've always been nuts, since the first moment we met you." She looked like his Abigail—the sweet, happy young girl without a harsh word—but she sounded more like Christine, who, despite having every advantage, felt disappointed with what life had given her.

"What happened to you to make you so hard?" he asked.

She frowned. "I had to get hard in a hurry. It's not easy to survive a rape, lose my dearly beloved husband, and raise a baby on my own."

He pushed himself to sit. "I loved you."

She said nothing, but her jaws clenched. Eventually she spoke. "Your nephew said Nora would be at the cabin?"

"She was on her way back from the reservation."

The rear of the Caddy fishtailed so she pulled her foot off the accelerator and coaxed the steering wheel in the opposite direction. They righted and she pressed the gas pedal. "You're sure?"

"My nephew wouldn't lie," he assured her.

He grabbed a plastic grocery bag and leaned over to wretch. Specks of blood and a tiny stream of foamy bile oozed from his heaving belly. His throat burned and his abdominal muscles ached with effort, but his stomach contained little. He heaved again, the sweat puddling in his armpits and filming his cold face.

He fell back on the seat and pushed the button to roll down the window. Warren forced the nearly empty bag through it and it was swept away by the rush of wind and rain. He rolled up the window and lay panting.

"What are you going to do with Nora?"

More questions. He closed his eyes, the effort it took to speak exhausting him. "I want to see her."

"You've already seen her."

He heard the weakness in his own voice. "I want to see her with the eyes of a father."

"You aren't her father. And even if you were, she wouldn't do what you want her to do."

He opened his eyes. "And what do you think I want her to do?"

She didn't take her eyes from the road or loosen her grip on the wheel. "I don't know. Take over your businesses? Be some grand poobah of the Mormon Church? I can't imagine what you want with her, but I know Nora and she won't have anything to do with you."

"I can offer her more than wealth," he began.

She frowned again. "It doesn't matter. I told her what you did to me."

Warren had been dragged through every bit of muck throughout his very public life. When a person acquired as much success as he had, it made him an easy target for resentment. Yet, no accusation hurt him the way Abigail's lies now ripped at his heart. The daughter he longed to see hadn't been conceived in anger or by force. Why couldn't Abigail realize that?

She slowed to a crawl and leaned so far forward her nose practically rested on the dash. She turned the wheel and they started up the road to Castle Valley. "Oh. Oh." She sounded so distressed Warren pulled himself up on the seat to see what was going on. He strained to see through the darkness outside his rain-streaked window, but finally he understood.

The valley below roiled and raged in a flash flood. What was once a peaceful sprawl of scraggly trees and homes was now a vengeful river, the red of the mud lightening the water so the flood's violence was even more obvious in the moonless night.

Abigail drove along the road to the turnoff that led down to Castle Valley. Of course, the road had been washed away. "The cabin … " It sounded like she wanted to say more but couldn't form words.

He gripped the door handle and fought the terror pooling in the pit of his stomach. God wouldn't give him a daughter only to take her away at the last minute. Be calm and believe.

Abigail gasped. She pointed down the road where the headlights caused the raindrops to spark in the reflected glow. He squinted and saw a figure staggering in the rain. He reached for the glove box to pull out the gun he kept there. He prayed it was Nora but needed to prepare for the worst.

Abigail shoved her door open and scrambled into the storm, running toward the person. What if it was a looter or someone intending to harm them? A second passed before Warren identified it as a man making his slow progress in their direction. Warren gripped the dash as the man came into focus. Darrell.

This didn't feel right. He expected Lee, but hoped to see Rachel. He prayed Nora was safe. But he didn't know Darrell was out here.

Warren closed his eyes and summoned strength. There was so little left. His deepest desire was to lie down and stop fighting, let the good Lord have mercy on him and take him home. But it wasn't his time yet. First he needed to leave the kingdom in good hands. He pushed the door open. It felt like a stone blocking the entrance to a tomb. His legs shook trying to support his own meager weight, but he forced his feet to move. The rain dripped onto his bald head, cooling his fever but chilling him so that his teeth chattered.

Darrell shifted his focus from Abigail. Warren expected the man to rush to his side at the frail state of his leader. Instead, he waited as Warren staggered into the peripheral glow of the headlights.

Darrell's shirt clung to his chest, the tattered sleeves rippling in the wind. Blood and mud dripped from long scratches on his arms and his face was peppered with scrapes and bruises.

The storm was losing steam, but the flood continued roaring. The frenzied water surged past with destructive energy.

"Where's Nora?" Warren managed to ask.

Darrell's shoulders slumped as he looked at the ground. "I don't know. Rachel and Lee had her when the house collapsed. I only hope she survived."

Abigail gasped. "Oh my God! She's trapped in the flood?"

"I tried to save her. We would have been safe if we'd stayed in the house, even though it was badly damaged. But after Lee was injured, Rachel forced Nora into the water."

"Lee is injured? How bad?" Warren needed Lee. The colony needed his survivalist instincts, his faith, his intimate knowledge of the plan.

Darrell dropped his shoulders even more, his face a picture of sorrow. "I wish I didn't have to tell you this. But I shot Lee."

Abigail let out an alarmed gasp.

Warren stepped back a few paces to lean on the Caddy.

"He had Nora and he planned to kill her. I knew you needed Nora to carry on your legacy. There was no other way."

The firm grasp Warren had on the plan, the future, slipped from his fingers. Everything was spinning out of control. "You're brothers, a team. Together you were going to lead the faithful. You've always been my sons!"

Darrell's head shot up. "None of that is true. Now that you have a true heir, you plan on leaving it all to her."

Warren's knees buckled and he rested his bony rear on the bumper as the rain streamed down his face.

Darrell stepped forward, following the beam of light toward Warren. "Not brothers. Half-brothers. You know what that's like, don't you, Uncle Warren?"

Abigail stared at Darrell's sudden transformation. Warren should have known Darrell would break under the pressure. He usually had perfect instincts with people. But somehow he'd missed Darrell's weakness. And now his nephew was turning on him.

Darrell's feet sloshed in the muddy road as he continued his rant. "To be the son whose mother is not the favorite. The ugly mother. The one with the harsh tongue. The mother whose only son is kicked out when he's fourteen because there's only room for the favorite son at the homestead."

How could the situation be unraveling like this? "I took care of you. You never had to go through what I did. I paid for your college and law school and got you the best clerk positions. I helped you."

"Why? Was it because you loved me? Because you wanted what was best for me?"

Warren's skin burned and his eyes felt like flames. He wouldn't be able to hold his head up much longer.

Thinly contained rage packed Darrell's words. "It was because you needed me! Someone you could groom to follow in your insane footsteps. A captain to lead your troops and keep your crazy plan secret."

"Not crazy."

"I did keep it secret, though. I did everything you wanted. Did you know that on the morning I dealt with Lisa, Lee was on his way to save her? If I hadn't gotten there first, he would have helped her escape and she would have exposed you."

Warren struggled to maintain his breath. "Maybe she didn't need to die."

Darrell hardly paused. "I even played nice with Brother Lee and his disgusting family. Oh, you helped me with your contacts and a little money. But you could have done so much more. You never claimed me as you own."

Warren wretched into the mud, a thin string of blood dribbling from his lips before splashing into the road. "Couldn't."

"Right." Sarcasm soured Darrell's voice. "The polygamy. Can't let anyone know you came from that. You can cover up the past and help the young man of a single mother, but you can't admit he's from your family rooted in polygamy."

"What did you want?" Warren managed to ask.

"Money!" Darrell yelled into the night. "You have millions—billions, some say. And yet you couldn't buy me an election?

Couldn't get me a decent car? Couldn't build Lee and his tribe a house? You stingy bastard."

"I needed it for … " Warren was interrupted by another heave.

"For the plan. Building the bunker. Stocking it. Buying silence." Darrell watched Warren raise his arm in slow motion to wipe the blood from his chin. It was clear he was in pain. "But it's not all gone. I know. Even a lunatic like you couldn't spend it all. Somewhere in the back of your mind, you know this whole thing is a joke."

No. Darrell believed. He had to believe. He'd killed Lisa Taylor to protect the plan.

"There is no space ship. There is no mystic connection with the Hopi and they won't be coming in two days to take the faithful."

Warren tried to lift his head to explain but he couldn't raise his chin from his chest.

"So the faithful will wait and when nothing happens, they'll know you lied to them."

Darrell stood in front of Warren, but Warren couldn't raise his eyes to see Darrell's face. He focused on the red mud caked on Darrell's shoes and the filth clinging to his dripping jeans. With slow, deliberate movements, Darrell slid his hand into his pocket and pulled out a pistol.

"Rachel and Nora will die in the flood. Lee is probably still in the cabin, dead. You're not going to last long and neither is she." He wagged his gun at Abigail. "No one is left to expose me."

Warren felt the shame of begging. "No. Please."

"And you know that will I prepared for you? The one you signed? I changed it after the fact." With feigned gratitude, he said, "You really shouldn't have been so generous to leave me what's left of your estate. Minus a small stipend for Christine, of course."

He'd failed. His life's work had crumbled in the grip of the evil man in front of him. The space ships would come, but the pilgrims couldn't get to them. Lee, his one faithful nephew, lay dead. His daughter, too—he'd never speak to her, never hold her.

Betrayed. Like his brother Jesus, Warren longed to cry out, "My God, my God, why hast thou forsaken me?"

Mud splashed as he heard the sound of footsteps. Good. He hoped Abigail was trying to escape.

But Darrell took a few strides then lunged, pinning Abigail to his chest with one arm. Warren prayed for the strength to protect her. He prayed God would listen to him, recognize the voice of his faithful servant, and grant him one last request. He needed to save her, the woman he had always loved. Just long enough to give her a name she'd know. The name to listen for when he called her across the veil.

God didn't allow them to share this life, but surely He would grant them eternal life on their own planet. This had to be why He'd brought Abigail to him at this last moment. *God please. I'm trying. Please help.*

THIRTY-FIVE

NORA'S HEAD PLUNGED UNDER the frothing wave of muddy water. She strained her neck, lifting her mouth to the air and filling her lungs. Grit choked her but she was able to breathe before dunking underneath the water and flipping herself over. Her spine scraped the desert floor and snagged on roots and branches. Sharp talons scratched at her face and the water tumbled debris against her to batter every part of her body.

She quickly lost contact with Rachel. She could only hope the surging water wouldn't drown them or smash them against a boulder or fence post and break them in two. The crushing pace of the water didn't diminish, but Nora choked back panic to form a plan. She dragged her rear on the sand, head pointed downstream. The water gushed around her chin and lapped into her mouth when she sucked a breath. She coughed and stretched herself flat so she could float along the surface. Kicking her legs and paddling with her hands, she worked her way to what she hoped was the north side of the flow.

The cold water penetrated her skin. If she stayed in the water much longer, she'd risk hypothermia. She lifted her head and opened her mouth for another gulp of air.

Nora couldn't see in the blackness that surrounded her, but the water felt more shallow here. She planted her hands in the sand behind her, with her feet out in front of her. She struggled but held her own against the current. Ten seconds ago, she hadn't been able to resist the deluge as it carried her toward destruction. She kept maneuvering herself to the shallower water, assuming she'd eventually reach the edge of the flood.

Nora pushed against the thick water, positioning her legs under her in a squat. Still facing the current, she resisted with her hands and legs, the water now to her knees and shoulders. Centering her weight, she stood and started to plow out of the main current. Planting her feet one step at a time, she made her way out of the river of muck. The rain had tapered to a few drops and the wind, while strong enough to make her teeth chatter with the cold, wasn't shrieking in her ears.

The black night closed around her as she felt her way around, sloshing in the ankle-deep mud, hoping she was headed for the bank that led to the road. She'd been tossed and tumbled so much she couldn't tell if she walked east or west.

Had Rachel made it? Maybe she shouldn't be so concerned with the fate of a woman who intended to kill her. But Nora didn't want to write Rachel off as an evil murderer just yet.

She kept picturing Rachel and Lisa together. A person couldn't fake the light in their eyes when their lover unexpectedly entered the room. Rachel never ignored an opportunity to touch Lisa and that kind of unconscious affection was hard to manufacture. Sure, people fall out of love. But that didn't lead to murder. Earlier, when Rachel spoke to Lee about Lisa, she had had the tone of a woman deeply in love.

The darkness in front of her solidified into the bank leading to the road. Saturated as it was, Nora struggled to climb. Her feet slid and she scraped her chin on the gravel and clay. Slowly, she crawled onto the road. Nora spotted lights about a quarter of a mile away. Headlights, she realized. Someone was out here and it meant help, warmth, and shelter.

She wanted to run, but her legs were too weak and she shivered so violently she did well just to keep moving, however slowly. She began to make out shapes in the headlights the closer she trudged. One very large person stood in the middle of the spotlight. It looked like another sat on the bumper. A few steps closer. The large person turned out to be two people standing close together, one holding the other up. An arm extended from the two person group.

Nora slowed her turtle-like pace and listened. "There is still time for you to do the right thing."

Oh my god. Abigail.

The dripping man holding her mother jerked her closer to him. "The right thing is that I get my reward for the humiliation and slave labor I've given him all my life."

Nora slid down the embankment so she could hide her approach, but kept her focus on the figures in the headlights. She crawled through the mud, her fingers numb and her teeth clenched against her trembling.

Darrell?

Darrell pointed his gun at the man slumped against the bumper. Warren. He didn't raise his head. His knees melted and he plopped into a puddle, whacking his head against the bumper.

The man who'd warned her against going to the cops. He'd told her he was taking care of Lee and Rachel. He had the gun trained on Warren. That was good. But he also threatened Abigail. Definitely not good.

Darrell lowered his gun. "You're finally getting what you deserve. Dying in the mud. How appropriate for the tenth richest man in the world." Darrell looked down at Abigail. "Come on." He jerked his head toward the bank and Nora ducked. "I think there's still enough water for a tragic drowning."

Had he heard her? Her heart hammered and she held her breath. Nora heard a scuffle in the mud and she poked her head above the rim of the bank. Darrell yanked Abigail toward the side of the road, only twenty feet from where Nora hid.

Abigail fought against him. "What do you hope to gain by this?"

"Your silence." He grunted in effort as he dragged her along.

"Even if I'm gone, Rachel and Nora will stop you."

"Rachel's had her chance. And Nora isn't going to make it through the night."

He succeeded in getting Abigail to the lip of the bank, but she didn't make it easy. Nora crouched well within his peripheral vision, but between the darkness and his struggle with Abigail, he didn't notice.

"I'm sure Nora has already called the cops." Abigail sounded strong for the fight.

"They won't help her. Most of them are packing their bags to join the faithful in the bunker."

Abigail freed one arm and swung her hand up to smack his face, but he dodged the blow. Nora waited until he had one foot down the bank, throwing off his center of gravity and making him unstable. She pushed off the thick mud to hurl herself at Darrell and send him sailing down the bank. But the mud sucked at her feet and she never got off the ground.

Her foot slipped and she tumbled backward, sliding down the bank with a grunt. Darrell spun toward her, pulling Abigail with him.

She lost her footing and shoved against Darrell. They toppled forward into the steep embankment. The turbulent water rushed below them.

Darrell lost his grip on Abigail and she rolled down the bank toward the flood. She wasn't as strong as Nora and she'd be swept away.

"Mother!" Nora's hands sank into the saturated hillside. She shoved with her feet, propelling herself toward Abigail. Abigail stopped rolling ten feet above the waves. Slathered in mud, she blended with the bank. She twisted her head up and Nora swore she could read panic in her eyes, though it was impossible to tell in the dark.

"Hang on!" Nora yelled.

Lightning flashed, with a crack of thunder following. The rain resumed, falling in solid sheets. Darrell pushed himself to his knees as he raised his gun toward Abigail.

The slight ledge that had stopped Abigail's fall began to break loose and slide into the rampaging water. Abigail screamed and flailed her arms, looking for anything to grab hold of.

Nora didn't have time to think things through. She could either lunge for Abigail and hold her on the bank, letting Darrell get a shot off in close range, or dive for Darrell and leave Abigail to save herself.

Flash! Boom!

Abigail screamed. Her feet slid in slow motion and brushed the edge of the water. She slapped at the muddy bank, her fingers clawing at air.

Rain battered at them, carving mini-culverts of icy water in the bank. A deluge of liquid mud ran down Nora's face and into her mouth as she fought to stand. In one fluid motion, Nora dove headfirst down the bank, her arm outstretched and her eyes focused on Abigail's frantically waving hand. She smacked into the mud, her fingers closing around air. Her mother's hand was just out of reach and slipping further away by the second.

Nora laid her head down, the rush of the flood splashing into her eyes and mouth. Abigail's legs kicked in the water as Nora saw her slide in past her knees. Her mother's sharp shriek sent lightning through Nora's veins and she scrambled through the mud, desperate to feel her mother's flesh. Nora had to concentrate in order to move her arms, legs, feet, and hands. The mud dragged on them, making them feel like leaden attachments instead of her own flesh and blood.

She inched forward. Abigail slid another foot as the bank gave way beneath her hips. "No!" Not knowing or caring where she got the strength, Nora lunged forward and this time, she felt the grasping answer of her mother's fingers close on hers. Nora braced her free hand underneath her body and pulled backward. At first, they remained mired in the muck, the rain stinging against their skin. Nora gritted her teeth and doubled her effort.

Darrell's bullet would rip into her any second. She'd die drenched in mud, never seeing Cole's face again. Abigail would slide into the torrent, not possessing the strength to fight it.

Slowly, though, they moved up the bank, fighting for each inch until Abigail's feet were no longer submerged in the swirling river. Nora struggled into a sitting position, hauling Abigail to her and hugging her close. Abigail gasped and sobbed and flung her arms around Nora. The mud made it feel like a sandpaper embrace, but the love flowed strong. She knew this would be their last hug and tried to shield Abigail with her body.

Darrell stood above them on the bank. His arm held the gun steady, aimed at Nora. Why hadn't he shot them while they struggled on the bank?

He shook his head. "Nice rescue. But it won't save you. You should have let her drown. Now I'll have to break her neck to look like she died from flood injuries."

"You have experience with that," she yelled at him, desperate to keep him talking until she could figure out how to stop him.

"I didn't enjoy killing Lisa. I offered her a compromise and lots of money. But she had her principles."

"Maybe my mother and I are less principled." Nora kept her voice above the noise of the storm.

"I will not … " Abigail started to say. Nora tightened her arm around her and cut off the rest.

"Liar." He steadied the gun and took a deep breath.

This was it. The bullet would rip into her heart. She thrust Abigail behind her and squeezed her eyes shut.

The shot rang in her ears.

She waited for the shock to wear off and the pain to hit.

She inhaled her last breath.

And waited.

"Oh, thank god!" Abigail cried.

Nora opened her eyes.

Darrell lay face down in the mud. His gun arm extended above his head, the gun flung down the slope.

Nora's eyes moved up the bank.

Warren stood on the edge of the road. His head hung down on a neck too weak to keep it up, and his eyes were closed. His arm was limp at his side, a gun dangling from his finger. A second later, it dropped into a puddle with a splash. He opened his eyes and found Nora with what appeared to be grueling effort. His lips moved as pinkish foam bubbled from his mouth. He sank to his knees, his mouth still opening and closing.

Maybe it was the rain or maybe tears streamed down his face. He finally croaked one word.

"Daughter."

He folded in on himself and splashed onto the road.

EPILOGUE

BRIGHT SUNSHINE TOASTED THE top of Nora's head and warmed her arms. The wrens twittered along with the sparrows. Humid air rose from the damp red sand under her boots where pinpricks of green already battled their way through the flood fallout.

Nora breathed with care, making sure not to pant after the short hike up the washed-out trail. The doctor assured her the ribs were bruised and not broken, but the difference seemed negligible. She couldn't move without pain shooting through her. Even with a black eye, a purple bruise the size of a Volkswagen on her thigh, and more sore muscles than she thought possible, she still fared better than Rachel.

Rachel leaned heavily on one crutch, her head hanging down with her thin blonde hair shielding her face. Along with her fractured ankle, Rachel sported a bandage wrapped around her forehead. She hadn't complained much, but the doctor told Nora that Rachel's headaches had to be epic.

Still, Rachel had insisted they come here this morning. Before them, the creek burbled on a calm and happy note. Two days ago, while Nora and Rachel had been tossed like marbles in a box down the raging flood in Castle Valley, this canyon at Moonflower had also exploded in floodwaters. The tough willows and cottonwoods survived, red silt covered the ground, and now the creek flowed in denial of the incident.

Abbey had waited out the storm in the cabin. Terrified and alone, he'd come through without a physical scratch, though Nora figured storms would always be an ordeal for him. He rested under the shade of a willow.

Rachel didn't look up. "The last of the immigrants left this morning."

Nora focused on a tiny yellow bud poking through the sand, amazed it fought back so quickly. "Did they get their assets returned?"

Rachel's shoulders drooped. "Lee's not a monster, you know."

Nora didn't know whether she agreed.

Rachel defended him. "Why wouldn't Lee believe Warren's lies? You don't know what it's like to be raised in isolation, where you're told only what they want you to know. Whatever they don't like, they label as sin and fill you with such terror of Hell, you don't dare rebel."

Nora said softly, "That's what happened to you?"

A sob caught in Rachel's throat. "Until I met Lisa. She saved me." They stood in silence, then Rachel continued. "I knew about Warren's plans. I could have stopped it. But I felt loyal to my family. And I honestly didn't think it would hurt anyone. The immigrants would wait, the space ships wouldn't come, then everyone would go home." More silence. "I should have known Lisa better. It's my fault she's gone."

The box Nora held felt too heavy.

"But that doesn't mean Lee was bad. He has a good heart. Warren and Darrell's death have broken it, maybe even broken him."

They stood in silence for several moments.

Rachel lifted her chin. "Okay. We came out here to say goodbye. We might as well do it."

Nora set the box of ashes on the sand. She pulled the screwdriver from the back pocket of her shorts and worked at prying the lid off. Abbey stood and trotted over to stick his cold nose on her cheek.

Rachel bent over and scratched his ears and he sat back to lean on her legs.

Nora set the screwdriver down and pulled the lid off to reveal a plastic bag. "Thank you for letting me be here."

Rachel's throat worked before strained words came out. "I couldn't do it alone."

Nora closed her fingers on the plastic bag full of course gray ashes. She lifted it and stepped toward the creek.

Rachel hobbled after her and they stood together on a smooth rock on the bank at a bend in the creek. Nora slid the top of the bag open and offered it to Rachel.

Tears streamed down Rachel's face and she shook her head. She mouthed the words "I can't" and broke down in sobs.

Nora pictured a laughing Lisa, her vitality and passion clear on her face. She considered the creek and slowly let Lisa's ashes sift into the running water and dissolve.

When the bag was empty, Nora wadded it up and stuffed it in her pocket. Rachel's sobs tapered off, and her fingers tentatively brushed Nora's hand.

Nora closed her hand on Rachel's and they stood together, watching the creek. Finally Rachel stirred. "My ankle is hurting and I need to rest. Can you bring Lisa's box?"

"Of course." Nora ached to think of Rachel picking up the threads of her life alone. She'd turned her back on her upbringing and now had no family.

Rachel hobbled down the trail, leaving Nora and Abbey. A few minutes later the rumble of voices pricked their ears. Abbey's tail wagged. If Nora had a tail, hers would be doing the same.

Footsteps on damp sand kept tempo with her heart. Nora limped a few feet from the creek toward the trail. She couldn't stop the goofy grin she knew was spreading over her face.

Cole's sandy hair and broad shoulders emerged from the cottonwoods along the trail. Nora was barely aware of her swollen knee and bruised hip as she shuffled toward him.

Cole squinted into the sun and searched the clearing. When he spotted her, he broke into a wide grin and jogged toward her. In mere seconds, he threw his arms around her, lifting her into the air and crushing her against him.

Pain from a hundred wounds zapped through her. She didn't care. She clung to him with all her strength. She buried her face in the warmth of his neck and breathed in his comforting scent.

They pulled apart and he bent to pat Abbey. "Your mother told me where you were."

"You didn't need to come all the way out here, but I'm glad you did."

He slid his arms around her again. "I had to make sure you're really okay."

"I'm sort of okay. Lots of bruises, and of course, I have major work to do if I'm going to present Canyonlands' case to the board."

"Of course." He chuckled. "But first, can I buy you some lunch?"

"A girl's gotta eat, right?" She hurried to retrieve Lisa's box. She leaned down to heft it up when her gaze was drawn to a splash of blue showing through the sand. Her breath left her lungs and she stood motionless for several seconds.

When her heart resumed, a smile danced on her lips. She brushed the sand away. The bright blue of the sash, as well as the feathers secured in his hand, identified the fist-sized kachina as hers.

She didn't bother looking around for who might have left the doll. She reached for the wooden figure. Energy surged through her fingers as she grasped him.

She belonged.

The End

© Kelly Weaver Photography

ABOUT THE AUTHOR

Shannon Baker (Flagstaff, AZ) can often be found backpacking, skiing, kayaking, cycling, or just playing lizard in the desert. From the Colorado Rockies to the Nebraska Sandhills, the peaks of Flagstaff and the deserts of Tucson, Western landscapes play an important role in her books. Visit her online at Shannon-Baker.com.

ACKNOWLEDGMENTS

I owe a huge thanks to Laura Kamala, who inspired this story. Laura and I sat on the patio at The Eklectica Café in the bright Moab sunshine and she told me all about the film project she initiated and produced through The Grand Canyon Trust. Normally calm and serene as a mountain lake, Laura burst with passion for this project. Midway through our conversation I stopped her and asked, "Who would want to kill you for doing this?" A true mystery lover, Laura never skipped a beat. In the way of the world, nothing turned out as we planned. While I ventured off on a whole different plot line, Laura's project was ripped from her grasp. Sadly, she didn't get to complete the work she'd given her heart to create.

Again I must thank Jessica Morrell for trying to teach how to be a real writer. And for throwing out a grappling hook and dragging me back to the ground when I wanted to include the strange conspiracy theories surrounding Denver International Airport and the giant ant-like creatures who have ventured from the center of the planet to take over the world. I thought it worked. Jessica was right, as she usually is.

Kate Watters filled me in on some botanical details. Alan Larson and Karen Duvall are beta readers of the first order. Without the help of the Sisters of the Quill, Janet Fogg, Julie Kaewart, and Karen Lin, I probably would have quit writing and taken up needlepoint. And I hate needlepoint.

Rocky Mountain Fiction Writers has seen me through from the very beginning. There isn't a step along this crazy writer path I've taken without RMFW leading the way.

The folks at Midnight Ink have taken good care of this series. I owe an enormous thanks to the best editor in the world—and that is not hyperbole—Terri Bischoff. You've changed my life for the better in so many ways. Thanks to Lisa Novak for another rocking cover.

To my daughters, who constantly inspire me with their amazing accomplishments, their fearless spirits, their paralyzing wit, and their uncanny ability to always keep me accountable.

Mostly, a deep, abiding thanks to Dave. You make the sun shine warmer, the colors brighter, and keep me laughing every day.